CW00493337

Specific State '89

Ian 'Snowy' Snowball
&
Centreforce Radio

NEW HAVEN PUBLISHING LTD

Specific State '89 ☺

Published 2018
NEW HAVEN PUBLISHING LTD
www.newhavenpublishingltd.com
newhavenpublishing@gmail.com

Cover design © Pete Cunliffe
pcunliffe@blueyonder.co.uk

Specific State and Snowy would like to put a big shout out to Centreforce and all of the DJs and its supporters, Andy Swallow, Rooney the Roonsta, Carley Denham, Dean Lambert, Nicky Black Market, Keith Mac, Dean Foster at Future Past Clothing, Loz wife-to-be, Colin Hudd, Keith Davis, Danielle Montana, Grant Fleming, Lisa Loud, Adamski, Slipmatt, Jumping Jack Frost, Jack Bass, Nicky Brown, Jazzy M (Mervyn), Ashley Beedle, Andy Barker,Lee 'Lust' Priest, Perry K, Jon 'Mr Music' Fleet, Jonny C, Danny Swallow, Peter 'P' Poyton, Mickey 'Star' Lewis, Tony Wilson,DJ Connie, Wayne Anthony, Roger The Doctor, Matt Early, DJ Seeker, Jim EP, Chris Lavish, DJ Hermit, Marshall Jefferson, Todd Terry, Screamin' Rachael Cain, Sterling Void, Virgo, Derek 'Smokin' Joe, Tony Grimley, Bobby Parry, Daddy Chester, Jonny Eames, Gary Dickel, Steve Proctor, the Maidstone Crewand Penenden Heath Posse (you know who you are and much love) and my main three drivers Craig Stead, Steve Sparkes and Steve Mepham, who often led the convoy as we charged around the M25, the back streets of London and country lanes as we pursued the promised land. And to Teddie and the New Haven Publishing team.

Content

INTRODUCTION

By the end spring of 2016 I had written the stage play RAVE. My vision was to create a show that included a DJ spinning records from the acid house/rave scene of 1989. There'd be the actors (only a handful), there'd be lights and strobes and lasers and shed loads of dry ice. Behind the stage would be screens to project footage from raves of the summer of love. There'd be anything that helped to recreate the feel and the buzz of being at a rave back in 1989. The stage play was intended to be a trip back in time when thousands of young people came together to dance (and yes, take illegal substances) and listen to great, great house music. It was a way of life for many and whilst the illegal parties lasted, it was amazing.

However, finding a theatre company to share my vision wasn't coming easy, so I decided to adapt the stage play into a novel, rather than the normally accepted way of turning the novel into a stage play.

Rave was my punk. It was 1989 and I turned nineteen. Along with loads of mates from school and others I had got to know from around the local discos, we got caught up in something that turned out to be one hell of a ride. It was great fun and it also gave us experiences beyond our wildest wet dreams AND friendships were forged.

We had rebel spirits, strove for pleasure and a good time and we embraced the thrills, pills and bellyaches. At the heart of it all was our love of house music and this drove us forward.

We also loved the buzz of locking onto Centreforce and it was the thought of this pirate radio station that partly inspired this novel Specific State '89. Centreforce and some of the other pirates like Sunrise were our rave-vine to what was happening. They played the best house music and those DJs told us where the meeting points were - and this information was vital if we were going to be successful in getting to a rave.

I grew up in Maidstone, Kent. The first record I bought with my own money was That's Entertainment by The Jam. I was eleven years old. The Jam would become my band. My mates and I were into the mod thing, which in time morphed into the casual thing, but as quick as the change came, it wasn't overnight. I can still recall the transition period where I was strolling around in a Pringle jumper, Levi 501s and a pair of desert boots. Not being loaded, it was going to take me a while to replace my mod wardrobe of Harrington's, Fred Perry's and Sta-prest with a Patrick Kagool, Lois cords and a pair of Diadora Gold Elites. During this period football had also started to become important. I had been supporting Chelsea since I was twelve years old and this was only because I had heard they were Paul Weller's favourite team (it took me nearly thirty years to discover that this was in actual fact true).

For many teenage lads, the mid-80s was a great time to be into football, into being a casual and being into new styles of music. I used to go to a disco called the Kent Hall. It was in there around 1987 that I first started to hear Chicago House records. Move Your Body and House Nation were played every week alongside records by De La Soul and the Beastie Boys. I also had a close friend called Craig. He had moved to Kent from Leeds. When he arrived at our school in 1984 he was already very clued up regards being a casual and hip hop music (and in time we both really latched onto the Go Go because of bands like Trouble Funk).

By 1985/86 were taking trips to Manchester's Underground Market and returning to Kent with Adidas Samba's, corduroy hooded jackets and flared jeans (and this was three years before the Madchester look). We certainly looked out of place back down south, alongside our mates who were dressing in Fila, Lois and Lyle &Scott. But what we all had in common was the excitement we felt when we purchased a new jumper, tee shirt or pair of trainers.

In Specific State '89 I have mixed up some of my own recollections of what was happening in 1989, like nights out in Clinks, a range of raves in an assortment of venues dotted around London-some of which were very basic dens, visits to Mash and Black Market Records, meeting points on Blackheath or South Mimms Service Station or the night the police turned our carsinside out at the Black Prince Interchange, or the night the police closed

8

the Dartford Tunnel because they wanted to prevent ravers getting to the party. There is also the day out for the Freedom To Party demonstration and the rave that evening in some warehouse in Radlett, Herts and how, when we ventured out from the warehouse in the morning, we found that Craig's motor had a flat tyre, but a copper helped us change it (he must have failed to notice our flying saucer eyes).

My memories work okay alongside other facts and figures that I have either researched or nicked from other people's hazy memory banks. And I have many hazy memories. Whilst writing the book I recalled the first acid house party that I attended. It was 1988 and myself and three mates took off in a Ford Estate (we all slept in it for three nights) to go and visit another mate, who I think was staying down Portsmouth way. This meant that somewhere between Maidstone and Portsmouth we ended up at the party which was in a warehouse. I don't recall much at all other than the DJs played just acid house, just like the acid house cassette tape that we played in the car, tracks like This Is Acid, Acid Thunder and Acid Tracks.

Going into the following year there was game changing tunes like Voodoo Ray and Fools Gold and we got deeper into the rave scene, the music, the clothes, the little helpers. And it was brilliant, until it started to turn dark - and for a period it did. I remember seeing my first gun at a rave. A group of lads dressed in black leather jackets surrounded one of our gang; they searched him and took what they wanted. As I moved closer one of them opened his jacket to reveal his gun. I, of course, backed away. That was at the Freedom To Party rave that followed the demonstration on that January day.

It did feel to me that some of the unity, the love and the buzz was getting overshadowed by the seedier aspects and the new people the parties were starting to attract. The sense of rave being underground was disappearing. Plus, the police were really cracking down on the raves and were starting to wise up to what was really happening.

A series of events soon followed. I got punched up by half a dozen fellas outside the Slammer nightclub in Gravesend and subsequently missed a Primal Scream gig in Tonbridge. Things just started to get moody and dull. It had been a great ride, but for me the trip had ended and I backed away for a period of timeAlthoughI still crammed in events like the first KAOS weekender and anEnergy event in the London Docklands. It included Adamski with an appearance from Seal to perform Killer, Guru Josh, 808 State and Snap amongst others.But thankfully most of my memories of 88, 89, 90 and 91are great memories and I am glad that I experienced it. And I still deeply love house music, some thirty years later.

You will notice I have massaged the timeline around a bit in some places and have included some tracks which may have not have actually been releasedat the time they are mentioned in the novel or stage play script.But hey, let's not allow the truth to get in the way of a good story eh!

FREEDOM TO PARTY PART 1

Patch noticed a discarded copy of The Sun on a bench in Hyde Park and, not being one to miss out on a freebie, snatched it up before anyone else could. Clocking the date: January 27 1990 and the price of the paper he fingered his way through the pages of the scum with his long nail bitten fingers, a habit he'd been dragging along with him since he had nails hard enough to chew on. When he was younger his parents had tried all sorts of things to 'cure' him of his addiction. Shouting and yelling at him constantly had worn them down so they'd tried some medical nail varnish that tasted disgusting and, of course, hadn't worked. Patch had long since surrendered to his vice and in the context of his other vices, biting his nails was hardly anything to worry about.

On leaving Hyde Park, Patch agreed that the page three model was well-formed and looked incredibly proud of herself about it. He lingered on the page for far longerthan he really needed to. Shrugging his shoulders and reassuring himself that his memory wank was secured for the next morning, he hastily flicked through the pages until he got to the sports section. His eyes immediately locked onto an article about West Ham's recent signing and hopeful Trevor Morley. The journalist was singing Lou Macari's praises regards Morley being a good signing for the club and also how he scored a fantastic goal away at Hull City the Saturday before.

The article excited Patch because he'd been a Hammer since he was seven years old. His dad and uncle had taken him and his older brother to their first match and, like all first matches, he believed he could remember everything about the day: the chatter of fans discussing what the manager should have done; the smell of burgers and horse shit; the mean-looking police officers and the meaner looking West Ham fans dressed in their flared trousers, with their long scruffy hair and their claret and sky blue woollen scarves wrapped around their wrists. And once inside Upton Park, Patch also remembered the roar of the fans as the goals went in and the tackles which ensued and the mandatory fighting between the rival fans around the Chicken Run terrace. Patch also remembered how his dad and uncle had laughed and encouraged the West Ham fans as they ploughed into the rival fans. Patch knew the memories of his first football match would stay with him until his last breath left him. He'd also remember how he'd got his nickname. It had been an away match - West Ham's finest taking the Ordinary to Liverpool for the Everton game. Everton were riding high, feeling confident that they'd be the sure winners for that season. Their firm were also reaping the benefits, strutting around, chests pushed out, twiddling their moustaches. It was after the game that the real battle commenced and, on the way back to the train station, a fight had broken out. It hadn't been anything too violent and the clash certainly didn't go down in any hooligan history book, but Patch did take a hell of a blow to his right eye. He never saw the punch coming but he remembered dropping to his knees and bracing himself for the next blow.

It took several weeks for the damaged eye to heal and even then, the socket area never quite looked the same. Along with a small scar, the impact of the blow had left a shadow around the skin and it was this that led to him being called Patch. He'd been Patch since the 84/85 season and now it felt strange and unusual if anyone called him by his real name, which was a boring John. Hand on heart, Patch was happy with being called Patch; it was unique and at least it had come about because of a football related incident and he could use this to trade off.

Just as Patch was finishing the newspaper article, a gush of cold wintery wind hit him in the face. He shuddered and pulled his baseball cap down as far it would go over his forehead. As he did so, he heard someone hurl some abuse at a posh-looking woman being hastily ushered into a Mercedes outside The Dorchester Hotel. He instantly recognised the offender's voice. It was Mancunian. It was his best mate and co-offender Tat. Tat was born and bred in Manchester, with a family history that had once included a longstanding family business in the textile industry; an uncle who been hung for murdering the man who'd been shagging his wife; and, from the 1950's onwards, there wasn't a time when at least one of Tat's family hadn't spent a period in Strangeways.

When Tat was eleven years old he bought his first 7" single. It was That's Entertainment by The Jam. He'd used some of his birthday money to buy the record. He retained vivid memories of the day he bought the record. He'd opened up his cards and presents, readily putting to one side the socks, shirt and jumpers that family members had got him, and which were possibly stolen, and he raced off to Woolworths. Once inside, he made a beeline for the records section, dived into the J's and fished out That's Entertainment. Years after, Tat could still picture himself feeling on top of the world as he's handed over his fifty pence in coppers and silvers, watched the girl at the counter drop the seven inch into a bag and pass it back to him. Tat literally ran back home, he couldn't wait to play *his* record. He'd pushed open the front door (it was always unlocked in those seemingly more safer days), climbed the wooden hill to his bedroom in the converted attic, making sure he spat some abuse at his Abba-adoring sister as she applied more mascara to her eyelashes and fell to his knees, booting up his record player as he did so. He removed his record from the bag, took the 7" single from the pink and white picture sleevewith the images of the pound sign, police car and so forth and carefully placed the record into position. It was at that moment that Tat's heart sank back down to the basement. The record was missing the middle bit which held it in position. Tat swore, replaced the record back into the sleeve and the Woolies bag and retraced his footsteps back into the city centre, where he'd then explained to the woman behind the counter that he couldn't play his birthday present because it had no middle. Thankfully for Tat, she'd been sympathetic and had signalled to another Woolies' worker to go and fetch the missing part. The issue was resolved and once back home, Tat had played the record over and over again.

Buying That's Entertainment opened up a whole new world for the boy Tat. From that day on, he scrimped and saved what money he could and spent it all on buying records. That's Entertainment was also Tat's gateway into The Jam and within weeks he'd saved or stolen enough coppers to purchase a copy of The Jam's Setting Sons album. It was a song on that album called Thick As Thieves that was to become the reason why he picked up his nickname Tat-Thick As Thieves - because whenever any of his friends visited him, he'd always have the song playing on his record player. And Tat was more than pleased with his nickname, especially when he compared it to names bestowed upon others like Piggy, Bully Spud, or just cunt.

The Jam was something that Patch and Tat had connected over. They'd met in the school classroom five years earlier. It was Tat's first day at his new school, having moved down to London with his mum, only the week before. As the two boys sat at their desks Patch had noticed Tat's Adidas Samba trainers and the black Farah strides and he'd approved. They'd got talking and before their first conversation had finished they'd established that they both loved football, albeit one was West Ham and the other Manchester City, clothing labels like Lois, Pringle and Lacoste and The Jam. From that day on, they both felt they had found someone who understood their passion for the Holy Trinity of football, fashion and music. Also, from that day on, Patch and Tat became thick as thieves and were always seen in the company of the other. The only days they weren't seen together was when they went to football. Both followed their teams up and down the country, home and away on cold wet and windy days. For them, football also provided opportunities to have a dig, a laugh and even on occasion an argument, but they never came to blows; they knew they loved each other too much to allow even something as important as football to come between them.

Smiling, Patch leaned against what looked like a newly painted white wall and waited for his friend to catch him up. Tat took his time, he seldom rushed anywhere. Patch noticed Tat was wearing the new red Kickers he'd recently bought from the Boot Store in the King's Road. Hewas wearing a new baseball cap too which Patch vaguely recalled Tat telling him over the phone that he picked up from Mash.

'Here you go,' said Patch shoving the copy of The Sun he'd been reading into Tat's hands, 'Get a load of the bird on page three.'

'Heavily loaded is she?' asked Tat.

'Not half mate,' laughed Patch.

Although the two friends knew their way around the streets of the city, they instinctively found themselves following an ever-increasing larger crowd of ravers, who were evidently also making their way to Trafalgar Square. Ravers snaked their way through the streets passing Green Park Tube Station and onto Jermyn Street, their numbers swelling by the minute. Soon a colourful throng of young people dressed in brightly coloured jackets, some with psychedelic patterns and equally brightly coloured Kicker and desert boots, flared jeans and dungarees soon descended on the already large crowd that had swooped upon Trafalgar Square.

The sight of seven to eight thousand ravers in such an iconic location was thrilling. Each and every raver was feeling the buzz and the excitement of the occasion. And each and every party goer was able to justify their reason for being present.

News that there was going to be a Freedom To Party demonstration had reached Patch and Tat weeks earlier and from the first moment they'd caught wind of it, they knew they'd be offering their support come the day. Initially meeting in Hyde Park, thousands of the most hard-core ravers had come together, intent onmarching into Trafalgar Square to protest at the recent Bills that the government was imposing and fighting for their right to party.

As Patch and Tat dodged and ducked beneath umbrellas, pony tails and perms, they felt grateful that the leading party promoters like Wayne Anthony, Jarvis Sandy, Dave Roberts and Tony Colston Hater had teamed up to rally their raving troops.

Pushing their way deeper into the crowd, both Patch and Tat's attention was drawn towards the familiar voice of the Centreforce DJ coming from a ghetto blaster that some ginger haired female, wearing a garishly coloured taqiyah, had taken the trouble lug around with her. As the DJ provided updates regards the progress of the demonstration to all those ravers driving around in cars in the city streets and the Home Counties, OochyKoochy played in the background.

The tune was a monster tune for Patch and Tat and, as if someone had pressed the start button, at exactly the same moment both lads could be heard chanting Oochy Koochy over and over again. In fact they kept it up, their voices getting loud and louder as they pushed their way nearer to where a modest stage had been erected.

Patch and Tat scanned the faces of the ravers that surrounded them. In the sunken eyes and glazed eyes, they saw themselves. In those eyes they were reminded of the parties they'd been to over the past twelve months. In the eyes of those other ravers they remembered the highs and lows, the meeting points, the convoys, the hours spent tuning into Centreforce, the hours spent trying to avoid the Old Bill and stay that one step ahead. For Patch and Tat, 1989 had been a year they'd never forget or regret. Rave had been their punk and they didn't want it to end. But Thatcher and her cronies had other ideas and they'd brought in laws to put an end to the parties.

The two lads halted twenty yards from the stage where one of the promoters was attempting to deliver his speech, which wasn't an easy feat by any means when faced with an excitable audience who held aloft banners with slogans painted on them such as Peace, Love and Unity, Freedom To Party, We Want To Party and there were even smiley faces with sad smiles, which said so much about how people were feeling.

Patch felt Tat elbow him in the ribs, which was followed by him pointing his chin in the direction to the right of the stage.

'That's your brother's mates from Echos ain't it?' said Tat.

Patch spotted them instantly and nodded.

'Is your brother with them?' asked Tat.

'No, I don't think so. I think Gary was meant to be working today. I've not seen him for ages though,' replied Patch

'Who d'you mean?' asked Tat.

'Rob. I don't know if your paths have ever crossed. Hard as nails he is. One of the older ICF boys. He and Gary got into a lot of scraps together. He used to run a market stall on Romford Market but I'm sure he does anymore. He found ways to make a better crust if you get my meaning.'

Tat grinned, fully understanding the meaning as there were countless tales of hooligans who had carved out alternative careers that didn't need to include travelling the length and breadth of the country smashing people's noses and taxing their designer label clobber.

And Patch's older brother Gary was no angel either. Being six years older than Patch he'd spent chunks of his teenage years in and out of borstal and fighting his way through the various football terraces since the late seventies. He'd been a skinhead before boxing away his Harrington jacket, tonic sta-prest trousers and Dr Marten boots with their yellow laces and taking on the casual look of Pringle jumpers, Lois cords, Fila tracksuits and topping the look off with a pair of Diadora Elite Gold's and a mullet haircut.

Gary was also a regular face in Echos, a club in Bow by the flyover and he'd been part of the group that had purchased plane tickets to go to Ibiza and see for themselves what was starting to explode out there.

It was Gary's acid house record collection that had initially attracted him to house music and it wasn't too long before Patch too found himself stomping his way across the dancefloor at Echos, along with his brother and his brother's mates. For Patch and Tat, it had been a natural progression from the terraces to the dancefloor and they loved acid house music and the feeling and vibe that the music left them with.

Patch and Tat's attention was drawn away from Rob and the Echos boys when they heard Debbie Malone treating the demonstrators with an accapella version of Rescue Me. Malone's singing was well-received by the crowd and people started to cheer and dance.

Tat and Patch joined in with the cheering whilst they weaved their way in and out of the crowd. It felt good to be part of something and they had been feeling part of something special since they first started going to Echoes and going to raves.

As they continued to zig zag their way through ravers, they heard more pirate radio DJ voices. One in particular could be heard clearly because the person who was carrying the ghetto blaster held it above the crowd and the volume was turned up as much as it could go.

Patch and Tat locked onto the DJ's voice. *'You knew it was coming London so get yourselves down to Trafalgar Square ASSSAP because that's where the Freedom to Party demonstration is happening right now. And keep paging in those updates. Word is there's already 7000 ravers on site. C'mon London have your say.*

We know Beggsy and the Lambeth crew, Sappy and his Northolt mob, Loud Wendy, the Lewisham Tarts and representatives from Genesis, Sunrise, Weekend World and Biology are already down there-so big shout going out to all of them. This next track is for you. Keep it locked London and Rave on!'

'Fuckin' hell Patch, what a turn out,' Tat shouted excitedly.

'Brilliant ain't it! Black people, white people, people from the working classes and upper classes, North London, East London, South and West and plenty representing the Home Counties, a fair amount of the 'love thugs' too. This lot are the cream of the rave scene, this lot are hardcore.'

Quoting from one of his favourite tunes Can You Feel It, Tat responded with 'You may be black, you may be white, you may be Jew or Gentile-it don't matter in our house.'

Both lads started to laugh.

'That's typical of you to come out with something like that,' replied Patch before adding, 'But yeah, good one... *and this is fresh,*' which made them laugh even harder.

'Yeah look, its brilliant and the Old Bill can't do anything about it,' Tat continued, just as a lad in a baseball cap with a pony tail poking through the gap in the back pushed a flyer into Tat's hand.

'It's for tonight. There's gonna be a rave that's linked to the demonstration,' the raver said.

'We'll make sure we'll let our mates know. Any idea where the party is going to be mate?' asked Tat.

'I don't know for sure, but from what I've heard it might be worth your while heading in the direction of Hertfordshire.'

'Hertfordshire eh! We've not been up that way since Biology was on back last summer,' shrieked Tat.

'And that was a mental night wasn't it. The good old days eh! Yeah, the goooood old days! You know the score. Anyway, I've got to hand these out, so catch yer later. Have a good one yeah!'

'Yeah you too mate. Have a good one,' Tat replied as he watched the raver slip away into the crowd.

'Here look Tat, over there, that lad's got one of those Stone Island jackets on.'

'Where? Oh yeah!' said Tat clocking the garment.

'It's just like Darren's. It's one of those heat-sensitive jackets. It's mental the way it changes colour with the heat. Darren's went from green to white. Mental!'

Seeing the jacket served as a reminder that Patch and Tat has set their hearts on also possessing similar jackets and even though they knew they cost a small fortune, they also knew they'd been owning their own jackets very soon. They'd been at the cutting edge of what to wear since their casual days and they weren't going to stop being at the vanguard now.

Patch and Tat felt themselves being alerted to some nearby hustle and bustle.

'It's the Old Bill, looks like they've spotted a dealer,' Patch observed.

They hadn't seen it for themselves but they'd heard that MC Chalky White had been arrested by the police. As the afternoon progressed, the police presence had increased and they'd started to throw their weight around ordering ravers to calm down and turn off any ghetto blasters. This of course was starting to rattle the ravers.

Not quite twenty feet away, Patch and Tat could see three Old Bill surrounding a raver who they'd targeted as being a dealer. One officer was rifling through the lad's jacket pockets, another was trying to speak to the lad, who was doing his best to look disinterested and the third officer was arguing with some females who looked like they were trying to tell the officers to leave the lad alone. It was clear that things were getting heated.

As Tat and Patch got closer, Tat started to cry, 'Acieeed, acieeed' and it wasn't long before Patch and other ravers started to join in. The choir were soon joined by another raver who switched his ghetto blaster back on. A moment later Adamski blasted out which ignited the crowd, setting them off like a firework. People started to cheer and dance. The police officers looked nervous, but being dutybound, one officer pointed his finger at the raver with the ghetto blaster and threatened him with arrest if he didn't turn off his ghetto blaster immediately.

Tat was now standing beside the police officer. 'Fuck off will ya, leave the music alone. If you wanna arrest anyone, go and arrest that girl over there with that umbrella – man, look at the size of it, let alone the colour.'

The police officer glared at Tat as he grabbed the ghetto blaster and angrily turned it off. Tat leaned forward and turned it back on. The police officer wasn't expecting that and turned it off again as he warned Tat not to touch it again. Tat of course paid no heed and stretched out his arm in the direction of the ghetto blaster. The officer intervened and grabbed Tat's arm, at which point Patch, who had been standing behind Tat waiting for the officer's next move, grabbed the officer and pushed him.

The other two police officers noticed what was happening and, in an attempt to bring some order to the inevitable, stepped in. As they did, so did another twenty ravers. More pushing and shoving ensued but Tat managed to struggle free from the officer's grip and he and Patch made their escape. Today was not a day to get arrested. They'd had their fair share of run ins with the law and, besides, they had a party to attend that night.

Strolling towards Soho, Patch and Tat talked about the Freedom To Party demonstration, the crowd, the promoter's speeches and their conflict with the Old Bill. They felt something was changing. The mood was shifting. 1989 and their second summer of love really was well and truly coming to an end!

BACK TO THE FUTURE

The Happy Monday's Bummed was spinning on Tat's record player as he sat in his favourite chair, positioned so he could look out of the window from his twenty-third floor flat in another grey and offending high-rise building in East London. Yet another hot rock fell to the floor as he'd taken in another long draw on the joint he'd been smoking.

Tat sucked in the smoke deeply, allowing it time to really fill his lungs to full capacity, before slowly pushing out the sweet smelly smoke through his nostrils and in the direction of the partially opened window. He watched on as the smoke merged with the polluted London air and disappeared. The February sky was grey, cold and unwelcoming.

From Tat's window he had a clear view of the surrounding area. To his left he could see the rooftops of the terraced houses that stretched out as far as the eye could see. He could even see into some of the narrow gardens with their patches of grass, sheds and washing hanging on lines. To the right there were several high-rise blocks of flats that looked just the same as the one he'd lived in for three years and occupied with people just like him. Only some of those people had lived in those flats for twenty years or more. For some of them, it had seemed a good idea at the time. The view straight ahead took in the city with its office buildings, churches and cathedrals and other notable venues that helped to draw in tourists to the nation's capital.

London was where Tat lived, but it wasn't home. For nearly five years he'd tried to make it his home. He'd built a reasonable social group since living in London; he had respect. His teenage years in the city had been fun. School had been a laugh and had never been taken too seriously. But Tat missed football and especially since getting involved in the acid house scene, he had seldom managed to get to matches.

Tat still had family in Manchester and he was still in contact with some friends who he'd grown up before moving down South. He also kept an eye on what was happening up North and got excited by what he had heard happening in the infamous Hacienda Club and with Manchester groups like the Stone Roses and the Happy Mondays. And only recently he and Patch had talked about blocking out a weekend and getting up to Manchester so they could go to the Hacienda and see for themselves what all the 'noise' was about.

Just as Tat took another pull on his joint, he heard the sound of a key being pushed into the door lock and a few clicks later, the sound of the flat's front door being pushed open. He knew it was Patch because Patch was the only other person who possessed a key to Tat's home.

Without saying a word Patch walked straight over to Tat, removed the joint from Tat's mouth, put it in his own mouth and plonked himself down on a large cushion that was littered with hot rock burns. He then rifled in his coat pocket and pulled out a torn packet of Rizlas and some fags. He looked up at Tat and held out his hand. Tat understood and tossed him a small cellophane bundle that contained some hash.

Patch stretched out his hand and pulled towards him the Bummed album sleeve, which he knew would serve as a surface upon which he could build his joint. Lazyitis was playing which meant the album was coming to an end.

'Ere bung us your Zipper,' Patch demanded.

Tat playfully dangled the lighter in the air before throwing it to Patch. Patch caught the lighter with ease and continued with his task of removing three Rizlas, tearing and sticking them together to form a shape he could then sprinkle in the tobacco which he'd removed from the cigarette. He opened the small bag Tat had handed him and broke off a small bit of hash, then proceeded to burn some off using the Zipper and carefully sprinkling the hash along the length of the Rizla papers. Building a joint was a process Patch had been doing since he was fourteen and he could do it with his eyes closed and in any state - and he'd certainly been in some states.

WIth the task completed, Patch popped the joint into his mouth and lit it. As he did so he put the Bummed album sleeve that was now covered in bits of tobacco and Rizla to one side and made himself more comfortable on the cushion.

'I bumped into The Ozzard of Whizz around the cafe. I could have done without him really. I mean I had only just sat down to crack on with my full English.'

'I s'pose he looked like he'd been up all night, did he?' asked Tat.

'Too right he did. Eyes sunk so far back into his head, his eye lashes were probably tickling his arsehole. Anyway, he sat down and started waffling on about that Genesis party he went to back in December. He must have described that warehouse in Aldgate to me about a dozen times before handing me this flyer, nicking one of my sausages and fucking off. Ere have a butchers,' said Patch leaning towards Tat to hand him the flyer.

'Let's have a look then,' said Tat. 'Yeah, it looks sound. It's a Biology party.'

Tat studied the flyer, admiring the artwork before accepting the joint which Patch had offered him.

'Do you remember the first time we met The Ozzard?' asked Patch.

'It was at the Trip wasn't it? Purple Ohms or maybe Window Panes if I remember right?' recalled Tat.

'Na, Micro-dots and strong, weren't they?' Patch corrected.

'Oh yeah! You nicked a torch off of some girl and spent most of the night running on the spot and shining the torch in people's faces. You were definitely having a good one that night.'

Tat eased himself out of the chair he'd been sitting on and ambled over to the record player. He dropped to his knees and removed Bummed because it had ended and the room was silent, and Tat didn't like a silent room. He started to flick through his collection of vinyl.

'I don't remember any of it mate. I was outta my tree. But I do remember we did some more micro-dots the week after too and you spent most of the night just staring at your hands. Yeah it wasn't wise to drop too many of those little fuckers. I'm sure there must still be people getting flashbacks off of them.'

'Have you ever had any flashbacks Patch? I mean like a proper freaky flashback moment, where you're like what the fook is going on?'Tat asked, feeling chuffed he'd found his Frankie Knuckles album on Trax; an album he'd recently bought but thought had loaned out and not had it returned.

'Only once! I got some work where I had to deliver some boxes of 'I don't know what the fuck was in them' down to Maidstone. It wasn't even like the day after I had taken some acid. It wasn't even a Monday morning; it was a Wednesday I think. I remember that all of a sudden, and without any warning, everything went a beautiful pink colour. I mean it was lovely, the sky was pink, the trees, the fields, everything went pink. It only lasted a few seconds and then everything went back to being normal again. But it did freak me out and for a few seconds I did feel a bit strange. But that has been the only time and that'll do 'fuck' you very much. Acid is good, great even, but it's not wise to take too much of it. You know I've heard stories that there are old hippies from the 60s who have permanent smiles on their faces because they took too much acid andit made them smile and grin so much that it fixed their faces. I dunno if it's true or not. It's just what I've heard.'

Tat shrugged his shoulders, unsure how he should respond to Patch's story. Instead he handed the joint back to his friend. Patch had now sunken deep into the cushion and was also wearing one of Tat's bucket hats.

'My brother phoned last night. Said he'd been to see The Stone Roses again. That's about the fifth time he's been to see them now. He literally does rave about them,' Tat informed.

'Well, yeah, them and the Happy Mondays.'

'We have to make sure we get tickets for the Roses when those Alexandra Palace tiks go on sale. I'll be proper pissed off if I miss it.'

'We'll sort it, you know we will,' Patch assured, as he grabbed Elephant Stone and started to check out the record's cover.

'Fuckin' mental cover isn't it? Not only is John Squire a top guitarist, he's also an artistic genius.'

'Yep, can't deny he is pretty handy with a paint brush. I'd imagine on acid you'd end up staring at the record cover for hours.'

'For sure, but then the same can be said of any of Pollock's work.'

'Who the bollocks is Pollock's when he's at home then?' asked Patch looking confused.

Tat rifled through a pile of magazines and books until he found what he was looking for. It was a book about Jackson Pollock. He slung the book in Patch's direction, which landed on the Bummed album scattering bits of tobacco and Rizla paper everywhere. Both lads ignored the mess.

'Jackson Pollock was an American artist. He did a lot of paintings in what they call Drip Painting. John Squire is very much inspired by him.'

'How comes you know so much then? This book is mostly just pictures.'

'I don't sit around here all the time just getting stoned. I go down the library and read books too sometimes,' Tat protested.

For no particular reason, Patch removed the bucket hat from his head and launched it at Tat.

'He died in the 1950s. Car crash! He was only 44,' said Tat who suddenly looked sad and reflective.

'Fuckin' ell, really! So, it was bollocks for Pollock's,' Patch laughed as he flicked through the pages of the Pollock book which didn't interest him at all.

'So, we're going to this Biology rave yeah?' Patch enquired.

Tat studied the Biology rave flyer again.

'For sure-it'll be mental. We gonna need to see The Ozzard though. Do you wanna do acid or ecstasy tonight?

Patch shoved his hand into the pocket of his jeans and pulled out what cash he had. He counted it out loud so that Tat could hear.

'Sweet! I can stretch to an E. How about you?' Patch asked, smiling.

'Sound! You know the score,' Tat replied smiling back, and then he turned up the volume on the record player a notch or three.

Patch hung around Tat's flat for the remainder of the morning. He needed time to allow his breakfast to go down and he wasn't in any rush to be anywhere; after all there wasn't any football to go and watch. Instead Patch was content to amble through the day, grab a swift pint on his way back home and catch the scores as they came in on the tele in the comfort of his parents' living room.

Following a short kip and some tea comprising fish fingers and a jacket potato, having a shit and shower and getting dressed, he was back in his motor and had driven the five minutes back to Tat's flat.

Tat hadn't left his flat all day. He was more than content to just play records, smoke more joints and gaze out of the window. His afternoon had only been interrupted by the sound of the couple in the flat above him having a row, a bath and some beans on toast.

When Patch returned to Tat's flat he found his friend kneeling on the floor in front of his stack system twiddling with some knobs. Patch could hear that Tat had tuned into Sunrise; there was a tune playing and a DJ putting some shouts out but the sound was distorted. Tat wasn't the most patient of blokes and Patch could sense that he was getting more and more frustrated.

'Here get out the way, let me have a go,' Patch suggested.

Tat surrendered and moved to one side.

'Come on...,' Patch spoke calmly as he managed to lock onto the pirate. 'Tune DJ. Go on my son!'

Numero Uno started to play. Tat, who by now was busy building a joint, nodded in agreement. Feeling pleased with himself, Patch stood up and walked over to the cushion he'd been sitting on only a few hours earlier and plonked himself back down onto it.

There was a knock on the door. Patch frowned wondering who that could be. Tat took his time to answer the door. It was The Ozzard of Whizz. The Oz had been a source of all sorts of 'goodies' for years. Although older than Patch and Tat, he'd gone to the same school as them and, even during those not so innocent school days, he'd been pushing amphetamines. It was the speed, the whizz, that earned him his nickname. The Oz had a keen eye for an opportunity and by '87 he was dealing LSD and making connections with people in Amsterdam who were now supplying him with large bags of ecstasy. The Oz was the go-to man for the pills, thrills and bellyaches.

'Hey up Tat, here comes the nice!' cried Patch, pleased to see who it was.

'Come in mate? It's fookin' cold out there tonight and you must feel it, there's no meat on your bones,' said Tat inviting the visitor in.

'Less of the cheek, but no I can't hang around, plenty of others to get around to tonight before everything livens right up. You're not my only customers you know...even though you might be two of my greediest,' The Oz replied.

'If you don't want our dollar Ozzard, you just have to say, there's plenty of others now serving up ya know,' Patch replied jokingly.

'Again, less of the cheek, and feel free, I've been that busy lately I might have to start taking on some extra members of staff.'

'That so?' asked Patch.

'Too right! There are house parties popping up all over town now. I'm like a house doctor on call six nights a week and it's doing my nut in. D'yareckon you two might be up for helping out with a bit of business? What you'll make will pay for your weekends and put a lot more vinyl in your boxes.'

'Na, not for us mate we're gonna be too busy with our own pirate radio station soon,' announced Tat.

'Our what?' Patch laughed.

'Is that so? Sweet! What's it gonna be called?' The Oz said, sounding curious.

'We haven't got as far as a name yet,' Tat replied, gathering the tools he needed to build himself another joint.

'We haven't got as far as having a conversation about it yet you Northern monkey,' Patch coughed.

'Sounds like you two need a team meeting. Anyway, I can't hang about so what d'ya want?'

'Two Eeeeezzzpleeeeezzzzeee,' said Patch, pulling out some tenners and handed them to the Oz.

'Ere you go! Forty dollars it is,' The Oz said, accepting the money and handing over the small white pills. 'I take it you're heading to Biology later?'

'Too right. We're keeping it locked to the pirates to get the latest about meeting points and what have yer,' Tat revealed.

'What have you heard? Any idea where the party is?' Patch asked, knowing full well that the Oz more than likely did know. He was well connected with what was happening, but also preferred to keep some things to himself. It was business related.

'All I heard is that it'll be over the West. I dunno anymore than that. If I did I'd tell yer.'

'Yeah thanks pal, appreciate it,' replied Patch trying to sound appreciative.

There was a moment of awkward silence as the radio reception dipped out. The silence seemed to outstay its welcome.

'So, there you go and here I go. Have a good un.'

And with that, Tat saw The Oz to the door and he was gone. Tat made a beeline back to where he'd spent the afternoon sitting and searched for the Biology flyer, which he found stuck between some pages of the Pollock book. He had no idea how it had got there and, for a moment, that bothered him.

'I only looked at the picture earlier,' Tat mumbled before he started to read out aloud the information printed onto the flyer. 'Biology 1989 World In Action. The DJs include Trevor Fung, Paul Anderson, Paul Oakenfold, Lisa Loud and Norman Jay. Location film studios and with a VIP room and Lounge. Tickets available from Black Market Records, Red Records and Vinyl Zone.'

Patch perked up and snatched the flyer from Tat's hand.

'And it's at Linford Street. I know where that is. It's one of the roads just offWandsworth Street in Battersea. I remember being on the run from some Chelsea after one match back in '86. There are some studios down there...the Linford Film Studios.'

'There you go then. Sorted! What's the time now?' asked Tat.

'Half nine,' Patch replied after checking his wrist watch.'It's a bit early. But let's go and start the motor up and let's head over that way anyway.'

Patch was standing up now. He looked excited and vigorously rubbed his hands together, a habit he had when he got fired up about something. 'And as soon as we park up I'm gonna swallow that E.'

'We've got plenty of time. The party won't get going until midnight. Roll one for the journey.' Tat handed Patch his gear which Patch willingly accepted.

'Anyway-pirate radio station-our own pirate radio station! What the fuck were you going on about?' asked Patch.

'Oh yeah, I was meaning to talk to you about that.'

'I'm sure you were. So, go on then, what's on your mind?'

'The pirates are gonna get big. Proper big! There are gonna be the ravevine for many a raver. For many it will be the only way they'll get to find out about meeting points, where the raves are gonna be held and also hear the latest imports and all the best new records. Whilst I've been sat in my chair, I've also been pondering on another idea.'

'I'm listening. I'm all fuckin' ears mate.'

'What I'm thinking is that we can set up the equipment in my flat and run the station from my flat. It's high up enough, so it should work well enough, you know get a decent signal and all that. We could put the transmitter on the roof. No one will ever know. I've never known anyone to go up there.'

'And what's this other idea then?' asked Patch as he rolled the joint.

'Ravestock!' replied Tat with a sparkle in his red eye.

'Ravestock!'

'Yeah Ravestock. We use our pirate radio station as a means to promote what will be the biggest rave that had ever happened. I mean a party that will be so epic it will go down in history as one of the greatest events of all time. I mean this will be our answer to Woodstock.'

Patch was used to Tat's mad hare-brained ideas and what he was hearing now was up there with the best of them. But Patch would never burst his mate's bubble, so he just nodded and went along with it.

'And what about a name for the pirate station? You got any suggestions?'

'Well I have a few-Resurrection FM, Ignition FM, IndepenDANCE FM, Eclipse FM...'

'Eclipse FM sounds alright. How did you come up with that?'

Tat, who had now sat down in his chair by the window, leaned forward so that his face was just two feet from Patch's.

'Yeah sounded like the better one to me too. It came to me after I remembered a hairdressers my sister used to work in called 'He Clips', and that made me laugh.'

Patch put the joint in his mouth and checked his watch.

'Okay mate. Well we can natter more about your ideas in the motor, I've got a tape I want to put on, it's got Adonte's Dreams on it. C'mon then, it's time to get going.'

And with that Patch stood up, grabbed Tat's bucket hat, placed it onto Tat's head and pulled it down hard.

'Let's go mentalllllllll,' Tat cried as he grabbed his coat.

THE FRIDAY NIGHT SHUFFLE

March had been a quieter month for Patch and Tat. Both had picked up some labouring work in Kent, so their days were full and knackering. But, being twenty years old and feeling bulletproof, most of the mid-week evenings were spent either smoking joints in Tat's flat or sipping a few beers in the Victory pub that was located near the estate where Tat lived.

The Victory was busy most nights and the majority of its clientele were tough individuals. They were a mix of tradesmen, printers and market stall holders. They also spanned three generations, which meant you had you had dads and uncles who'd been mods in the mid-sixties, older brothers who'd been skinheads and then suedeheads in the late and then boot boys and smoothies going into the seventies, and then punks and then skinheads and mods again. By the early to mid-eighties the new young generation were casuals and by 1988 most were already heavily into acid house. If anyone happened to dip into any of these chaps' prized record collections, they'd be packed full of gems covering such labels as Tamla Motown, Blue Beat, Trojan and artists and groups from Georgie Fame to Judge Dread, David Bowie to roots reggae, to The Clash, The Jam and a plethora of jazz funk, soul and disco. From '87 onwards it was about Chicago House music and the best of hip hop. And of course, going to football and being dressed in the latest terrace fashions was paramount.

It had been one Wednesday night in The Victory whilst Tat and Patch were kicking back with a pint and playing pool that they bumped into one of Gary's mates. The three of them got chatting about the various acid house parties they'd attended and the ones they'd heard had been popping up, and this led to them debating the rights and wrongs of the recent trouble that had occurred at a Labyrinth party over in Canning Town. They had all been at the party on the night and each had witnessed some of the incidents.

They concluded their conversation by agreeing it was a good idea for the promoter to move his club night to the Four Aces Club in Dalton as it was licensed premises and they'd have better security to back them up.

That same night, on their way back to Tat's flat, Patch and Tat agreed to go to Labyrinth that coming weekend. They also agreed that they needed a shopping trip too.

The labouring job that Tat and Patch had been on was finished by midday on the Friday. This meant they had their opportunity to spend a relaxing afternoon in The Victory, talk about their pirate radio station and what to call it, and be bright eyed and bushy tailed come Saturday. West Ham were away but Patch had decided not to go as he and Tat had agreed on other plans.

It was approaching 11am when Patch arrived at Tat's flat. He found Tat sitting in his usual place smoking a joint. Sterling Void's Runaway was being played. Patch tossed Tat a pair of Timberland boots, removed the joint from his friend's hand and waited whilst Tat put on his boots.

A few minutes later they were on their way to the bus stop that would take them into the West End. The journey went quickly and they mostly talked about how they'd get their hands on the equipment they'd need to set up their own pirate radio station.

With time on their hands and the fresh sense of spring in the air, they decided to jump off the bus at Oxford Circus and take a casual stroll to D'Arblay Street. It took them fifteen minutes to get to Fish. Fish was a hairdresser's they'd been going to since it opened in 1987. They had come to know Paul, the owner, well and they always looked forward to seeing each other and having a catch up.

It was Patch who entered the shop first.

'Awright mate, how's tricks? said Patch sounding chipper.

Fish, dressed in a sweat shirt from Mash, baggy jeans and some green desert boots was sat at the counter near the door. He had been flicking through an edition of Boys Own. He instantly looked up as he recognised a familiar voice.

'Sweet, it's all good Patch, Tat, how's it going mate?'

'Sound, keeping busy. You know the score,' replied Tat, also sounding pleased to see Fish.

'I hear you are starting up your own pirate. Is that right?' Fish enquired.

'Blimey word gets around fast. That's right though,' Patch moaned.

Patch and Tat could see that Fish's interest had perked up. He put down the copy of Boys Own and, keeping his eyes on his visitors, took a sip of his coffee.

'Nice one. So, what are you gonna call it?' asked Fish.

'Eclipse,' announced Tat. 'What d'ya think?'

'Yeah, I like it lads. It's got that ring about it. You know like the name of those acid house parties that have been going off all over London.'

'Anyway, how did you hear about our idea? I mean we don't want every Jack and Jill knowing about our plans. Gotta be discreet, yeah!' Patch said placing his index finger on his lips.

'The Ozzard of Whizz popped into the shop a couple of weeks ago. He had a delivery. You know what I mean,' Fish revealed.

Tat frowned and Patch screwed up his nose.

'Well I hope he's not telling every one of his customers. The last thing we need are the Old Bill closing us down before we've even played our first record,' Tat grumbled.

Fish took a large gulp of his coffee and smiled.

'No, it'll be fine. Give the Oz some credit. Anyway, what are you doing around here today?'

Patch picked up the Boys Own that Fish had been reading and thumbed through the first few pages. He usually bought copies of the fanzine but for some reason hadn't purchased that particular issue.

'We're gonna pick up some bits from Black Market and have a nosey around Duffer too,' Patch informed.

Patch resumed looking at the Boys Own but continued to speak to Fish, 'So how's the Friday night shuffles going Fish?'

'Still happening! The lads come in here after work on Fridays to get their hair done, then they shuffle along to Duffer to buy some clobber and then they dive into Black Market to pick up a couple imports-you know something new to whack on the turntable to help build up the buzz before they head out on a Friday night. I tell you lads, London is buzzing at the moment. You can feel something's really building up. It's gonna explode. It's gonna be mental.'

'Yeah, its brilliant ain't it? It's the Second Summer of Love,' Tat almost cried.

'And it'll be wilder than the first one,' Patch added.

Patch had had enough of the Boys Own and attempted to hand it to Tat. But Tat's attention was drawn elsewhere. At the back of the shop was a female sorting out some bottles. She looked to be in her late teens, had short-ish dark brown hair and was wearing a white tee shirt, some black dungarees and wore Converse boots that matched her tee shirt and dungarees.

Fish and Patch noticed Tat's interest but remained quiet whilst they observed Tat studying the girl.

'So, who's the new girl then?' asked Tat keeping his eyes on the girl.

'Her name's Kim. She's my new stylist. Lives down Lewisham way.Her older brother's a bit of a known face around The Den. Still fancy her then do you?'

'She's a looker for sure. How did you find her?' Tat replied unconcerned about the Millwall connection.

'She came to one of my rent parties last year and I was introduced to her. I remember she'd just come back from Ibiza. I think she'd been hanging out there with that lot that are involved with Shoom. She's a lovely girl, big into her House music too.'

Before Tat had an opportunity to probe further, Fish cleared his throat.

'Kim, come and join us, I want to introduce a couple of mates to you.'

Kim acknowledged the invitation and stopped stacking the bottles that she'd been wiping clean and putting into some kind of order. She smiled as she strolled towards the three males. As she got closer, Tat got a clearer look at her features. She had long dark eye lashes, large brown friendly eyes, bright red lipstick, high cheek bones and her dimples showed as she smiled. She was a stunner.

'Kim this is Tat and this is Patch. Tat, Patch this is Kim.'

'Fish tells us that…'Patch began, but Tat butted in.

'Fish says you're big into your House music. That's sound that. Got any faves at the mo? Fish says you've been to Ibiza too. How was that? Where did you stay? What's Amnesia like? Did you…'

'Slow down mate. It's not a police interview,' said Patch waving his hands in the air.

'Nice to meet you Patch, nice to meet you too Tat. Strange names! How did they come about then?' Kim spoke softly.

'Well his surname is Egbert. Fuck knows where that came from. But as a kid he loved reading stories about pirates.' Kim folded her arms. She wasn't convinced.

'He's called Tat because it sounds like twat and he's from Manchester and I think up north that means cunt. But we try not to hold the northerner thing against him,' Patch giggled.

'Ah OK,' Kim nodded, before continuing with 'Yes, when I was in Ibiza I did go to Amnesia. I got to know quite a few lads from Manchester. They were a laugh. And yes, I do like my House music and if I had to choose a few of my fave tracks I would have to say Voodoo Ray, Lack Of Love and Your Love.'

'Sound choices those. I would put all three of those in my top ten too,' Tat agreed, sucking up to the pretty young thing.

'We're sure you would,' Fish and Patch mumbled in unison, which Kim heard. She could also sense some embarrassment rising in Tat.

'Fish tells me you're thinking of starting up your own pirate radio station. Is that right?' Kim said stepping in.

'Yes, we are. It's gonna be called Eclipse and we're gonna run it from my flat,' Tat answered.

'Again, slow down mate. Walls have ears you know. If you wanna broadcast what we're doing, just page everyone or get some flyers printed with your name and address on it.'

Tat looked at his best mate and shrugged his shoulders.

'Don't worry. Your secret is safe with me,' Kim stepped in again and made an action that was meant to say she was zipping her lips. As Tat focussed on Kim's lips, the door opened and a customer entered. Patch, Fish and Kim looked to see who it was. Tat's eyes didn't leave Kim's lips and Kim caught this.

'This is my 12.30 so I had better see to her. Hey, nice to meet you lads. Maybe I'll see you again,' said Kim with a big friendly smile.

'We will be at Clinks...' Tat rushed.

'Right lads I'll see you later yeah. Have a good un,' Fish said placing his hand onto Tat's shoulder and grinning.

'Yeah catch you later Fish,' replied Patch as he started to push Tat out of the shop.

'Yeah see yer later mate,' said Tat to Fish, before yelling out to Kim, 'See you later Kim.'

Kim sent Tat on his way with a wave and a smile and, leaning over to a radio, turned up the volume as Right BeforeMy Eyes started to play.

Tat felt like he was walking on air as he followed Patch to the Duffer shop, which was only a few steps away from Fish's. A monster of a hit from the FPI Project was playing as they entered the shop.

The shopkeeper, a man in his mid-twenties wearing a baseball cap was standing by the shop counter folding some sweat shirts. There were four other people in the shop who were checking out what was being sold.

The shopkeeper glanced up as Patch and Tat entered the shop and nodded. A rack of sweat shirts caught Patch's eye and he raced towards it. Tat watched on as Patch removed various garments and checked them out. Patch found one that excited him and held it up for Tat to see.

'Yeah I like this one. This would go perfect with my green desert boots.'

'Sound,' said Tat, 'but this would go with your red Kickers, your blue Wallabees or those purple desert boots you got the other week. In fact, there's so many colours in this, it'll probably go with every item of clobber that you've got mate.'

Patch laughed. He had to agree.

'Ere this is a piece of you mate,' said Tat tossing Patch a baseball cap which he promptly put on his head and checked in the mirror.

'Yeah it's alright that. I'm gonna get it. And this is a bit of you,' Patch replied handing Tat a yellow bucket hat with Duffer written in big letters on it.

'Too right, yeah that's a bit of me. I could do with another one,' Tat agreed.

'You bet you do. That other one stinks of sweat. Every time I enter your flat it's the first thing that I can smell...well that and hash. But look at you now mate. I remember when you first moved down to London. Your wardrobe consisted of a few Fred Perry's, some flares, a snorkel parka and a beaten up old pair of Adidas Sambas.'

'That was a sound look. It's what we wore on the terraces for a while. We had left behind all that Pringle jumper and Fila tracky look. Although we did hold on to the Cecil Gee G2 range-that was quality gear,' Tat shot back.

At this point the shopkeeper piped up. He'd been tuning in to Patch and Tat's conversation.

'Bollocks mate! Ere what's your mate going on about? You couldn't fault all that Fila, Sergio Tacchini, Kappa, Lacoste track suits and kagools, Lois cords and jeans, Pringle and Lyle &Scott jumpers - all topped off with a smart pair of Adidas Forest Hills, Trim Trabbs or Diadora Golds. Quality-Sweet!' the shopkeeper argued.

'Quality Street! Is that what you said?' questioned Tat.

'The whole casual thing, all that football terrace wear took its lead from the London clubs. Everybody knows it,' The shopkeeper continued.

'Well that's a load of bollocks and you Southerners know it. The whole casual thing started up North on *our* football terraces. You all know the stories of the Scousers venturing into Europe, robbing from their sports shops and bringing them back to Liverpool to sell to their mates down the pub. There weren't any London clubs playing in Europe so they didn't even know about the labels like Kappa and Fila.'

'And you continue to believe that, but I tell you what, before I worked here I worked in Stuarts in Shepherds Bush and on match days the shop would be packed full of Northern lads, lads from Manchester, Stoke, Derby, Hull and Leeds buying up...well sometimes nicking...bright coloured electric blue Lois cords and even brighter yellow Pringle jumpers.'

'It's true mate. Me and my mates were always lurking around Stuarts on Saturday mornings and the place was full of Northerners. We used to wait for them around Shepherds Bush Market Station and then chase them up the side streets and tax them. I remember one occasion when we chased a group of Burnley lads up Loftus Road. They were outnumbered and had clearly eaten more pies than us throughout the season-and it was still only November- and we caught them, had a rumble and then taxed those that hadn't legged it off. I got myself a new pair of faded blue Fiorucci jeans and a white Fila roll neck out of it. One of my mates even nicked the lad's trainers. We left him crying on some doorstep. We didn't steal his money though, so he could have gone back to Stuarts to get some clothes…or the market for that matter…they used to do snide range of Lacoste gear. They were good times,' said Patch offering support to the shopkeeper.

'You horrible bastards! Mind you, you all got the same treatment when you came up North. Although I also knew a few lads from my area that would go and wander the streets and nick clothes off people's washing lines. There would have been many angry lads returning home from a day's work only to discover that their mams had washed their favourite bloodied jumpers and polo shirts, hung them on the washing lines and had them robbed by some scally. It's just the way it was then.'

The shopkeeper sat on a stool by the counter and grabbed a box of JPS. He popped one into his mouth and offered Patch and Tat one, which they accepted. The shopkeeper continued.

'It's always been like it. I used to think it was just something that happened to us casuals, but it wasn't a new thing at all. There was some fella in his mid-forties who came in here a couple months back. I think he was lost or something coz the gear in here is hardly up his street. But we got talking and it turned out he had been a Mod in London in the 60s. He was right at the heart of it too, buying clothes from Carnaby Street, spending his nights in the Marquee watching The Who and riding his Vespa down to places like Margate and Brighton on bank holidays and 'avin it out with the rockers. And he told me stories of the pills they used to take-you know French Blues and Purple Hearts - and also how they used to nick clobber off other Mods. Only they called it rolling back then rather than taxing. So, it's always gone on. It's just part of our culture. The way it is. It's just a bit of fun really and nobody ever gets really hurt-just their pride most of the time.'

Sensing some boredom arising in him regards the topic of their conversation, Tat decided he'd had enough. He had lost count of the amount of conversations and arguments he'd had regards the origins of the football casual.

'And a few blisters on their feet. Ere mate I'll have this off of yer,' said Tat fishing out some five pound notes from his back pocket.

'And me this,' added Patch also handing over a bundle of pretty green, which the shopkeeper happily accepted and mumbled back, 'You know the score.'

Patch and Tat said their goodbyes to the shopkeeper and left the shop with their new hats on their heads and still some hard-earned cash burning in their pockets.

The first thing that grabbed Patch and Tat's attention as they entered Black Market Records was the pleasing sound of Krush's House Arrest, the tune had been one of the reasons why both Tat and Patch had got into house music and even though it was a couple of years old, it still sounded as fresh to them as it did when they first heard it in various clubs dotted across London.

Venturing deeper into the small record shop, they headed straight for the counter where a male, known to the regulars as Spinner,wasdressed head to toe in Rat Pack clothing that he'd recently purchased from Mister USA in Woodgreen. Spinner stood sticking price labels on a stack of imports which had been delivered that morning. He vigorously chewed gum as he engrossed himself in his task and failed to even notice his new customers standing in front of him. Patch coughed.

'Awright mate, Nicky not in today then? asked Patch.

Spinner looked up and, seeing who it was, he smiled. He had got to know a lot of ravers and record collectors whilst working at Black Market. Patch and Tat had become familiar faces due their frequent visits and parting of cash, as they purchased the latest imports and any old house classic that helped to boost their ever-increasing record collections. Black Market was also one of the major outlets to pick up flyers for raves and buy tickets for them too.

'Alright Patch. No mate, Nicky's not here. He's got some other business to attend to but he might be in later. I know he's deejaying at some rave tonight too, so he might just avoid Soho altogether today.' Spinner took a break from his task and appeared to be relived to do so.

'Fair nuff I suppose. Anyway, so how are tricks and what's new in? Tat enquired.

Spinner pushed to one side the stack of records he'd been pricing up and, with effort and sighs, dragged a box of records out from under the counter. With more huffing and puffing he plonked the box onto the counter and opened the box lid. Diving in, he pulled out two records.

'Here you go,' he said, 'And have a listen to this one.'

He made a gesture with his hands which invited Tat and Patch to dip their hands into the box. As they did so, Spinner removed a record from its shiny black sleeve, wiped the vinyl with a cloth and, removing Krush from the turntable, placed the new record onto the deck. As the tune crackled and started to play, he nodded his head in time with the bass drum beat. It took only a glance up at his two customers and grin before Tat and Patch also joined in with the head nodding.

'You know the score,' said Spinner, noting his customers' approval.

Patch and Tat listened to the song as they continued to nod their heads and search through the records in the box, some of which grabbed their attention and were put to one side.

'What's it called then?' asked Patch.

'It's Paradise,' replied Spinner, getting deeper into the beat and embracing the vocals.

'I'll take that,' said Patch flashing a look at Tat, who in turn nodded.

More ravers entered the shop and Spinner nodded to them. As they passed the counter, one of their group grabbed some of the flyers that were there for the taking and could well inform where they'd end up that night.

For the next thirty minutes Tat, Patch and Spinner chatted and played records. Ravers came and went and cash was exchanged as records and tickets for raves were bought.

'So how long has the shop been here now? Must be coming up to its first birthday?' asked Tat.

'Yeah not far off. There's been some talk of having some kind of a party.'

'It's something to celebrate. The shop's been doing really well. It's always full of people, especially on Saturdays,' Patch pitched in.

'This last year has been mental,' said Spinner. 'We have people coming in from all over the place now: London, the Home Counties and even further really. Since the raves kicked off, they come in to buy their tickets for the parties. They know that we're an official outlet for buying tickets for the raves and the various promoters like us and trust us, and the punters know it's all kosher. So, everyone's a winner and long may it continue. Plus, there are more and more people taking an interest in house music so they come here to pick up the latest tunes. If I had a quid for every time some raver came in here on a Monday morning asking for some tune they heard at some rave on Saturday, I'd be buying my first Lotus by now.'

Patch and Tat laughed. They'd been in the same situation themselves, where they'd heard a tune at a rave but had had no idea who the artist was or the title of the track, and this would especially annoy Patch. But they also liked the thrill of the chase and the efforts to seek out what the song was - and the staff in Black Market had done them a turn on many an occasion.

'Like we do!' laughed Patch.

'Ha, not exactly. You usually know what you're after. Most of the time some kid comes in here and begins with '*I heard a tune on Saturday night, I dunno who it's by, but it goes something like this*' and then they start humming it and then within seconds they're dancing in the middle of the shop. I usually know the tune they've been trying to hum but sometimes it's just impossible, so I just say '*yeah, I know, it's this one*' and I hand them some import which they buy, take it home, whack it on their home system and love it anyway. It's all good.'

Patch and Tat laughed.

41

'What's this like?' asked Tat handing Spinner a record that he'd selected from the box.

'It's brilliant. 'Ere have a listen,' he replied and put You Are My One And Only by Seduction on the turntable.

As the record spun, Spinnertold Patch and Tat that he'd heard on the rave-vine that they were putting plans in place to start up their own pirate radio station. Tat and Patch knew they could trust Spinner, so told him that his information was correct and that they'd be sourcing the equipmentthey'd need like pagers and transmitters and how they'd be needing to add more records to their collection and getting the latest imports was going to be paramount for them, especially if they wanted to be a credible pirate station that could keep up with the other pirates like Sunrise and another new onethey'd heard about that was due to start up in East London called Centreforce.

Patch and Tat explained that they intended to set up the equipment in Tat's flat and install the transmitter on the roof of his block. Their theory was that their operation would go unnoticed by the Old Bill and any other nosey parkers and they'd serve the underground ravers with the latest tunes and information about meeting points and so forth for the raves. When they spoke, they did so with all the buzz and enthusiasm that reflected the feel of what was going in London at the time.

By the time Patch and Tat left Black Market Records they were stoked up and thrilled with their new purchases which included the Seduction record, alongside a bunch of others that included Index, Impedence, Raven Maize and of course the Ellis D track 'It's Paradise'.

YOUR LOVE

A group of ravers clustered around a burger van that had positioned itself just a few feet from the entrance to where Clinks was located. Tat and Patch had heard the rumours that the burger van not only cooked up a mouth-watering burger, but the owners also served up some of the finest E's in London. Knowing this, ravers chancing their luck, bought their burgers and pills and washed them down with a gulp of Lucozade before they headed off into the club. There had also been rumours that sometimes the security firm who manned the entrance would search the party-goer and, when they found any hash, they'd break it in half and give one half back to the raver and keep the other half for themselves - and being that they are mean-looking blokes, no one argues with them. Besides it's a small price, however unlucky, to pay just to ensure entry to the Clinks club - and Clinks is one of the liveliest places to be in London on a Saturday night.

'Who knows what ghosts and memories hang in the dark cells and corners of this place,' said Patch, as he and Tat followed a few steps behind some ravers from Kent, who had also paid their entrance fee and were heading towards the door of Clinks.

'What you going on about mate?' asked Tat who was feeling the apprehension and the buzz that awaited him inside the club.

Tat and Patch had started attending the RiP events the previous year and each time they went, they'd had the time of their lives. There was never a bad night when the likes of Mr C and Evil Ed had control of the decks. Nights at RiP ensured a wild crowd that loved to blow their whistles, cheer, hug, smile, sweat and dance, dance, dance - and of course partake in the LSD that was easily available to get their hands on.

'This was once one of London's most notorious prisons,' Patch continued.

'That right?' replied Tat not sounding particularly interested and checking the time on his wristwatch, which reminded him it had gone midnight.

'It's said the prison's name came from the sound of the blacksmith's hammer closing the irons on the wrists and ankles of the prisoners.'

Patch was still trying to provide Tat with a history lesson as Tat pushed him into the dark club. There were bodies crammed into every available space, most danced, happy to live for a few hours in a world of their own, and world they wanted to be a part of.

The music, a mix of Sterling Void's Runaway Girl, was very loud which gave the impression that the room was shaking. Patch pointed his chin in the direction of some known Chelsea Headhunters who appeared to be happily conversing with some of the top boys from Arsenal and Tottenham's firms.

'I heard someone use the term 'love thugs' the other week,' shouted Tat leaning into Patch so he could hear. 'That's what some people are calling the football hooligans that are now getting all loved up, going to raves and dropping pills instead of having punch ups.'

Tat and Patch took another moment to observe the firms coming together. The spectacle provided a clear sense of the bond that acid house music had brought together. The benefits of unification and spending time with like-minded people was second to none for the hardcore raver and, of course, Ecstasy and LSD had been helping this along. After all, some wise person had once said 'make love not war', which wasn't a bad shout at all, especially compared to how things had been on the terraces in the previous years.

'Yeah, it's good to see,' said Patch, 'I dunno how long will last though. At some point it'll go back to how it was-back to battles on the terraces. We're British, it's what we do. We love a punch up. But all the time the E's are being popped it's all okay.'

'Hallelujah-not sent to save ya,' Tat chanted.

'Just here to spank ya, n'play a game,' Patch returned with a big grin on his face.

'Bet your brother misses it though,' Tat continued.

'I don't know if he does,' shrugged Patch, 'He's been at it since he was fourteen and I think, like a lot of his mates too, he was getting bored with the punch ups. The buzz he's been getting from acid house has served as a good substitute.'

Just as Patch finished talking, Kariya started to be played. Tat and Patch had to join in with the dancing. Just like everyone around them, they got lost in the music and sunk deeper into their own private worlds. They remained in their bubbles whilst the DJ spun tracks by Frankie Knuckles, Phase 11 and Dion. With each track they were elevated to new heights and, the higher they got, the higher they wanted to be.

It was only the need to take a sip of water from the bottle Tat had been clutching that temporarily burst his bubble. As he gulped down the warm liquid he scanned the room and the sweaty, smiling faces. Tat felt great! And then a girl caught his eye. He had to focus to ensure it was who he thought it was. He felt himself light up. It was Kim; the girl he'd been introduced to at Fish's.

'Look, it's that Kim from Fish's shop,' Tat said whilst nudging Patch, which brought Patch back down to earth with a thud.

It took Patch a few moments to find Kim in the darkness of the room.

'You need to go and speak to her then mate. She is a bit tasty. Get in there mate - before one of those Millwall lads do.'

'Too right! Yeah bollocks to that!' Tat yelled, 'I can't let that happen.'

'Go on then mate. Crack on-she won't bite…maybe just gurn a bit.'

With effort, Tat used the sleeve of his Mash t-shirt to wipe the sweat from his face.

'OK, right, I'm going in,' he said, taking another sip from his bottle of water and heading off in the direction where Kim was dancing.

As Tat navigated his way through the crowd, the strobe lights flashed aggressively again and he also got a whiff of some hash. He eventually reached Kim who was looking sweaty, but still gorgeous, and shaking a bottle of Lucozade as she danced.

Kim caught sight of Tat approaching and with a smile on her face, stopped dancing. She took the opportunity to take a swig of her Lucozade. She welcomed the sensation of the bubbles hitting the back of her throat.

'Alright Kim,' said Tat, adding, 'Funny seeing you here.' He realised this sounded corny.

'Hi Tat. Nice to see you,' said Kim

Tat felt relieved that Kim appeared willing to chat, which also meant that she wasn't entirely off of her tits yet.

Kim's eye sparkled as the lights in the club shot across her face. She continued, 'Yeah we don't usually come to Clinks, we prefer Shoom. But, you know, it's good to have a change of scenery sometimes and besides the tunes are good here too.' As she spoke she glanced over Tat's shoulder and strained her sparkling eyes.

'Yeah, you're not wrong there,' said Tat, 'A change of scenery is good.'

'Are you with your mate? What's his name again? Something to do with pirates wasn't it?'

For some reason, Tat felt pleased that Kim had remembered his name but not Patch's.

'Ha, yeah it's Patch. Yeah, I'm here with him. I don't go anywhere without him-he's my wing man.'

'Your wing man eh. Where is he now then?' asked Kim.

'He's right over there. You can't miss him when he dances.'

'Oh yeah, why's that?'

'Coz he dances like he is crushing grapes with his feet whilst shaking some maracas.'

Kim started to laugh, took another gulp of her drink and offered the bottle to Tat. Tat liked that, but declined as he held up his own bottle of water. They both took a sip of their drinks and focused their attention on Patch, who was now well into his trip.

'He looks like he's right on one too,' said Kim leaning into Tat ensuring that he could hear. As she did, he caught a whiff of her perfume, which sent a thrill through his veins.

'Yeah he will be by now. He dropped a tab about half an hour ago, so he'll be well on his way by now.'

'Mental! And what about you-have you taken anything tonight?'

'Nothing yet, but I've got an E in my pocket which I was about to swallow just before I saw you,' said Tat tapping a pocket on his jeans.

'Are they good ones?' asked Kim.

'Yeah they're good alright. I get them from a reliable source. Do you want half?'

'Yeah alright then!' Kim was the sort of raver that didn't need asking twice.

Tat was pleased that she'd accepted his invitation and handed her his bottle of water. He fished in his jean's pocket and pulled out the small white pill. He grinned at her as he broke it in half.

'There you go-a cheeky half,' said Tat, noting that SL2's Do The Dance was starting to kick in.

Kim popped the pill and washed it down with a gulp of water from Tat's bottle. This didn't go unnoticed by Tat and he hastily placed his half of the E onto his tongue and grabbed his bottle of water. He knew it was probably going to be the nearest he'd get to Kim's lips on this night. But, in that moment, both boy and girl knew some mysterious union had been formed and they both felt pleased about it.

The DJ had started to delve back into some of the best in acid house and for the next fifteen minutes treated the Clinks' crowd to tracks from Jolly Roger, Maurice and Humanoid. Kim and Tat embraced every acid sound and beat until their legs could take no more. They could feel the E starting to rise up and needed more sips of their drinks.

'So how are you getting on with setting up Eclipse?' asked Kim, fanning her face with her hand, in a pointless attempt to cool herself down.

'You remembered the stations name,' replied Tat feeling chuffed.

'Yeah it's a good name. It'll stand out.'

'We're doing alright. We have got pretty much all the equipment that we'll need. Patch knew some people who turned over some electrical shop in Sidcup. He knows someone who can set it all up for us too. Then we just have to flick the switch and broadcast our first show. It's gonna be mental. I already know what records I'm gonna play for the first show and Voodoo Ray, Lack Of Love and Your Love…I mean the Eclipse debut broadcast has got to have some Frankie Knuckles in it.'

'It sounds good. I'm sure you'll make it a success,' said Kim, blowing out her cheeks and adding, 'Phew! I've just had a bit of a rush. This E feels like it'll be a strong one.'

'Yeah, me too! And can you smell that?'

'Yeah amyl,' said Kim screwing up her nose.

'Yeah - someone did this the other week. I think they must pour a bottle into the smoke machines or something. The place will be full of the smell of amyl in a minute.'

'Well it'll help to kickstart the E. Not that I need it, mine's really coming on now.'

'Mine too now. Have a good un,' said Tat, and with that they both launched back into dancing as the wonderful bassline to Your Love began.

MY HOUSE

Tat still couldn't believe what he was reading, as he again tried to digest the article telling the story of the events from a few days earlier. As Tat sat in his chair by the window in his flat, he read about the tragedy,whichhad happened at the Hillsborough Stadium, home of Sheffield Wednesday. It had been 15th April, day of the FA Cup semi-final between Liverpool and Nottingham Forest and Tat, like a nation of football goers, knew what had happened would be remembered as one of the darkest days in the history of English football.

The article told of how ninety-six football fans had died and over 700 more were injured due to over-crowding and failures from the authorities to manage the large crowds,whichswelled the Hillsborough Stadium. Tat read on as the article described how only six minutes of the match got played before being stopped but, by then, fans were already being crushed to their deaths. Tat found the information very hard to stomach. He put down the Texan bar that he'd been trying to eat.

He read on as the author of the article described how some fans had tried their best to help and how they had made stretchers from advertising hoardings. Tat knew that the Hillsborough disaster would touch the hearts of the people of Britain and he hoped that in the years to come the victims of that day would not be forgotten.

Tat sat in a quiet state for a long time after reading the article. He stared out of the window, looking at nothing in particular. He didn't notice the birds that flew by his window or the aeroplanes which flew high in the sky, leaving their white trails behind them. It was only the knock on his door that shook him out of the reflective, sad, state that he was in.

Tat checked his watch and a much-needed smile formed on his face. He opened the door and welcomed Kim in. It had been a week since they'd both been in Clinks and Kim had been around to Tat's flat on three occasions. The awkwardness and inhibitions they'd both been initially feeling had mostly lifted as they had started to feel comfortable in each other's company.

'D'ya wanna cup of tea or something?' asked Tat following a kiss.

Kim removed her bomber jacket and hung it on the back of a chair near the kitchen area. She then plonked herself on a large green and yellow cushion on the floor and started to remove her red and white Converse boots.

'Nah thanks. I've still got some Lucozade left,' she replied holding up the bottle with the orange fizzy fluid inside it.

'Can I get you anything at all? I've got some chocolate digestives left, or there's a box of Maltesers somewhere.'

Tat manically searched for the sweets.

'I'm okay thanks. Really, I had some lunch earlier.'

As Tat made himself a cup of tea Kim scanned his flat, taking notice of some of the items he possessed. This was the first time she'd been around to Tat's flat in the day time. Whenever she'd visited before it had been at night and the curtains had been drawn and the lights lowered.

'You've got a lot of books on art,' she observed, 'and a lot of records too.'

'Yeah I love art. It was the only subject I liked at school really. What about you...what did you like at school?'

'I loved history and English. I definitely wasn't one for maths, science or biology though.'

Kim had found the box of Maltesers under a pile of newspapers and had removed a few, popping them into her mouth, one at a time.

'I liked a bit of history too and like you I hated maths. I still can't see the point of algebra and that sort of bollocks,' said Tat carefully placing himself next to Kim so as to not spill any of his tea. She shoved a handful of Maltesers into his mouth.

'And what about all those records? You'll need them and more to become that pirate radio DJ.'

'Well funny you should say that because me and Patch are making real progress to set up our own station and we are buying new records weekly at the moment. He's got a load more that he'll be bringing round in the week.'

'Wow! That's brilliant. Where are you going to set it up?' said Kim scanning the room again.

'There,' replied Tat, pointing in the direction where his record collection was piled up. Only the day before he and Patch had rescued a table from some skip near Charlton and had lugged it up to Tat's flat. They'd also found a busted up old chair which just needed some TLC but, once done, that would be Patch's throne during the broadcasts.

'Yeah it should do. I have some friends from around here - a bunch of West Ham supporters - and they are going to start up their own pirate too.'

'Yeah, I know about that new pirate starting up. By the end of '89 there'll be loads. It's all good though. Whatever helps the parties yeah?' Tat took a large gulp of his hot tea.

Kim lay flat on her stomach and stretched out so she could reach some of Tat's records. She scattered a few across the floor and admired the artwork on some of the covers and took a note of the labels that the records were on. She chose one record she especially liked - My House by Rhythm Control - and passed it to Tat. He put the record on, but not too loudly.

'This is one of my faves,' said Kim, 'This brings back memories of Ibiza. I just love Chuck Roberts' vocals on this. 'In the beginning there was Jack and Jack had a groove...'

Tat agreed and joined in.

'...and from that groove came the grooves of all grooves...'

Kim picked the baton she had been handed and continued.

'...and Jack declared-let there be House...'

Tat replied, '...and House music was born.'

Both rolled around on the floor in each other's arms; it felt great.

'You've been to Ibiza then?' asked Tat after some kissing.

'Yep! There was a group of us that went out there at Easter time last year. Originally it was just going to be me and my mate Lisa going on a week's holiday. Lisa also works in Fish's; she's also a stylist. But word got around and in the end six of us went. We stayed in San Antonio. The very first night we were there we heard about some DJ called Alfredo who played all the latest house music and other stuff that had people dancing all night long. It sounded like a laugh so went to find him in some club called Amnesia which was in San Rafael.'

'That's the club that doesn't have a roof isn't it?' asked Tat, reminding himself that he really needed to get himself out to Ibiza and see for himself what the hype was about. He had heard plenty. Patch's brother and his Echos mates had been out there, and they were some of the first to do so back in the summer of '87.

'That's right. It's an amazing place with an amazing vibe. And everyone was so friendly. We had a fantastic night. We danced all night. We then went back every night that week. It was in Amnesia that I tried my first E too and I loved it. But whilst we were there, we got friendly with a bunch of lads who were from London. After that holiday I went back two more times that year and each time was better than the last. It was obvious some scene was developing too. More and more people from London went and then there were gangs of lads from Manchester too. There was a real party vibe.'

Kim sat up and popped another Malteser in her mouth. She washed it down with a mouthful of Tat's tea.

'Those Mancs you met were probably part of the Hacienda scene and linked to the Happy Mondays.'

'Yeah, I know that now, but back then, I had no idea. They were just Northerners joining in with the party. It was later that year that Shoom opened. I went to the opening night; it was the first time I saw Carl Cox deejay. The Genesis parties also started up, but back then it was all bandanas, whistles, white gloves and smiley t-shirts. I was at the Lee Valley Ice Centre party in December and I went to the Genesis Hedonism and Against All Odds parties too. Did you go to any of the early Genesis parties?'

Tat sat up too and gathered the things he'd need to make a joint.

'Me and Patch went to Hedonism and we did the 'New Year's Eve: The Final Party' in Clapton and we went to Shoom a few times in its early days.' Tat started sticking some Rizla's together, pondering, 'We might have even danced beside each other.'

'Ha, we might have done. The parties had more of an intimate sense then, but you can feel that's changing now. It's getting bigger every weekend. Places like the Trip and Spectrum would never be able to cater for what's coming.'

The tone in Kim's voice changed, something that Tat picked up on.

'Don't you like that it's getting bigger and reaching more people then?' he asked.

'No, it's okay, I don't mind. It feels good, but I think something will get lost when the underground element goes and it will-these things always do.'

Tat stopped what he was doing and moved towards the record player. He shifted some records, it was clear he was intent on finding something. He eventually found what he was looking for.

'Here you go. This one's in honour of DJ Alfredo, the father of the Balearic beat,' said Tat as placed Let The Music (Use You) by the Night Writers onto the turntable and turned up the volume.

ECLIPSE 89.9FM

For the first two weeks in May, all Patch and Tat talked about was Centreforce. The pirate radio station had been creating a buzz that was second to none. For Patch and Tat, Centreforce was an inspiration and they locked on to 88.3 whenever the show was being broadcast. They'd even bumped into one of the station's leading men at a rave called Back To The Future. That rave had gone off only a couple of days before Centreforce had gone live. At the rave, Tat and Patch had engaged in a lengthy conversation with the guy from the station and he'd given them a few pointers as to how they could run Eclipse and avoid getting noticed by the Old Bill. The tips passed on were gems. Patch, Tat and the guy could have talked for hours, but the tunes were banging and they couldn't resist the urge to dance. Plus, where they stood, the stench of animal feed was overpowering so they had to move to a different spot. So, they'd shaken hands and parted company, but not before the guy handed over some telephone numbers for some up and coming aspiring DJs who'd probably jump at the chance of being part of Eclipse.

The following afternoon Patch and Tat started contacting the various DJs and a team of like-minded people started to build. Alongside DJs, Tat and Patch, the team included DJ Need All, who was a ginger haired fella, approaching mid-20s and intent on growing dreadlocks. He had a deep love of roots reggae too.

Then there was DJ Buzzlines. He was from Lewisham and had also grown up listening to ska and reggae that his Jamaican family played at the house parties they regularly provided for their neighbours. DJ Buzzlines was cool in many ways. He seldom spoke and, out of the Eclipse team, he was the quietest, but when he got behind a microphone you just couldn't shut him up. Patch especially warmed to him.

And then there was DJ R.E White. He was the oldest in the team and had served his DJ apprentice lugging boxes of records around for some of the soul and jazz funk DJs from the Kent Soul Mafia. He was born and bred in Dartford and he knew he'd die there too. His passion was for the more soulful end of house music and he loved lemonade, which worked out just fine because in between playing records he liked to whisper over the mic 'and that was…and this is DJ R. E White the secret hot lemonade drinker.'

The Eclipse team also included two duos. DJ Spank E and DJ Sensible Simon were a force to be reckoned with once they got going. Their show would always be kicked off with Phuture's Spank Spank and this was intended to get the listeners' hearts beating fast. DJ Sensible Simon served as Spank E's neutraliser. He'd keep things on the ground when needed. Both had met in Shoom and, from that night, a brotherly love type bond had been formed. They had also put themselves forward as the DJs who'd keep Eclipse broadcasting on Saturday nights and into the early hours of Sunday morning. And then at 2am, they'd turn everything off and go and find a rave somewhere. This arrangement suited Tat and Patch and the rest of the Eclipse team.

The other duo were two females. Sandra and Anita, otherwise known as DJ Smile and DJ Jewels, were East London girls and they didn't take any shit. They were funny and fun to be around. They loved their house music, loved banter with the listeners and they both sounded as sexy as fuck over the microphone. Their show was bound to be a hit amongst the hardcore.

And lastly, there was DJ Lenny Mash. His tag line was 'Let's get smashed with the mash'. He was a tough looking black guy, thick-set with fists like hammers. He was old school West Ham too and had held himself well on the terraces. He had been part of the Echos firm and had made Ibiza his second home. He boosted his income by shifting bags of E's and most of his earnings went on buying records. He loved anything on Trax and records released on the label made up the bulk of his personal collection. He was keen to do a tribute to Trax show and Tat and Patch had agreed that would be a spot-on idea. A date had been identified too.

Two more weeks had passed and more meetings held with the Eclipse team which now numbered ten. Rules were also established and these included never turning up at Eclipse Towers, as Tat's flat was now fondly being called, clutching record boxes because some nosey parker might give the game away to the Old Bill. So records were to be only carried in ordinary bags. Safety for the station was paramount. They all understood and accepted that what they were doing was illegal and if they got rumbled by the authorities, there would be consequences. But this illegal also contributed to the buzz that they felt.

The various DJs and an ever-present Kim helped to turn Tat's flat into a studio. All the equipment needed to broadcast a radio show was set up and all that was left to do was for Tat and Patch to press the 'go live' button and launch their debut broadcast into the homes, cars and clubs of London and the Home Counties. They felt confident they'd invested in the right equipment which meant they could reach ravers in the deep and dark corners of Kent, Surrey and Essex.

'Here we go then Patch mate,' said Tat glancing around the flat at the anxious and excited faces of the Eclipse team, and their number one fan Kim, 'Everything is ready is go, but let's do one last check list?'

Patch puffed away on a joint as he twisted knobs and checked buttons and levels. His heart was pounding.

'Electricity on!' Patch mumbled through the smoke.

'Check,' replied Tat.

'Records ready?'

'Check.'

'Joints rolled,' yelled DJ Lenny.

'Check!' laughed the team.

'Then let's have it,' roared Patch.

'Check.' nodded Tat, accepting the joint that DJ Buzzlines handed him with a huge grin spread across his face.

'Right then. Countdown time,' said Patch turning to the Eclipse team.

'Do it!' Tat added, motioning to the team to join in.

'10, 9, 8, 7, 6, 5, 4, 3, 2...'

'1...hit it!' screamed Tat. A light went green and Eclipse pirate radio station 89.9FM got launched with 808 State's Pacific State, which somehow seemed fitting because they did indeed feel in a specific state in their minds, bodies and souls.

Tat and Patch allowed the majority of Pacific State to play whilst they tried to get settled in their chairs. The nerves they felt were a thousand times worse than trying to get out of the Den in one piece on a bitter cold Saturday afternoon.

Tat twisted a knob and the record dropped low. Patch gulped, coughed and leaned into the microphone.

'Welcome to all you hardcore ravers out there. You've heard the rumours and they're all true. Eclipse is the new pirate station that will be rocking the capital. We're going to be ripping up the airwaves London, so keep it locked to 89.9.'

Patch sat back and Tat grabbed the second microphone.

'We've got all the updates on the whereabouts of tonight's raves, we know which warehouses have been cracked and which haven't, so keep it locked to 89.9 to hear all the announcements as we shout them out.'

Tat breathed a sigh of relief. He'd broken the ice and was off. He nodded to Patch, who in turn picked up the baton.

'To send us any info or shouts, just page Eclipse on 08550 32020, that's 08550 32020.'

Pacific State was pumped up again and played to its end, which got mixed in with the arrival of Sterling Void's Runaway Girl, which was dipped in and out as Patch introduced the Eclipse team.

'Yes, your Eclipse DJs will be yours truly along with my partner in house DJ Tat, who, you'll have noticed is from oop North, but let's not hold that against him.'

At which point Tat butted in.

'And yes, as you can probably tell, I'm not from 'down sarth', I'm from Manchester, so be prepared to hear plenty of tunes from the likes of 808 State and A Guy Called Gerald and not forgetting the Stone Roses and the Happy Mondays. You know it makes sense. You know the scorrrrre.'

Patch took a draw on a joint and took over.

'And we also have DJ Need All; DJ Lenny Mash 'let's get smashed with the mash'; the terrible twins-DJ Spank E and DJ Sensible Simon; the two ladies in the squad - DJ Jewels and DJ Smile and be assured they will light up your lives London; and then we have DJ R.E White 'the secret hot lemonade drinker' and last, but not least, DJ Buzzlines.

Tat turned up the volume, the studio started to rock and the Eclipse team fell about hugging and laughing. They all felt they had achieved something special just to get to the stage of going live.

For the next thirty minutes, Tat and Patch treated their listeners to tunes from the Trax vaults and some of the game changers from A Guy Called Gerald, T-Coy, along with other meaningful monsters such as Ride On Time, S'Express Theme and We Call It Acieed. There were also shouts out to other pirate stations like Centreforce and Sunrise and the respect and love flowed.

As the show progressed, it became apparent that more and more people were locking onto Eclipse. The Eclipse team tried to keep up with the messages which got paged in.

'And yes, we got your page Kenny and yes, you are the first to page in. You'd win the prize if we had one,' joked Patch.

'And we've had another page and it's a message for The Ozzard of Whizz from Mandy. Oz, she wants to know where you are going to be around midnight. Get back to her mate-you know she needs you tonight.'

More pages flew in and the banter between broadcasters and listeners flowed.

'This is mental mate,' said Tat nudging Patch, 'The pager is on fire.'

'Brilliant ain't it. Eclipse is gonna light up London,' replied Patch.

More records got spun along with more shout outs.

'This is a shout out from Vanessa. She says she'll see you in Hypnosis later,' said Tat.

'Ah 'Manipulation of the Mind' at Dungeons on Leah Bridge Rd,' added Patch.

Tat increased the volume so that London could rock to the Jungle Brothers. He then searched for the Sunrise 5000 flyers that he'd picked up in Black Market Records a couple of weekends previously. Kim realized what Tat was trying to do and lifting up her bum cheek,she produced two triangle shaped flyers and handed them to Tat.

Tat grabbed the microphone and started to read out the information on one of the flyers.

'So it's finally here, it's Sunrise 5000 Once In A Blue Moon. There's going to be fairground rides, bouncy castles and a 20k sound system for Paul Anderson and Eddie Richards.'

'And remember this is a private party for ticket holders only,' said patch, pushing his way in.

A few more records got played and a couple of announcements issued informing ravers where the meeting points were going to be, before Patch announced that he and Tat were going to be handing over the show to DJ Spank E and DJ Sensible Simon, because they too were going head to the Santa Pod Race Track in Bedfordshire.

Patch felt a weight lift off his shoulders. He knew that Tat and himself had pulled it off and they had their very own pirate radio station that could help keep the ravewaves fed and watered. He looked Tat directly in the eye and, in that moment, they both knew they were onto a winner and they knew they were going to enjoy the ride.

Patch took hold of the microphone for one last time.

'Message here for Battersea boys Andy and Tim - Sally says she's been waiting for you both for over an hour. She needs picking up as soon as because she wants to go raving. So, this one goes out to you two fellas...have a good un! Let's go mental.' And with that Let Me Love You For Tonight fed the ravewaves of a thousand ravers who were hurtling along the M25 on their way to Podington.

ENERGY

Eclipse had been broadcast three more nights during the week that followed since going live. Eclipse Towers was a hive of activity. Tat felt tired but was still buzzing and he was forever having to nip into the local Co-op to stock up on tea bags, coffee and Rich Tea biscuits. Kim and himself hardlyhad any time to be together, but it was okay, they were both enjoying themselves-the whole Eclipse team were too.

Tat's flat became a meeting place, a den where stories were told about the various parties that people had been to and the latest gossip was shared. And music got played all of the time. There'd even be times when one of the DJs would just swing by for a couple of hours. They would smoke joints, play new records, pour themselves over the flyers that were now coming thick and fast. Patch and Tat had also caught the attention of the various party promoters and there were mutual benefits to be had. Patch, Tat and the Eclipse team got trusted with sensitive information regards where the parties were going to be, the meeting points and for supporting the promoters. In return, Patch and Tat were being sent free tickets for the raves. They had no reason to complain, things were going great.

Saturday 27th May had been a magical night for Patch, Tat and Kim. Patch and Tat had done their Saturday night slot from 8-10pm. They'd mixed in some of their latest purchases from Black Market Records with a fine collection of early acid house. They'd finished their set with Can You Party and then handed over the mic to DJ Spank E and DJ Sensible Simon, who both looked more stoned than they ever had done. They were enjoying life too.

Patch had driven to the Westway Studios in Shepherds Bush and Tat and Kim travelled with him. They had their tickets to the Energy rave in their pockets. Whilst they drove, they locked on to 89.9 and listened to their Eclipse comrades having a ball.

The venue was amazing. It was clear that a lot of energy and effort had been poured into the event. There must have been some very creative minds on the Energy team too because the five rooms within the venue had been turned into themed rooms for night only. Patch, Tat and Kim spent most of the night in either the Greek Temple room or the room which looked like a scene out of the film Blade Runner, which just happened to be one of Tat's favourite sci-fi films. They never got as far as the other rooms which were the Sushi, Pyramid and Stonehenge ones. But they did bump into Jeremy Taylor, who was one of the organisers. Patch and Tat knew about his background as being the key organiser behind the Gatecrasher Balls for the Hoorah Henries. They'd had a brief chat before going their separate ways and disappearing into one of the dark corners of the Blade Runner room.

The rave had gone off without any obvious hitches and there'd been much smiling and laughter and, of course, a great deal of dancing. In fact, once the rave had ended, people still wanted to dance and they'd headed over to Clapham Common, where more music got played and people raved on for a few more hours. It was a sight to be seen and even the Old Bill couldn't really get their heads around what was going on. Being on Clapham Common with those like-minded raving souls turned out to be a fitting end to a great weekend and Patch, Tat and Kim went to their beds that Sunday night grinning like Cheshire cats. They also felt they were truly apart of the second summer of love.

Ever since DJ Lenny Mash had said he wanted to do a tribute show to Trax Records, other Eclipse DJs had said they wanted to do themed shows too. Someone had suggested a Balearic show and another just pure acid. All suggestions had been agreed and Tat wanted to do a show where he'd only play records linked in with the Madchester vibe.

Word had been reaching the Eclipse team that rave had spilled out from the Hacienda and other areas in the north were also starting to rave. Blackburn was getting mentioned in a lot of conversations.

For some reason, DJ Buzzlines couldn't do his Friday night show so Tat decided he'd sit in and do his Madchester thing. Patch had other business to attend to, so he took a night off from being in the

Eclipse studio. This meant that Tat and Kim could have the flat to themselves, do the show and enjoy each other's company.

Kim rolled the joints and made cups of tea whilst Tat spun tunes from the Stone Roses, Happy Mondays, 808 State, Guy Called Gerald and bigged up the Ruthless Rap Assassins and MC Tunes. He kicked the show off with Voodoo Ray and two hours later, stoned out of his mind and buzzing, ended with Wrote For Luck.

There'd been plenty of banter between himself and the listeners which had paged in with messages. There were countless stories from people where they reminisced about the night they'd gone to the Hacienda and how much they'd loved seeing the Northern bands doing their own unique thing in amongst the ever-increasing rave culture. The Madchester show had been a success and Tat signed off promising a part two at some point in the near future. He went to sleep that night with his home town and the Hacienda very much on his mind.

Children of the Night tickled the ravewaves the following night. Patch had wanted to open that evening's show with the song. It had been running around his head all day and he needed to get it out of his system. He sat in his chair and picked some dry skin on the sole of his foot; his blue kickers had been discarded at the flat's front door. He'd taken to doing the shows barefoot for some reason only known to himself. Tat sat beside Patch trying to pretend he couldn't smell his feet. Kim had made herself comfortable on one of the many cushions that were now a necessary feature in Eclipse Towers. She marvelled at the various flyers that had been collected and rolled joints for the DJs.

'Alright London, DJ Patch and DJ Tat are back in the house for another Saturday night Eclipse broadcast. We've got plenty of updates on the Biology rave that'll be going off tonight and a whole load of shouts going out too. Keep paging them messages to us here on 08550 32020 and a bunch of our tunes tonight are going out for Jonny C, Lust, Jazzy M, Jack Bass and Nicky B. We love what you do!'

Patch sat back to make way for Tat to take over. Tat had been digesting the information that he balanced on the palm of his hand. He liked the imagery of the Vitruvian Man and had studied it for a long time whilst puffing away on a joint. He'd then read on:

Panorama, Biology 2, No Surrender. Heflipped the flyer over and read through the information, taking note of the DJs: Paul Oakenfold, Trevor Fung, Nicky Holloway and Lisa Loud amongst many others. The part about the rave being a 'private party' and 'admission strictly ticket holders only' always made him chuckle because he understood the smoke and mirrors game that the promoters needed to play with the authorities. He and Patch had also spent the last couple of weeks telling the Eclipse listeners to go and get their tickets from such outlets as Vinyl Zone Records, Red Records and of course Black Market.

Patch nudged Tat, instructing him to take over as Children of the Night was coming to an end.

'The first big shout tonight goes out to Jermaine deep down in Deptford. Nice to hear from you again, it's been a while mate. Good to know you're keeping it locked to Eclipse on 89.9 FM."

Patch put on Blackout (Phase 2) which, along with French Kiss, was one of his favourite tunes by Lil Louis. He also started to screw his nose up at the amyl odour that filledthe flat.

'Fuckin 'ell Tat I can hardly breathe and my eyes are stinging like fuck,' he moaned.

'Yeah alright, I've said I'm sorry. I've tried to wipe it up-what d'ya want me to do…get on all fours and lick it up?' Tat spat back.

Patch shrugged his shoulders.

'Do you remember that night you spilt that bottle of poppers in the back of Sparksy's Metro? He went fuckin' mental, complaining that his dad will string him up by his bollocks and leave him hanging there for a week.'

'Yeah I do,' replied Tat, 'Funny as fuck. Anyway, I didn't spill the bottle - I dropped the bottle on the floor then trod on it with my Timberlands. It took days to get the stench off those boots.'

'And that was the night of the Sunrise Guy Fawkes party,' Patch remembered.

'5th November 1988. That was the night the Old Bill tried their best to prevent party goers getting to the venue. That 'orrible old gas works in Greenwich.'

'It was also at that party where that lad had some sort of pipe and basically became the pied piper for the rave. There were times throughout the night when he had thirty plus ravers dancing behind him, as they followed him in and out of the crowds.'

'That was a mental night. And if I remember, Vanessa was one of them - that bird you were seeing for a while…the one that didn't last long coz you started to shag her best mate.'

Patch started to laugh. He couldn't defend himself.

'We had a right run around that night too didn't we? Good job Sparksy was our designated driver that night. He knows his way around town. And that was the night the Old Bill closed off the Dartford Tunnel wasn't it?'

'Yeah it was. They also threatened to arrest the coach drivers if they tried taking the ravers to the venue. It was definitely a night of chaos and one to remember. We were one of the lucky ones. They reckon there was about 3,000 ravers trying to get to the party, but in the end only half managed to get there. At least that was enough to stop the Old Bill shutting the party down. They knew they'd have a riot on their hands if they tried.'

'Yeah, it was a sound night,' Tat agreed, 'One of the best from that period. I think it wasn't too long after that that Tony Colston-Hayter set up his TVAR system Telephone Venue Address Releasing. Fookin' genius idea really! That was also the same night your brother told us that story of when he was in Shoom one night and how he spent an hour talking to his own reflection in one of the gym's mirrors.'

'Well he did say he had dropped a micro-dot and those little fuckers are strong,' replied Patch.

'We only went to Shoom half a dozen or so times, didn't we? Didn't we stop going because of your brother?'

'Yes, well that and also having to charm our way past the woman on the door,' laughed Patch.

Tat turned to look at Kim, who looked back rolling her eyes. Tat, stretching out, passed the joint to Kim and continued.

'Oh yeah! She was certainly particular about who she did and didn't want in the club. That Fitness Centre down by Southwark Bridge was just right for Shoom too. Easy to get to but off the beaten track and in a basement that would get really hot and sweaty and all those mirrors everywhere, but the music was just brilliant, some of the best house music ever got played in Shoom. I suppose it was London's answer to Chicago's Warehouse.'

'And most of my brother's mates were too dodgy for us really. Because they were a few years older than us, they'd always be giving it the big I am coz they'd come up the route of the jazz funk soul scene, go to the Goldmine in Canvey Island weekly, the Caister Soul Weekenders and followed the Soul Mafia around, and coz they'd been part of the Wag Club's 'in crowd' and hung out with the likes of Norman Jay and Barrie Sharpe. After the Wag closed, then they used to go onto the illegal parties held in cinemas, gyms and even swimming pools. He used to go to the Demob parties down Roseberry Avenue and Nicky Holloway's Special Branch club nights,' Said Patch, searching through a bag of records as he spoke.

'And all looking the same in their Wag dress code of a black MA1 flight jacket, stone-wash jeans with turn-ups high enough to show off their black and white stripy socks and black Doc Marten shoes.'

'That was us too though. We wore all that gear. But then we loved all that Rare Groove stuff - still do. Every time I hear Maceo Parker's Cross The Tracks or the Jackson Sisters' I Believe In Miracles, I get a nice tingly rush pass through me.'

'That's just wind mate,'chuckled Tat.

Patch found the record he had been searching for and got it ready to put on next. That done, he checked the pager and read through some of the messages. There was one about DJ Spank E running a bit late, with an estimated arrival time at Eclipse Towers, being nearer to 10:30 than 10:00. Patch read the message out to Tat and Kim, who both complained because they knew they wanted to be on the road straight after the show, so they could get to the Biology rave that they knew was kicking off in a field near to the Elstree Studios in Hertfordshire.

Patch grabbed the microphone and started to read out the messages.

'We have a message just come in from Julie asking us to let Kimberly know that she has the bottles of Lucozade so Brian only needs to bring the burgers and they'll be setting off at ten. She says she can't wait to get to Biology.'

Tat grabbed the pager and continued.

'We got your message Debbie from Highbury and yes we will play that tune for you within the next half hour.'

Patch took the pager back.

'And thanks for the page from the Kent crew. Seems there's been a rumble at the Black Prince Interchange and a few ravers' cars have been turned inside out by the Old Bill. Good luck with that one geezers and do your best to get to the rave once you've handled that.'

Sharing the pager between them, Tat and Patch managed to read out most of the messages that had been paged in whilst they played tune after tune. The buzz had been building as they'd started to feel more and more excited about the prospect of getting to the Biology party.

'Hopefully you're still keeping it locked Debbie coz this one's for you,' said Tat as he spun the last record of the show before handing over the headphones to DJ Spank E, who looked flushed and apologetic. And then Patch, Tat and Kim grabbed their gear and rushed off to the rave.

TRAX

Kim slowly flickedthrough a newspaper whilst Tat flicked through his record collection. The Biology rave had been a blast. They'd popped their first E and then a second around 4am. It had seemed like a good idea at the time. Tat and Kim had then danced, side by side, for the next few hours and by the time they crashed through the door at Tat's flat and slumped down onto the bed, it was nearly 10am. As they lay in the bed they could hear the streets outside getting busy with the religious rush-hour, but within ten minutes they were both fast asleep.

It was the sound of the early evening religious rush-hour that woke them up. Kim was awake first and went and made some coffee and toast. She was starving and she knewTat would be too.

By the time Tat started to come back to life, Kim had had a bath, washed her hair, put on her make-up and was sitting in his chair that looked out of the window, whilst reading the previous day's newspaper.

'It's terrible what going on in China at the moment,' she said not looking up.

Tat entered the room rubbing his eyes and scratching his arse.

'I've not read the paper yet and haven't watched much news lately. Why what's been going on out there?' asked Tat, his voice hoarse and weak.

'Well, from what I can gather, a lot of Chinese students have been protesting since April,' Kim replied, 'They initially gathered to mourn the death of one of someone called Hu Yaobang who was the Communist Party General Secretary. From what I can understand, he was very vocal in standing up for the Chinese people and, especially vocal about the corruption he insisted existed in some of the higher levels of the Chinese government. There were then student-led demonstrations where they have been protesting for the freedom of speech and the freedom of the press. Hey, maybe one day we'll have to protest for the freedom to party.'

Tat plonked himself down onto one of the cushions and popped a cigarette into his mouth.

'Nah, I can't see it coming to that,' said Tat shrugging off the idea of ravers needing to come together to demonstrate for their right to party.

'It seems that the government are starting to get heavy-handed too. Back in May, martial law was declared and the troops have been out in force. Some students have even been doing hunger strikes and gathering in numbers in places like Tiananmen Square. It's all looking pretty desperate and edgy out there. I have a bad feeling that something *really* bad is going to kick off out there.'

'I like it that you care,' Tat said noticing that the article resonated with Kim. He liked that she had a strong sense of injustice and cared for the wellbeing of other people. She was a rescuer too and at several raves she'd been the one who'd notice if someone was having a bad trip or struggling for some reason. Kim would go to them, take care of them, be with them and assure them that everything was going to be okay. People warmed to her good-natured soul and the rave scene needed people like her in it.

'Don't you care then?' asked Kim, 'I mean those students aren't much different to us. They are opposing the authorities and making a stand for what they believe in. We believe in the raves don't we- the freedom to do what we want to do and have a good time?'

Tat stubbed out his cigarette and started to search for his stash of hash. He went on.

'Even if that means descending on some sleepy village somewhere on the edge of the M25 and keeping the villagers awake all night, parking our cars on their doorsteps and then spending the next eight hours screaming, dancing, cheering and refusing to go home, despite the police vans gathering in force and chasing us across some field?'

'Yeah, I see your point but I still care. There's definitely something in the air though in 1989; something is stirring here in the UK and in Europe, as well as China.'

'I do care too…just not at the moment. My head is banging and my eyes are sore.' Tat took a large gulp of the coffee that Kim had made him. He then took a big bite of his toast and washed that down with an even larger gulp of his coffee.

Tat and Kim lounged about the flat for the next few hours until DJ Need All turned up to do his Sunday evening show. Tat asked him to play The Eve OF The War by Ben Liebrand.

The next few days seemed to go very fast. The roofing job that Patch and Tat had been doing out Bromley way turned out to be a hard graft. They were glad to see the weekend in sight, but had the Thursday night broadcast to enjoy first- and this was to be DJ Lenny Mash's tribute to Trax show.

Most of the Eclipse DJs descended on Eclipse Towers for the show. They'd been getting excited about it for weeks and it had been all that DJ Lenny Mash had talked about. He'd even brought along a few of his mates. Eclipse Towers was crammed and there was a good buzz going around, along with the joints that DJ Lenny's mates constantly rolled.

DJ Lenny's show kicked off at 8pm. He had to open up with Marshall Jefferson's Move Your Body. This had been a game changer in 1986 and had defined the way house music was heading. With its distinctive piano part, the tune jacked everyone's body and brought the house down every time.

Towards the end of the song, DJ Lenny Mash took control of the microphone and introduced the show. With the mic in one hand, and a Rasta-sized joint in the other, he began.

'Hello London! DJ Lenny Mash is in the house tonight and as promised last week, I'm going to give you a two-hour set of the biggest and best tunes of '86 and '87 - and this means Trax Records. So, let's get smashed with the mash. This is the great man himself, Marshall Jefferson with the house music anthem and this goes out to Ashley Beedle.'

The record played on and everyone in Eclipse Towers rocked. Seven minutes later, turning a switch, DJ Lenny eased out Marshall to make way for Frankie Knuckles' Bad Boy and Jamie Principle's beautiful vocals were released into the Eclipse ravewaves.

'Trax Records is where it all began for so many of us,' DJ Lenny continued, 'Because of our Chicago theme tonight, we'd like to hear your requests and any stories of your visits to such legendary clubs like the Paradise Garage, the Powerplant or The Warehouse.'

DJ Lenny dipped out allowing Bad Boy to continue. He took a long draw on the joint that he'd been smoking and blew the smoke out slowly through his nostrils. He went on.

'I wanna hear from you - what it was like being baptised with sets of house music from the likes of Ron Hardy, Marshall Jefferson, Frankie Knuckles and, if you go back even further, the genius that is Larry Levan. Page us here at Eclipse 89.9FM on 08550 32020.'

DJ Lenny Mash continued with the show, tossing in Phuture's Acid Trax, Mr Fingers' Washing Machine and Robert Owens' Bringing Down The Walls. Raising the roof even further, he played R U Hot Enough and spent the following minutes raving on about how much he loved the bubbling bassline sound. He played Spank Spank too and gave a big shout out to his fellow Eclipse DJ. Ride The Rhythm also went down well and this provided DJ Lenny with an opportunity to praise Ron Hardy.

Pump Up Chicago took the show to another level and DJ Lenny especially enjoyed dropping the song out and replacing the song's lyrics with some of his own, which included shouts out to the hardcore ravers from the north side, east side, south side and west side. This had the Eclipse DJs in the room rolling about with laughter.

Baby Wants To Ride was an opportunity for DJ Lenny to join with the 'na na na na na's, you can't hurt me', which also had the people in the Eclipse studio falling over laughing and joining in.

DJ Lenny took the Eclipse listeners on a nostalgic trip back to the mid-80s and threw in Farley Jackmaster Funk's Farley Knows Best and he quickly followed this with Sleezy D's I've Lost Control, No Way Back by Adonis and some Jungle Wonz.

The Trax Records tribute show rolled on, digging deeper and deeper into the roots of house music. The likes of Frankie Knuckles, Marshall Jefferson and even Jesse Saunders and Chip E were mentioned several times, their names spoken with a kind of religious reverence. DJ Lenny also put a big shout out to Larry Sherman and thanked him for helping to make Trax Records happen. Dub Love was the track that DJ Lenny Mash chose to wind up his show.

'This is the sing off track for tonight London. I hope you've enjoyed the show delivered to you by yours truly, DJ Lenny Mash, at Eclipse 89.9FM; let's get smashed with the mash.'

As the record faded out, he listed some of the great artists that had had releases on Trax: Frankie Knuckles, Marshall Jefferson, Adonis, Virgo, Screamin' Rachael, Kevin Irving, Willie Wonka, Ron Hardy, Mr Fingers, Phuture...

A MIDSUMMER'S NIGHT DREAM

Now that summer was really starting to lift off, it seemed as if every other person Tat or Patch met wanted to tell them what a lovely summer 1989 was going to be. The older folk shared their fond memories of holidays on the hop farms of Kent; others talked about days spent in the seaside towns of Southend, Margate and Hastings. For Patch, he'd grown up with summer holidays at Butlins in Bognor Regis and for Tat it had been Blackpool; it was only ever Blackpool.

Tat and Kim hadn't been up long when they heard the sound of Tat's front door being opened. As much as Kim loved Patch too, she had asked Tat to get his door key back because she just knew one day Patch would burst into the flat and catch Tat and Kim at it, or Kim wandering around naked. She knew she'd never live it down. Of course, her requests fell onto stony ground, despite Tat's continued agreement.

Patch plonked a bag of bacon rolls onto a table and started to boil the kettle. Tat and Kim soon joined him and they each tucked into their breakfasts. It was nearly midday and their plan was to take a drive out to north London. It had been Kim's idea to visit the Sunrise shop in Islington and get some Sunrise memberships for some friends she had made at work.

With their belly's full and their bowels emptied, they jumped into Patch's motor and made their way north. As they drove, they played cassettes of Eclipse shows. DJ Buzzlines had been keen to capture as many shows as possible and the tapes were starting to pile up.

Surprisingly for a Saturday, it didn't actually take them too long to get to Islington. They found a parking space a spitting distance from the Sunrise shop. A few moments later they entered the shop. Sueno Latino was playing as they did so. The vibe in the shop felt good.

'Toon!' cried Tat, 'This is what you want to hear when you enter a shop.'

'Yeah! Love this track. Love the way it builds and builds,' Kim agreed.

'It's one of those house tracks that takes you on a journey. It's a good track to come up on an E to,' Patch added before making a beeline for a rack of yellow and red t-shirts that had caught his eye.

'I thought my mate was working in here today. She's good friends with Tony Colston-Hayter, but she knows all the rave promoters and faces like Wayne Anthony, Jarvis Sanday, Anton Le Pirate, Dave Roberts, Jeremy Taylor and Quintin 'Tin Tin' Chambers. She is in with them all. She was one of the people we met when we were going to Amnesia and then we would see her in Shoom, the Trip and Spectrum and places like that,' said Kim as she studied the patterns on some sweatshirts that she liked.

'Sounds like she's a proper hardcore raver. And that's something I love about our rave culture, there's a place in it for girls. For years it was just lads. You'd go to football and it would be lads, when you went to see bands it was mostly lads, but raves invite everyone in. I've never spoken to so many girls, posh people, people from every quarter of the UK, Rastas, villains, gay people. The raves really are an open house to everyone and I think that's why the vibe is so good and friendly.'

'Do you remember that day we came here to get our membership cards?' asked Patch, who now stood with Tat and Kim, holding up a t-shirt which he wanted their approval on before parting with his cash.

'Yeah it was the same day we bought our tickets for the Sunrise 5000 rave which was at the Santa Pod Race Track. I've still got the flyer at home somewhere and intend for it to not end up being used as a roach. Sunrise 5000 'Once in a Blue Moon',' said Tat, 'And that 20k sound system -it was brilliant.'

'I remember seeing coachloads of ravers turning up. I always liked the bit on the flyer that said 'private party for Sunrise clubbers- and their guests'. Those 'guests' swelled the numbers that night...or morning should I say,' said Kim, joining in.

'Yeah, morning it was. We didn't get there until about 3am in the end, did we? We kept getting caught up talking to people at meeting points. We were trying to help out all those ravers who couldn't get through on the Dial-A-Rave number. Every meeting point we got to the Old Bill was lurking. Every public phone box en route had a hundred ravers around it, all trying to find out where the venue was. It was a right buzz. Loved every second of it!' said Tat, virtually bouncing on the spot as he recalled the events from that night.

'I remember you spent most of the night on some bouncy castle. You were tripping off your head, bouncing around in a world of your own with a massive grin over yer face. I wish I had caught a photo of you,' Tat reminded Patch.

'Yeah splashing out £25 on our Sunrise membership cards left me short that weekend. We work hard so we play hard, right?'

Tat had to agree, being involved in the rave scene didn't come cheap. Between them they'd spent a small fortune on records, raves, clothes and drugs, but they never dwelt on it, it was part of the deal. They certainly weren't regretting any of it.

They spent another half an hour in the shop talking to the girl behind the counter. They chatted about the shop, about the Sunrise and Back To The Future club magazine called Outrage, about the various flyers that were scattered across the counter and they talked about Eclipse, which seemed to impress the girl, and Patch liked this. He also left the Sunrise shop with a smile on his face because he had a new t-shirt which he intended to wear at the rave that night and he also had the girl's phone number.

'C'mon let's get a move on,' said Tat leading the way back to the car, 'There'll still be time to nip over to the Boot Store to see what desert boots they've got in and then I've got some business to sort with The Ozzard of Whizz.'

***

A few days later Kim sat in Tat's chair by the window again, only this time she was seething.

'What a pile of shit and waste of 22p.'

She was reading The Sun's 'Ecstasy Airport' story from Monday 26th June.

'Did you get around to reading this yet? It's about the Sunrise Midsummer's Night Dream rave on the 24th. That White Waltham

Airfield was a great venue for a rave. Definitely one of the biggest raves so far. Do you remember the tiny pieces of silver paper getting fire-worked into the air and showering over people? It was fantastic! What they've written about the rave and us is a load of bollocks.' Kim was angry and she wasn't one to swear much.

'Spaced out!' said Tat reading aloud what he saw in the newspaper, which he read for a bit, then tossed it back to Kim.

'The Sun cracks secret drug rave-up in hanger,' Kim continued to read on, 'Scandal of M25 parties. Eleven thousand youngsters go drug crazy at Britain's biggest ever acid party...11,000 go wild...the Hooray Henries are at it too-Oxford toffs brawl at ball...beheaded pigeons littered the floor.'

'Well you can rely on the media to introduce fiction into the facts. Wankers!'

'It's what they have to do to sell papers Tat. Always been the way. They never let truth get told.'

Kim threw the newspaper onto the floor and turned to look out the window. Tat got up from the cushion where he'd been relaxing and stood beside Kim. He kissed her on the head.

'I know that,' replied Tat, 'But why don't they write about that newly formed Police Pay Party Unit. I mean they're properly closing in on the raves now. They are getting serious about stopping us raving.'

'I heard that the police unit is based in Gravesend. I've got a cousin who lives down that way. Well, nearer Slade Green, but she knows someone who cleans the offices and that's how she found out about it. She then belled me and told me. I forgot to tell you. You're going to have to be really careful now with Eclipse.'

Tat shrugged his shoulders and placed the palms of his hands on the window and he gazed out across London.

'It's a waste of the tax payers' money. I mean where's the real harm? Okay, I get it that a few villagers lose a night's sleep and wake up on a Sunday morning to find the country lanes surrounding their homes all clogged up with cars and vans, but there's never any real damage. It's not like people are burgling their homes or breaking into their village shops. We just want to dance.'

'I suppose people feel threatened. People always do when they are faced with something they don't understand...'

'Or can't control,' added Tat.

'...or can't control and that's a big deal for Thatcher and her cronies. They don't like what they can't control.'

'...or make money off of. And that's another thing I suppose, why the Police Pay Party Unit don't like it -the fact that a handful of people are making a lot of money and they're not.'

'It's the drugs side of things too Tat. We've seen the amount of drugs being pushed around. It's big business and there'll be a side to it that the likes of you and me and most ravers don't see. And don't want to see. But we know there's an unsavoury element to it all. There's more to going to a rave and having conversations with strangers like 'Where you from? What's your name? What you on?''

'Yeah, I know and, yes, you're right. But there are ways to go about doing things but that new Police Unit will probably get it wrong. And, don't get me wrong, it's not that I've anything against the Old Bill, asI don't. Do you remember that time we left Clinks and we counted about a dozen car windows all smashed in and all had their car stereos nicked? The Old Bill were helping ravers that night. And there was that time Steady and his mates left that rave on that Sunday morning only to discover that they had a flat tyre. A couple of Old Bill stepped in and helped them replace the tyre with the spare...and that must have been a funny experience because Steady was still tripping.'

'So yeah, it's a bit of the good, the bad and the ugly really. It'll be interesting to see where it all ends up,' said Kim.

'Yeah it will,' replied Tat returning to his cushion, 'But for now I know where I want to end up and we've got an hour or so until Patch shows up.' And with that he beckoned Kim to go to him and they made love.

MOMENTS IN LOVE

The past few weekends had started to catch up with Tat because, when DJ Smile and DJ Jewels bounced through the doors at Eclipse Towers, he was huddled under a blanket on his chair. It turned out that he wasn't bullet proof after all. But he also knew it would only be a few days before he'd shake his cold off and be back to his usual self-all bright-eyed and bushy tailed. Tat had felt pretty shit though and, because of this, had even decided to take a day offwork. He'd spent the majority of his day watching shit programmes on TV and these included the Open University, which reminded him of the days when he'd been off sick from school.

Tat had also flicked through some of his Pollock books and worked his way through two tins of Heinz tomato soup. But the real highlight of his day had been the hour or so that he'd spent writing a letter to his friend Brendan. Brendan was still serving his prison sentence. He'd been one of the unfortunate ones to have been dawn-raided because of his connection to football hooliganism and, whereas most had gotten away without a conviction, Brendan hadn't been so lucky.

Tat had first met Brendan back in 1984 via Patch and some of the ICF firm and, even though Brendan and Tat followed different teams, they clicked and got on well. In fact, Tat and Brendan had been drinking in the Prince of Wales together only a few nights before he'd been nicked and carted off to the Old Bill station.

In Tat's letter to Brendan, he wrote about what he and Patch had been getting up to. He knew their exploits would make Brendan laugh and help him get through the hours he'd be spending staring at the walls in his cell. Tat wrote about setting up Eclipse and how his flat was now transformed into a radio studio and constantly smelled of sweat, Mandate and marijuana. He Told Brendan about Kim and described her as best as he could. Tat also wrote about the buzz lighting up London and how the parties were taking off. He knew Brendan would be gutted that he'd be missing out on what was happening, just like he was missing out on going to see West Ham. Tat finished up the letter by reminding Brendan to keep his chin up and that he'd soon see him back down the Prince of Wales again for a nice cool pint.

The letter was lying on the floor beside Tat when DJ Smile and DJ Jewels arrived. Both girls spent the first ten minutes tidying up Tat's flat, making him tea and giving him cuddles. But the girls weren't visiting Eclipse Towers to do housework or offer TLC-they had their Balearic show to broadcast to hungry ears.

Tat watched on as the two girls got themselves organised. DJ Smile really did light up the room just as she did the pirate ravewaves. Her long, bright blonde hair, that she often tied back, and her even brighter pale blue eyes melted everyone that she came into contact with. And then she had her voice. Her London tones took no prisoners and excited every male Eclipse listener.

DJ Jewels was equally as stunning with her jet-black hair and dark brown eyes. She had a great figure too and she knew how to dress and what worked for her...and for boys. She never left the house without her bright ruby red lipstick, multiple bracelets and necklaces and some big hoop earrings. Her family had gangster connections too and this she said was why she called herself DJ Jewels. Tat or Patch never pressed her for any more information.

Of course, their show was one of Eclipse's most popular. Both girls had a great relationship. They took control of the ravewaves and knew how to relate to the listeners. They also knew their house music and had been deep into the warehouse scene since the early days. They had been regulars at Planet Love, which was held in the Fridge in Brixton and they were always welcome at the Camden Palace. They knew the likes of Mark Moore, Colin Faver and Eddie Richards and it was by watching them that they'd learned how to deejay.

DJ Smiles and DJ Jewels kicked off their Wallabees and got themselves ready to do their show, which was to be their tribute to Ibiza and the Balearic vibe. Both had been frequenting Ibiza since the summer of '87 and, because of this, had got to know DJ Alfredo pretty well.

DJ Jewels fiddled with the mixer; it had been playing up. She looked at Tat as if asking for help but, having assessed that he wasn't in a good way and that he likely to be as useful as a fart in the wind, she decided to sort the mixer problem out for herself. Whilst she attended to the mixer, DJ Smile removed records from the bags that she and DJ Jewels had lugged into Tat's flat. Only after she'd done that did she roll a joint and fire it up.

'Hello London,' DJ Smile began, 'DJ Smiles and DJ Jewels here for our tribute to Ibiza show that we've been promising you. We hope you're locked on.'

'If you went to Ibiza and want any records played, please just page in those requests,' DJ Jewels invited.

'And you know you can page in any shouts you want sent out. The Eclipse studio pager number is 08550 32020 and if you need a taxi to get to any raves call Echos Cabs on 9807919. And to kick off the show, we have this for you. Smile and enjoy.'

DJ Smile eased in Dreams of Santa Anna and took back the joint that DJ Jewels had been sucking on.

'How's Kim? asked DJ Smile, offering Tat the joint.

'She's alright,' coughed Tat accepting the joint and forcing the smoke down into his lungs.

'I bumped into her down Oxford Street a couple of weeks back. We had a good chat. She's lovely. You're punching above your weight,' joked DJ Jewels.

Tat laughed. He believed her. The three of them shared what gossip they had whilst Orange Lemon played. DJ Smile checked the messages which had started to come in on the pager.

'Hello Earl, nice to hear from you. Hope all is well over there in Putney…and hello Sean, nice to know you're locked on to the show.'

DJ Jewels gripped the microphone with both hands, her bracelets rattled as she did so. She spoke slowly, telling the listeners that the show was going to include an eclectic mix of tunes which had been favourites at Amnesia. Before she introduced Camino Del Sol, she invited the show's listeners to page in any of their memories of going to Amnesia.

Over the next half an hour, DJ Smiles and DJ Jewels played tracks from the likes of Prince, The Wooden Tops and the

Thrashing Doves and these were mixed in with Salsa House and House Nation. Judging by the amount of messages being paged in, the show was apparently going down well.

'We got your request Louise. This one goes out to you. See you on the white sands again soon,' said DJ Smile as she put on Moments In Love by the Art of Noise.

'Do you want a cuppa?' asked DJ Smile, glancing over her shoulder at Tat. In response, Tat sat up and nodded.

'So do we. Put the kettle on will you?' said DJ Jewels waving her mug in the air.

Tat made three cups of tea whilst the girls sorted through records and read the pages.

'Look at this one,' said DJ Jewels, handing the pager to DJ Smile.

'Oh,its him again,' she replied.

'What's up?' asked Tat handing over the mugs of steaming hot tea.

DJ Smile held up the pager so Tat could read it. He rolled his eyes. He looked forward to the girls dealing with it. DJ Jewels took control of the microphone.

'We got your page Derek from Dulwich. Its good know that you have such a high opinion of yourself, and be assured that, yes, DJ Smile and me do come as a pair, but you'll never get to find out.'

And with that she flicked the switch and Jibaro Electra took the Balearic show to another level. Kaw-Liga by The Residents, City Lights by William Pitt and E2-E4 by Manuel Gottsching got air play too.

'Before we finish the show tonight, we just want to put a shout out to some of the KISS deejays. DJ Jewels and myself were only chatting the other night about how we used to love listening to KISS. We hope you do get your licence. This next track goes out to Norman Jay, Judge Jules, Jazzie B and the Madhatter Trevor Nelson.'

As Planet E fired up, DJ Smile and DJ Jewels huddled around the microphone and signed off the show with a 'Bye London and we miss you KISS' and they blew a kiss down the microphone.

NRG

'Oh, I meant to tell you something,' began Kim as she struggled to unlace one of her Timberland boots and pull it off. 'When I was at work on Thursday, I overheard two lads having a conversation about Adamski. They were arguing because one of them was insistent that Adamski's real name is Adam Ski. The other one was trying to tell him it was bollocks. They went on and on throughout my whole fag break. I couldn't be arsed to step in and tell him that we know him and his actual name is Adam Tinley.'

Tat, who was busy messing around with leads that hooked up the mixer with the record player, looked up and rolled his eyes. Although, on reflection, he thought it was plausible. He didn't dwell on it though because the leads issue was getting him hot and bothered. He was pleased when he heard the door open and saw Patch enter the flat.

'You alright?' asked Patch. He could see that Tat looked annoyed.

'There's a fooking problem with these leads. Here, you have a look.'

Patch carefully placed the bag of records he'd brought with him onto one of the cushions beside Kim. He smiled at her, tutted and told Tat to get out of the way and put the kettle on. Tat happily did as he was told and, a few minutes later, Patch was sipping tea whilst looking pleased with himself because he'd resolved the leads issue. He celebrated the victory by removing a Lion bar from his denim shirt pocket and, tearing off the wrapper, took a large bite of it. It was only whilst he was chewing the chocolate bar that he remembered he had intended to save the snack for later that night.

'I saw that geeza who has that Ford with the sound system in it in the week,' said Patch.

'The one we saw outside Spectrum that night?' asked Tat, casting his already hazy memory back to a Monday night the year before when he and Patch were stood in the queue outside Spectrum and some fella pulled up in a car, wound down the windows and pumped out Tod Terry's Bango very, very loud. It turned out that the owner of the car had installed an impressive sound system in it and took pride in driving around London blasting out house music.

'Yeah,' said Patch, 'He had everyone in the queue dancing like lunatics. It helped kill the time though.'

'Yeah I remember. I also remember hearing The Project Club's Dance With The Devil for the first time that night too.'

The recollection of The Project Club track prompted Tat to search through his vinyl until he located it. A few moments later, the track was opening up the Eclipse show for that evening and he and Patch were playfully mouthing the words 'dance with the devil' as they sang along with the record.

'That goes out to all those that went to Spectrum. Good days. Good days,' said Patch whispering into the microphone before backing off to allow Tat to take over.

'So, London, another Saturday is upon us-yes, it's Saturday 1st July 1989, just in case any of you have been sleeping since last Saturday. Now, straight after this next tune we have just what you've been waiting for. So, keep it locked to Eclipse and all the info you'll need about the Energy rave will be revealed.'

'And a big shout going out to some of the other pirates tearing up the airwaves-Sunrise, Centreforce and Fantasy-there's plenty of room in our ocean of black vinyl – dance, dance, dance!' Patch added as he turned up the volume as it got to the part where the chimes started on Dance With The Devil. This was his favourite part.

'This is a party-political broadcast on behalf of the Energy party. Here are the following requirements for this Saturday's DJ Convention and gathering of young minds,' said Tat, feeling amused.

'Yes, firstly you must have a Great Britain road atlas. Yes, that's a Great Britain road atlas,' Tat continued.

'...and secondly a reliable motor with a full tank of gas...' added Patch.

'...and lastly, you must have a ticket and you must be a member,' Tat pitched in.

'So now we end this party-political dance broadcast on behalf of the Energy party. Don't waste your vote: stand up and be counted, because ENERGY IS ON,' said Patch reclaiming the microphone and, with that, he gave out the Energy hotline number.

For the next two hours Tat and Patch delivered their show, playing requests which people had paged in, along with the various shout outs. They also updated their listeners that the police had shut off sections of the M4 in the Membury area and advised the ravers to seek out alternative ways of getting to the party. Tat was just providing an update regarding a police road block when The Ozzard of Whizz turned up at Eclipse Towers with DJ Spank E and DJ Sensible Simon. They all had red eyes.

The Ozzard made himself at home as Tat handed Eclipse over to the two DJs and Patch sorted out some business with The Ozzard.

'We've not seen you since that gathering on Clapham Common,' said Kim.

'Haven't we?' said The Ozzard, plonking himself down on a cushion next to Kim.

Kim handed The Ozzard the joint she'd been smoking, which of course he accepted.

'That was after Biology. That was mental, everyone making their way over to Clapham Common at that time on a Sunday morning.' The Ozzard spoke fondly of the occasion when a few hundred ravers descended on Clapham Common after a Biology rave. Dozens of cars wound down their windows, opened their doors and played house music. As the party continued, some police showed up by they didn't react in a negative way. They seemed to be more bemused. The party went on for a few more hours.

'That was good that we saw you there. We needed that pick up.' Kim was referring to the E's that she, Tat and Patch had bought off of The Ozzard on Clapham Common.

'People were still hungry for supplies,' said The Ozzard, 'Do you remember seeing that fella who was wearing that bright yellow top hat on his head. He had been going mental at the rave. He was the one who climbed right up to the top of the scaffolding and danced on top of that speaker.'

'I remember that girl who was dressed all in white. She danced on the stage all night. Amazing dancer!' Kim remembered.

'Sexy dancer you mean,' The Ozzard added.

'Yeah, definitely sexy,' said Patch, joining in with the conversation now that he'd conducted his business with The Ozzard and was now the proud owner of three E's. 'She was dancing like she was properly on one. I was still watching her dancing when The Beloved's The Sun Rising came on at dawn. That was a special moment. There's nothing like hearing that track at that time of the morning. It sums everything up about the raves and this Second Summer of Love.'

'So true Patch,' Kim agreed.

'Hallelujah Patch mate,' said Tat also joining in.

'And talking about characters, there was that white bloke with the dreadlocks. I keep seeing him around. I'm sure he used to go to Amnesia, but back then he didn't have his dreads. The dreads suit him.' Kim shook her head, as if waving dreadlocks around.

'Yeah, he looks wild, especially when he dances coz his dreads swish about wildly. He has a wild look in his eyes too,' Patch concluded.

The Ozzard passed on the joint and stood up. He needed to be on his way; he was in demand.

'The one that'll always stick in my mind was that bloke on crutches,' said The Ozzard leaving the Eclipse team to ponder the image as he waved goodbye and made his exit.

'Oh yeah! Now he is hard core,' said Kim waving off The Ozzard.

'That bloke with the crutches was mental. Wasn't he at that party we went to that had that mental pendulum ride?' asked Tat.

'That ride went so high it felt like it would just spin right over,' Kim recalled, adding, 'That's the one. He was there. I remember noticing him poking the air with one of his crutches like he was spearing a dragon. I dunno what he was on that night. Maybe in his trip he was seeing dragons.'

'My fave ride at a rave is the Tilt-A-Whirl,' said Tat.

'The one I couldn't get you off? You must have spent a pill's worth of dollar on it because you kept going back for more,' Patch recalled.

'Yeah, you were a right sissy that night,' Kim teased, 'You wouldn't go in the pendulum with me.'

'That was because that trip I took made me feel a bit paranoid. I don't often get bad trips but that night I did. Fortunately, it wasn't a fiercely bad trip,' Tat shot back to defend himself.

'My fave rides are the drop towers. You can't beat that feeling of the pit of your stomach hitting the back of your mouth just as an E is about to explode in your brain,' said Kim excitedly.

'For me, I'm just happy with the bumper cars,' Tat shrugged as he left the room to go to the toilet.

'Well you do need the driving practice mate,' Patch yelled after him.

Patch, Tat and Kim left Eclipse Towers in the capable hands of DJ Spank E and DJ Sensible Simon, who were preparing to pump the ravewaves for the next two hours with the latest Hip House tracks.

DJ Sensible Simon took control of the microphone and introduced himself and his partner in vinyl crime. He also shared their intention to be playing Hip Hop and Hip House, as they'd both been playing a lot of that in recent weeks.

'Hello London, we promise you some golden oldies tonight, tunes that will remind of the days when you spent Saturday afternoons spinning on your backs on pieces of cardboard,' said DJ Sensible Simon, kicking off the show with Hip Hop, Be Bop (Don't Stop), which certainly caught the listeners' attention.

DJ Spank E lined up the next three records, which he knew would blow the roof off. First up would be Let There Be House by Deskee, which would be followed by Silver Bullets' Bring Forth The Guillotine and The She Rockers' Get Up On This. The show was really starting to rock!

'DJ Spank E is manning the pager tonight. I know it's usually my job because I'm the sensible one in this outfit, but tonight its over to him. So, keep them requests and shouts paged in and we'll do our best with them. You know the score and you know the number here at Eclipse Towers: 08550 32020.'

Satisfied that the show had now lifted off okay, DJ Spank E slumped back into his chair and grinned at DJ Sensible Simon who was already on the case of checking the various pages that were beginning to fly in.

'This one's for you Lisa from Denmark Hill, what a tune,' said DJ Spank E as he put the needle on the record of Who Is It by Mantronix.

'And we have this request too,' said DJ Sensible Simon, responding to another page that had come in. 'This is a good shout Joel and Stacey, Eric B and Rakim's Paid In Full. Thanks for the page.'

Over the next twenty minutes, DJ Spank E and DJ Sensible Simon took their listeners right back, mixing in records from Grandmaster Flash and the Furious Five, Run-DMC, De La Soul, Afrika Bambaataa, alongside Public Enemy and Derrik May. They did all this whilst providing updates on the Energy rave that was going off near Membury in Berkshire. They signed off the show with Get On The Dance Floor, which felt just perfect.

THE HACIENDA

Tat, Patch and Kim were still buzzing two weeks after the Energy rave near Membury. Their night had turned into an adventure from the moment they left Eclipse Towers. Even though the Energy promoters had supplied all the Eclipse DJs with free tickets for the rave and told them the location of the party, Tat, Patch and Kim had decided to drop by Blackheath Common because they knew that was where one of the meeting points was. By the time they reached the Common, there were already hundreds of cars packed full of ravers. It was a sight to be seen as ravers danced on car roofs or wherever they were standing.

Patch parked the car on the Common in one of the few spaces left. It was Patch who had spotted one of the Energy team with a huge mobile phone stuck to his ear. He was surrounded by ravers who eagerly awaited to get the latest information as to where either the next meeting point was, or the where the actual rave was.

There was a real buzz on Blackheath Common and the atmosphere was electric. Ravers were full of excitement and anticipation, and it felt good as Patch, Tat and Kim snaked their way through the make-shift car park listening to cars pumping out the hip hop and hip house tracks that DJ Spank E and DJ Sensible Simon were pumping out back at Eclipse Towers.

They'd hung around on Blackheath Common for half an hour, chatting to people and having another conversation with The Ozzard of Whizz, who they had also bumped into. Of course, he was extremely busy so they didn't chat for too long.

And then, as if by some kind of special magic, cars started to fill up with ravers and speed away from the Common. It was clear that word had reached people as to where the Energy rave was and they were off to find it.

Suddenly the roads surrounding Blackheath Common became busy and blocked. It was chaos. Patch, Tat and Kim got caught up in the chaos until eventually spotting an opportunity to free themselves and head away from the Common. On at least three occasions, they had to take sharp lefts and rights in their attempts to evade police cars which seemed intent on pulling over cars full of ravers. Eventually they were racing down the M4 and enjoying every second of being locked onto Eclipse 89.9.

The night of the Energy rave had wiped out Patch, Tat and Kim for days. There had been a lot of driving but not so much dancing. The pills they had taken had been strong too and the come down was costly. Doing their day jobs was tough, their bodies and brains ached, but they eventually bounced back. It was in the evenings which followed the Energy party that Tat and Kim had lazed around and come up with the plan to go to Manchester and to the Hacienda.

It was Friday afternoon and Kim had spent the best part of two hours packing the things she thought she'd need for the trip to Manchester. Tat and Patch had packed their sports bags in a fraction of the time it had taken Kim, and it was looking likely that they'd be sharing a toothbrush.

Tat was especially looking forward to going back to his roots. He may well be living in London, but Manchester was his home and he knew it always would be. He knew he wouldn't have time to see any of his family and had resigned himself to this. Besides, he had other intentions and an impressive list of things he wanted to do - and spending some hard-earned dollar in Eastern Bloc Records was at the top of his list.

Patch had only ever been to Manchester for football. Jumping aboard an ordinary a few years earlier was where he'd partly served his apprenticeship in the ranks of the ICF faithful. On those train journeys, he'd learned to hold his own amongst often challenging company and he also honed his skill as a card player and would often be paying for his pre-match burger with handfuls of shrapnel. He also made good friends on those away days and they were loyal, he knew he could trust them and he knew each and every one of them would have his back - and there were many occasions when he needed his back watched.

Kim was still packing and unpacking as Tat and Patch prepared themselves for their Eclipse show, which they intended to be a tribute to the sounds coming out of Manchester and what they knew had been rocking the dancefloor in the Hacienda.

The Hacienda was something in which Tat and Patch had a vested interest. They were fully aware of the club's history and knew it had been opened in May 1982 by Tony Wilson-owner of Factory Records andthat the club was even given its own catalogue number FAC.51. Located at numbers 11-13 Whitworth Street West, the club played host to some of biggest acts of the 80s: The Smiths, New Order and even Madonna performed at the club in 1984, her appearance captured on film by Channel Four's The Tube. Tat and Patch also knew that in 1986, Lancashire lad Mike Pickering had started his Nude nights on Fridays and he was one of the first to introduce early house music to the Northern kids. Within a year he was joined by fellow DJ, Graeme Park, which helped take the Nude nights to a whole new level. And then, in the summer of 1988, Pickering began his Ibiza inspired Hot nights which he shared with Jon Da Silva and ever since then, The Hacienda, acid house and rave had become one with the Madchester vibe.

'What's the time?' asked Patch.

'Five to eight,' replied Tat, checking his watch as he flicked a switch on the mixer.

Patch nodded, reached for a record and removed the shiny black vinyl from the sleeve, admiring it, as always, and placing it carefully onto the deck. He seldom undressed a woman with such care, but records, well, they held a place in his heart that no woman was likely to ever compete with and which also explained why he was single most of the time.

A few seconds later and the crackle of the needle on the record kick-started the Eclipse Manchester tribute show. The intro on 808's Pacific State evoked something in Patch that he felt no words could ever describe; for him this track was of the reasons why he was loving what he was doing in 1989.

As the saxophone came in, Patch glanced at Tat and he knew his best mate was also falling under the spell of Pacific State - and it was a specific state to be in. Looking into each other's eyes, grins grew on their faces as the drums entered, their heads nodding in time. Joining in with the hand claps, they surrendered to the tune and the show had lift off.

Six minutes later the track nearly over; Patch took hold of the microphone.

'Hello London. Now there's a tune that needs no introduction. We love it here in Eclipse Towers and we know that you love it, wherever you happen to be. Tonight's two hour show is going to be our tribute to Manchester. DJ Tat and me have a pile of records to get through, and we know you're going to love it.'

Tat slid over to be nearer the microphone and as he replaced Pacific State with Magical Dream.

'And here's another from 808 State, it's one of my faves at the moment.' He let the record play for a few seconds, 'And you can still page us your shouts, but we're not taking any requests tonight, sorry. The Eclipse number is 0855032020, as always it'll be good to hear who is locking on.'

As Tat and Patch played such records as Wrote For Luck, FX and New Order's Confusion, the show got deeper entrenched in the Manchester vibe. Several times, Tat put shouts out and these included the Kitchen faithful in Hulme, MC Tunes and the Rap Assassins and he'd end each shout with a growling 'Manchester vibes in the area' and this had Patch doubled over with laughter every time.

'An' now,' Tat began, slowing things down, a serious tone in his voice, 'this next track was a game changer and will still be talked about passionately a hundred years from now. This one is for you Graeme Park.'

Pressing a button and leaning back into his chair, Tat was going to make sure he'd enjoy Voodoo Ray and he knew Eclipse listeners would do too.

As the show continued, Kim walked back and forth carrying various items like towels, shoes and bangles, and Tat was convinced he'd seen at least three different hair dryers.

Tat spun three Happy Mondays tracks. It seemed fitting and included: Holy Ghost, Hallelujah and of course Rave On. And Patch had followed these with three tracks from the Stone Roses: Fools Gold, Made of Stone and Waterfall. He'd also added that Fools Gold was another game changer and that it had certainly changed his life for the better. He couldn't praise the Roses enough and gave shouts out to Ian Brown, John Squire, Mani and Reni, who he considered to be of the best drummers of all time.

Towards the end of the show, Kim joined Tat and Patch, having finally deciding she'd packed all she needed for the trip. She relaxed with a joint and enjoyed the last track of the show, the mellower Emotions Electric 2 by A Guy Called Gerald.

As the last seconds of the track played out, Patch had already crawled onto the bed of cushions which Kim had made up for him earlier. He was staying there for the night because they'd all agreed to make an early start and be on the road by 7am. A flick of several switches later and Eclipse Towers went quiet and dark.

'Fuckin typical - when we left London the sun was out and the skies were blue, and now we arrive in Manchester and it starts to piss down. I don't wanna fuck my Wallabees up,' said Patch rolling his shoulders in an attempt to shake off the stress of driving to Manchester from London.

'Shut up with your moaning, that's all you've done for the past 100 miles. Look, you're in Manchester, the home of Joy Division, The Smiths, Stone Roses and the Happy Mondays and we are going to have a fookin top time in the Hacienda tonight. The Hacienda is the cathedral to house music in Britain,' Tat spat back whilst continuing to stare out of the window and suck in the familiar sights of his place of birth. He was happy.

'Can't argue that the Hacienda, the Roses and the Mondays are helping to put *our* music at the centre of the universe,' Patch huffed.

'It's Madchester Patch mate, Madchester!' yelled Tat, which awoke a sleeping Kim.

'Where are we?' she asked wiping sleep from her eyes and feeling the need to pop some Wrigley's into her gob.

Tat explained they were entering Manchester and as they got nearer to the city centre he pointed out significant landmarks that had had some bearing on his youth.

'Can we go to the Salford Lads Club whilst we're up here?' asked Kim as she searched for a brush and started to attend to her messed up hair.

'Doubt we'll have time, but maybe tomorrow,' said Tat knowing full well that Kim would be in no mood or shape to want to go seeking out locations of The Smiths. Plus, he wanted to avoid the

Ordsall area because he knew there were some naughty boys who lived there and he'd prefer to stay out of their way, especially as he had two southerners in tow.

Tat directed Patch to a street near the underground market and they parked the car. Tat then took them on a tour of the market and showed them the stalls where he had picked up flared cords and jeans, together with the corduroy hooded coats that he loved and which he thought was a terrace look that worked well with a pair of Adidas Samba's. However, it wasn't a look that caught on down south and, in truth, the northern casuals had only held onto that look for a few autumn months anyway.

Before heading back up into the streets of the city, Tat dived into a bakery and treated Kim and Patch to custard slices. It didn't take them long to wolf them down. Kim and Patch followed Tat as he led them through the old Victorian streets of Manchester until they got to Eastern Bloc Records.

More than hour was spent in the record shop and more than a hundred pounds was spent on a selection of 12 inches. Both Tat and Patch left the shop as pleased as punch. They strolled over to the café opposite Eastern Bloc and, once inside, purchased several bacon butties which they washed down with several cups of steaming hot sweet tea.

The remainder of the afternoon was spent trudging the streets of Manchester and getting settled in the B&B which Kim had booked for them. Once showered, and Kim and Tat had shagged, it was time to make their way to the pub opposite the Hacienda, have a few drinks and get themselves in the mood for some serious and energetic dancing.

By 11pm Patch, Tat and Kim found themselves standing in the queue outside the Hacienda. There was an undeniable buzz shared by the ravers surrounding them.

The queue moved slowly, but Patch was pleased with the copy of Freaky Dancing he'd found which someone must have dropped. He flicked through the pages with Tat and Kim looking over his shoulder. Patch had heard of the fanzine but had never actually seen a copy. The contents made him laugh and he was still giggling away when he found himself being pushed through the doors of the Hacienda.

The music was loud and T-Coy's Carino was playing. As Tat took Kim and Patch on a guided tour of the club, Sugar Bear, The Beat Club andTurntable Orchestra got the crowds rocking on the dance floor and every available space. Patch especially liked the yellow and black hazard stripes that made up the majority of the club's décor.

Finding a pillar to lean against, Tat searched for the E's that he had stashed away in one of his pockets and he dropped one into the hands of Kim and Patch. On the count of three they swallowed them.

'I was interested to see what this Hacienda crowd were like, you know. They are as mental as us down South,' said Patch, feeling the first rush from the E.

'I knew they would be,' said Kim also feeling the first woosh, 'Although those twins we saw at Sunrise 5000 might take some beating as being amongst the most mental.'

'Oh yeah them two girls. Identical twins, dressed exactly the same in some sort of customised boiler suits, exactly the same haircuts, both wearing Timberland boots.' Tat had a clear recollection of them.

'And both dancing exactly the same way. They were like mirror images of each other. And do you remember that boy who stood, just staring at them for ages. He was totally tripping off his head. Watching those twins must have been freaking him out,' laughed Kim.

'Mind you, it reminds me of being in Shoom one night. I had dropped some acid and there were two girls there that I couldn't take my saucer eyes off. They weren't twins as such, but they were dressed almost identical and looked like Mel and Kim...even had those funny Spanish cowgirl style hats,' recalled Patch.

As the E's started to work, so did the compulsion for the need to dance. Patch was the first to launch himself into the dancing. Tat and Kim followed; they couldn't resist, especially as Voodoo Ray was playing. They shared the dance floor with Manchester's hard core 24-hour party people. No-one in the club stood still. The music being played demanded that each and every person dance.

A solid hour of dancing passed. A drink of water was very much needed, so Tat disappeared off to the bar. He returned with three bottles of water.

'This is proper having it mate,' yelled Patch.

Tat nodded. The next moment Tat, Patch and Kim huddled together in a loving cuddle. They were having the night of their life and, what was more, Pacific Sate started to play. They were in rave heaven and in the most talked about club in the country of that summer.

RIDE ON TIME

Patch kicked off the show with Ride On Time. He loved the track and it didn't bother him that it had reached the masses and was partly responsible for bursting the underground bubble he had been living in for the best part of eighteen months. As the track reachedthe end, Patch - who had been happily pouring himself over the article from an issue of ID magazine that was already a year old on 'Amnesiacs' - snatched the microphone from the grip of Tat who was about to start talking.

'Big shout going out to the Penenden Heath car park crew down in Kent, that's Craig, Chang, Colin, Sparksy, Chris, Noddy, Justin, Tim, Tel, Jason, Smitty and not forgetting Pedro Pete and his chicken legs dancing. Get yourselves through the Dartford Tunnel quickish coz you don't want the Old Bill getting there before you - you remember what happened last time when they blocked it to stop you getting to South Ockendon. And keep it locked for updates on meeting points either side of the tunnel. You wouldn't want to be heading in the wrong direction, would you? It's gonna be a big one tonight, see you there...and lads...bring some girls eh!'

Having said his bit, Patch passed the microphone to Tat, who had been busy rolling a joint all the while Ride On Time had been spinning and had been mixed into Cry Sisco's Afro Dizzi Act.

'We have all the info about the location of tonight's party,' he began, 'and all the back-up venues if they need to be used. Energy is on and for those who still have their tickets from the last Energy party that got cancelled-your tickets are valid for tonight's party/ That's right-your tickets are valid for tonight!'

'The number for dial-a rave is 01-726 8845 or direct to 0860 212571 and become part of the best-kept secret in town.' Patch took the microphone back and chipped in.

Tat played The Beat Club's Security as he reclaimed the microphone and told the listeners that he had control of the ones and twos and that they were locked on to Eclipse 89.9.

'We have a page in saying that Shaun and four car-loads of his Bexley crew have had their cars stopped and searched down by the Black Prince. Cheers for the page Shaun. Its turning into a bit of a hot spot that area. Word of advice for party goers - avoid that neck of the woods and get to the meeting point a different way.'

'Yep you all know the score, it's essential to get to the party early coz we don't want the Old Bill shutting Energy down again,' Patch encouraged.

'Pass us that pile will yer Patch mate?' said Tat pointing his chin at a bunch of tickets and flyers that had been stacking up for weeks.

Patch stretched out and grabbed most of what Tat had requested. He put them on the table beside the mixer, decks and records. Between them they sifted through the pile. There were numerous flyers and tickets for parties they'd been invited to. There were simply too many going off for them to be getting to.

'It's good that promoters see us as being valuable assets in helping to promote their raves,' said Tat, marvelling at the artwork on one of the flyers.

'Yeah, for sure! It's been getting me thinking though. There's ways to start making some money out of all of this too.'

'What d'ya mean mate?' asked Tat.

'Adverts Tat. We should be getting the promoters and also record labels to pay us to make adverts for them.'

Tat's ears pricked up. It seemed to make sense.

'It's all good that we get free tickets for raves and that we're getting records sent into us, but I think there's other opportunities that we're missing out on. I've heard that some of the other pirates are starting to do the same.'

'Seems sound enough to me,' replied Tat, 'How do we go about doing it then?'

'Hold on a mo,' said Patch putting on another record, 'I've not thought about that bit yet, but we will sort that out.'

'I'll organise a meeting to let the other Eclipse DJs know. DJ Need All will have some ideas around this. He's good at that sort of stuff.'

Patch agreed that would be a good idea and left the planning to Tat.

'Where's Kim tonight?' Patch asked.

'She's making a night of it with some of her friends that she used to go to Ibiza with. A couple are back in the country. I told her where the Energy rave is, so they should be making their way towards the Heston Services about now.'

'It's going to be a big one tonight. You can feel that people are right up for raving.'

Tat agreed and, leaning into the microphone, put a few shouts out.

'This next track goes out to Stacey down there in deep dark Kent and to Julie Gilliland - thanks for the support darling.'

A promo copy of Quartz's Meltdown took the show to the next level. Tat and Patch loved the track but wished they'd broken it before Centreforce had.

The following Friday, Tat woke up with a banging headache. He was also annoyed with Kim because she had forgotten to fully shut the curtains and a slither of midday sun was penetrating the bedroom. He pulled the bed sheets over his head attempting to avoid the bright light, but it was in vain and, after tossing and turning for the next ten minutes, decided the sun had won and he threw the sheets off himself and Kim. Kim, who had been fast asleep, woke with a start as she tried to focus on Tat; her mascara and lipstick smudged across her face.

'What time is it?' asked Kim.

'Just gone twelve.'

Kim huffed and flopped her head down onto the pillow. The first memories of the night before began to flood back. She remembered listening to DJ Need All's show on Eclipse as she'd driven to Tat's flat. She'd then caught the handover as DJ Need All had passed the responsibility of the ones and twos to DJ Smile and DJ Jewels. Tat, Patch and DJ Need All and she had then made their way over to the Astoria for the Empathy 'State of Mind' rave. Mr Pasha at Centreforce had posted Patch some tickets for the rave and being that a great night was undoubtedly going to occur, Patch and Co.weren't going to miss it.

The Astoria was also one of Patch's favourite venues in London. He had fond memories of the Trip come Sin nights. The crowds were great and the music was amazing and those events certainly helped take the acid house experience in the city to new heights.

As Kim lay stretched out on the bed, her head aching too, she recalled how they'd made their way to the Astoria and, instead of having to queue up, they'd been allowed to walk in on their arrival. The doors had opened at 9.30pm, the event advertised as ending at 3am. The tenners they'd saved on door admission had gone towards paying for their E's and, from the moment they got inside the venue, Kim remembered how they'd danced and danced.

The five hours inside the Astoria had gone like a flash and it was Kim who had suggested that everyone carry on the party back in Tat's flat. Tat, who was still full of the love drug at 3am had agreed, and the party had indeed continued back at Eclipse Towers until the first sounds of the milk floats rattled and morning traffic started to flow. Kim had no recollection about going to bed; she just knew that Empathy had been a winner.

'Do you remember what Need All was going on about last night?' asked Tat, who had since got up, put the kettle on, made some tea and climbed back into bed holding two cups of the hot brown liquid.

Kim sat up and gratefully accepted the tea, taking a large sip. Unlike Tat, it always took her longer to come back to life following a heavy night.

'Twit...comes to mind,' she offered.

'WIT,' blurted Tat, 'World In Trance.'

'Oh yes, that's right. He wants to start up his own events. Did he mention something about finding some empty railway arch in Brixton?'

'Dunno about that,' replied Tat shaking his head.

'Good luck to him. He also said something about doing something with the Run Tings Crew, but I can't for the life of me remember what that was to do with.'

'Yeah, he was on one last night, wasn't he?' Tat laughed.

Tat and Kim finished off their cuppas in record time and felt pleased with themselves for taking the day off work. Their Friday was pretty much theirs to do what they wanted, but they knew it would include a trip to Fish's because Tat needed a haircut; a drop into Duffer because Tat had his eye on a sweat shirt he'd seen hanging up on their last visit; and a dive into Black Market because Tat had fifty dollars that he wanted to blow on exports. It was after the day of the Friday shuffle. With the thought of the day's plans in mind, Tat and Kim collapsed back into the bed, pulled the sheets over them and made gentle love.

THE FUTURE DANCE MUSIC FESTIVAL

'Pass us the sugar mate?' asked Patch who was already on his third cup of tea.

Tat pushed the jar of sugar in Patch's direction without looking up from reading his newspaper. He'd been engrossed in the story about the chief superintendent who had taken control of the FA Cup Semi-Final game at Hillsborough being suspended on full pay. The memories of the disaster were still raw for Tat and football fans all over the country.

By the time Tat had moved onto some story about a train derailing near West Ealing Station, The Ozzard of Whizz had entered the café and had plonked himself down next to Tat. As he stubbed out his fag in the over-full ashtray, he yelled out for a cup of tea to the old girl who was buttering some toast behind the counter. The old girl, not being swayed by his cheek, simply ignored him.

'Alright mate,' said Patch.

'Yeah, all good, busy and mental as usual,' replied The Oz as he fished into his dungarees for a small bag which contained some Strawberry Field acid tabs. The Oz had been shifting sheets of the stuff throughout July and he had plenty more that would see many ravers through August too. Tat and Patch had agreed they'd lay off the E's for a few weekends and content themselves with indulging in some acid trips instead.

The Oz slid the tabs across the table so that Patch could easily pick them up. Patch did so in one swift motion and the tabs were safely dropped into his shirt pocket. A moment later, The Oz was paying for his tea with the moneyPatch had slid across the table back to him. Everyone was happy.

'We heard you went up to that rave in Rochdale,' said Tat.

'Yeah it was mental.'

'How comes you went all the way up there?' asked Tat.

'Business as usual, plus I know the Donnelly brothers. I got the invite and took a drive up there.'

'I heard it was on some farm. That right?' asked Patch.

'Yeah, Stand Lees Farm. It was a good venue. The crowd were right up for it. Dozens of them dancing on stone walls and old farm equipment. Them northerners can rave you know.'

'What was the rave called?' enquired Tat.

'Joy,' said The Oz stirring more sugar into his tea.

The three of them sat chewing the fat and drinking tea for the next hour and it was the first that Tat and Patch had heard about some weekender called Woodstock which Centreforce were organising - and that sounded like a must do.

As the day rolled on, Tat and Patch were in no rush. They had hours before they needed to be back at Eclipse Towers and get the ball rolling for the Saturday night broadcasts.

Patch spent the afternoon in the Ann Boleyn pub with his Hammers pals before going to the match. Tat had lazed around his flat, mostly attempting to tidy up a bit and reading a new book he had found on Jackson Pollock. He was pleased to have had some time alone. He craved for peace and quiet and so far, 1989 had given him only a little of it.

By six o'clock, Eclipse Towers was back to its usual lively vibe. Tat and Patch got the decks working and played around with a new mixer they'd picked up that week. Now they were getting paid to broadcast adverts, they had some money to spend on upgrading the studio equipment.

Kim had brought two of her friends to the flat and they chatted away quietly in the background as Eclipse Radio 89.9 went live. Patch kicked off the show with his usual introduction which included the Eclipse pager number, the frequency and the invite for listeners to page in their shout outs. Three records were then played back to back, which helped get the Eclipse listeners in the mood for their Saturday night adventures.

'The Future Dance Music Festival is going to go down as the biggest Rave of all time. Of this we have no doubt. You can feel something big is happening tonight,' said Tat.

'And remember this is a Sunrise and Back To The Future party, so you just know it's gonna be proper - and it's Sunrise's 28th party.

They've got a 100,000-watt sound system and SNAP appearing for your pleasure. The numbers you need are 01-836 7846 or 01-247332. We have some pager numbers on their way too, so keep it locked to Eclipse 89.9. But, staying with 1986, here's some other much loved and much requested tracks that have kept us rooted to the dancefloors on many a sweaty night,' said Patch as he dropped the needle on The Nightwriters' Let The Music (Use You).

Two minutes into the Nightwriters, Tat took control of the microphone.

'Keep it locked into Eclipse party people coz this is where you'll get all the updates you need to get you to the party. Avoid the station that's telling you to go to Essex...there is no rave at Essex, any talk about Essex is coming from the Old Bill's fake pirate radio station.'

As the record played on, Tat and Patch talked about the rumours they'd been hearing about the police's Pay Party Unit setting up their own radio stations in an attempt to clamp down on the raves.

The Pay Party Unit had been ramping up their efforts and had been coming up with more and more creative ideas to stop ravers getting to the parties. There had been stories of police officers taking down road signs so people would get lost. They were using their radio stations to divert ravers to villages and towns in the Home Counties where there was no rave happening at all, and they were making their presence known in service stations around the M25. In truth, the Pay Party Unit they were losing the battle, but they had to be seen to be doing something to combat the illegal raves.

Over the next two hours, Tat and Patch pulled out house anthem after house anthem. They felt on top of the world and couldn't wait to get to the rave, drop their Strawberry Fields and have a great trip.

'DJ Patch and DJ Tat are at the controls in Eclipse Towers for only the next ten minutes and then we are off to the party,' Tat announced before handing the microphone to Patch.

'We have a backlog of messages, requests and shouts we just couldn't get through. Sorry London, so this is for all of you, this BIG BIG tune from '87 - and good luck finding the Promised Land.'

'So, it's just one more track from us tonight from our back to Chicago House mix. It's a personal favourite of mine and takes me back to many mental nights of clubbing around town. Good luck to you all with finding the party and have a good one. Remember its h..h..h..h house nation and this next one goes out to Guy and Malc and you can't help it being Spurs.'

And, with that Tat and Patch handed the reigns over to DJs Spank E and Sensible Simon. They then grabbed their coats and followed Kim and her friends who were already legging it down the stairs.

CAN YOU DANCE

Kim lay flat out on a bed of cushions she had made and picked away at some hot rock marks, whilst Tat sat in his chair that overlooked the city. So far, their day had been lazy. It had taken them a few days to get over the World Dance rave that had gone off near the village of Wrotham in Kent. Tat and Kim had merged their memories of that Saturday in an attempt to try and put the pieces of the jigsaw puzzle together.

Kim recalled how following Tat and Patch's Eclipse show, they'd set off in the direction of Wembley where there was a party happening. However, the police in one of their more zealous attempts, had intervened and were making a nuisance of themselves in the area, pulling over cars and setting up road blocks.

Fortunately for Tat, Kim and Patch, they'd been locked onto Eclipse and about a mile away from Wembley they heard the announcement from DJ Sensible Simon that there was a rave from World Dance happening in Kent.

The next thing, they find themselves caught up in a convoy of cars who'd also heard about the World Dance rave and were hammering it through the streets of London, onto the M25 and onto the M20. It had been on the M20, as Patch drove past the Wrotham Transmitting Station, that they'd lost connection with Eclipse. Tat played with the dial in an attempt to lock onto Centreforce and catch Keith Mac or Sunrise, but he didn't succeed. It didn't matter though, as a couple of miles further down the motorway they suddenly found what they were searching for.

Coming out of a haze in the distance to the right of them was a mass of colourful lights. It was obvious it was the location of the party. The excitement felt in the car almost lifted the roof off. It wasn't long after that, that Tat, Patch and Kim found themselves dancing in a field with an ever-increasing number of ravers. Reports following the rave said nearly8,000 ravers had danced in the field that night and Tat, Kim and Patch felt proud to have been part of it. And then there'd been the Genesis 88 and Biology party which had gone off near Meopham in Kent and this had also delivered.

Looking back on the events in August, Tat and Kim agreed it had been a memorable month. And then September had also delivered. Kim started off the conversation about the Genesis 88 party that had happened on the 9th. The warehouse in the East End that promoter Wayne Anthony had secured had been perfect for the rave.

Tat pushed himself out of his chair and went to the kitchen. He returned a few minutes later with mugs of coffee and a plate loaded with cheese and cucumber sandwiches, which he knew were Kim's favourites. He was awareshe'd been unhappy about something lately, however, he didn't quite know what and he hadn't found a way to ask her, which he knew he should be doing.

Kim took a bite of her sandwich and started the conversation about the Energy rave. She reminded Tat how, after leaving Odyssey at the Four Aces Club in Dalston, they'd spent a chunk of the night going from meeting point to meeting point, had got stopped by the police twice and had needed to think on their feet to talk themselves out of the situation and avoid the Old Bill turning the car inside out. They had then followed the instructions coming from DJ Spank E at Eclipse and Roger the Doctor and Mr Music at Centreforce and around 6.30am, they eventually found themselves dancing in some huge airplane hangar at Raydon Airfield in Suffolk.

The rave had been organised by Energy and word had spread around that some of the profits from the party were getting donated to the survivors from The Marchioness and the tragic accident that had befallen the Thames pleasure boat. The boat had been hired as part of the celebrations of a twenty-six-year-old male. In the early hours of 20thAugust, The Marchioness collided with a Thames dredger near the Cannon Street Railway Bridge. Fifty-one people drowned in the accident and some of the party goers were friends and known to members of the London rave scene.

Both Kim and Tat had been shocked when they'd read about The Marchioness the following morning. They hadn't actually known anyone who'd been on the boat, but they fully recognised how dreadful and sad it had been.

It was Tat who recalled how the Energy rave had then gone on well into Sunday afternoon and how thankful they'd been to bump into The Ozzard of Whizz, who was able to help out with supplies to keep them dancing and enjoying themselves. It was Kim who recalled how they'd then spent Monday, Tuesday and Wednesday suffering.

September had ended with a rave put on by the newly founded Helter Skelter. Tat and Kim had only heard about the party at the very last minute. They'd been in Eclipse Towers and the show was going well as usual and Kim recalled how DJ Lenny Mash had doubled up with Patch for a change and provided a history lesson on Trax Records and sharing his knowledge. Lenny had told the listeners how Trax Records was established in 1984 by Larry Sherman and Screamin' Rachael Cain. They based their brand-new record label in Chicago. The label's first release was Wanna Dance by Le Noiz and within two years was putting out house music produced by the likes of Adonis, Ron Hardy, Marshall Jefferson and Mr Fingers.

It brought a smile to Kim's face as she remembered how DJ Lenny had signed off the show by saying 'What Trax Records helped to do was introduce a generation of young people to house music and it provided the foundations upon which the rave culture built itself. Trax Records truly was the House that Jack built and many were given the keys to it.' And she couldn't agree more. The final tune of the show which DJ Lenny Mash spun, along with his tag phrase 'let's get mashed with the smash', was Wanna Dance, which he dedicated to two ravers from Kent, Stacey and Spencer. It seemed a fitting tribute.

However, Kim's memories of the 30th September were mixed. Helter Skelter was organised to be held in a field near Banbury, Oxfordshire and the party was attended by a modest few thousand and went off okay, but this was the same night as Phantasy which was held in a field near Reigate. A larger number of ravers found this party, as did the police, and there were violent clashes between the police and the event's security team Strikeforce. Kim felt that this wasn't how the Second Summer of Love was meant to be.

BIG FUN

Tat grabbed the policeman's hat, which had been occupying his favourite chair, and launched it across the room in the direction of the bedroom. The hat had been placed on the chair a few days earlier following an eventful night in South Ockendon. Tat had decided to leave the hat on his chair to serve as a constant reminder of that night. Several times a day Tat caught sight of the hat and it had triggered thoughts and feelings in him that felt confusing and uncomfortable. He was aware that something within him was struggling to understand what had happened in South Ockendon and, indeed, other disappointing events throughout October. And, on top of all this, things weren't going great with Kim and this also bothered him.

With a joint rolled and the smell of hash starting to fill the flat, Tat made himself comfortable in his chair and gazed out of the window. Somehow, the London outside that he'd looked down upon at the start of the summer now looked different - more drab, more tired and, quite frankly, more grim.

Tat inhaled deeply and, as he did so, the thought of those eight ravers getting arrested on the South Ockendon night entered his thoughts. He wondered what had happened to them. He hadn't heard if they'd been fined, let off, imprisoned. He could imagine they felt angry and, like him, disappointed. Taking another drag on his joint, Tat's thoughts moved onto another weekend's adventures and being in the car with Patch and finding themselves being diverted away from the Dartford Tunnel. They, along with many other cars packed full with ravers also trying to get to the party, had been stopped by the police. Some had had their vehicles searched, others were just given a bollocking by the boys in blue and told to 'fuck off home'.

Of course, Tat and Patch were not to be deterred and, after being turned away from the Dartford Tunnel, had weaved their way through outer London streets until eventually finding their way onto the M2 and heading in the direction of Chatham where the Paranoia 2 party was going off. And that was a night Tat knew he wouldn't forget. He and Patch had dropped acid that night and his most vivid memory was spending large chunks of the night dancing next to a raver dressed like one of the characters from the Clockwork Orange, who looked both menacing and lovable. Tat had thanked his lucky stars that the tab had been good and he'd had a nice trip rather than a bad scary one.

Continuing to study the life in the streets below him, Tat found himself reflecting on the two promoters who had been arrested and sentenced to six and ten years' imprisonment for 'conspiring to manage premises where drugs were supplied.' The harsh sentences dished out by the courts had made the rave community gasp. It seemed so unfair, so ridiculous-what on earth were the authorities trying to prove?

Tat had been aware that promoters and ravers alike had started to get more careful. The Pay Party Unit, working alongside the Department for International Trade, had ramped up their efforts to stop the party promoters and the illegal pirate radio stations. People were getting nervous, cautious and suspicious. Did going to a rave really need to cause so many problems?

And then news had reached Tat that Centreforce had been raided. The operation had also included the Old Bill making their presence known at Echos. Some of the main faces at Centreforce and Echos had been targeted and the authorities were trying to make a point and make certain things stick. As far as Tat knew they'd been unsuccessful, but the events had shaken himself and Patch and this had resulted in Tat going out and buying extra locks for the door at Eclipse Towers. He and Patch had even considered moving their station to another location and had spent a couple of afternoons searching the East End for possible alternatives. They were still looking.

Thinking about the trouble that Centreforce and Echos had encountered, Tat found himself remembering the news which came the day after. It was the day of the Biology party. Biology had intended to put on a rave near Guildford. They'd even had Public Enemy booked to perform. But the Old Bill had found out about the party. Maybe they'd seen the site from one of their helicopters?Maybe they'd been following members of the Biology team? Maybe some nosy parker walking his dog, or a farmer, had spotted the unusual activity and, casting their memories back to what they'd read in the Sunday newspapers, had decided to do the 'right thing' and report what they'd seen to the local bobby?

Whatever the truth was, the police did manage to prevent the party from happening and, on the night, the country lanes and streets in and around Guildford were chock-a-block with twenty plus thousand ravers trying to get to the rave.

Tat and Patch had been within the number of unsuccessful party goers and, feeling deflated after getting stuck in traffic jams in country lanes with nothing to do except locking onto Eclipse and listening to DJ's Spank E and Sensible Simon having the time of their lives, it had been boring and unrewarding.

In the end and about two in the morning, Patch and Tat just returned to Eclipse Towers, booted up the station and did what they loved to do-play house music to likeminded people.

Coming to the end of his joint, Tat stubbed it out in the ashtray. As he did so, he glanced over at the policeman's hat. He couldn't even remember how it had ended up in Eclipse Towers. However, seeing the hat made him shudder. He felt as if a dark shadow had wrapped itself around him like a cloak. Standing up as if to shake off the cloak, Tat was left with a sense that the Summer of Love really was coming to an end.

Whilst making another brew and trying to change the direction from where his thoughts and feelings had been leading him, Tat heard the sound of the key going into the door of the flat. For a moment he hoped it was Kim, but looking up he saw it was Patch and, for a second, he felt low again.

Patch must have sensed something wasn't quite right and made a beeline for his best mate who was stirring more sugar into his tea. He gave him a hug, something they never did. Of course, he followed this by giving Tat a punch on the arm and a ruffle of his hair.

'What you been up to today?' asked Patch, reaching for the West Ham United mug that he kept at Eclipse Towers. It had been a gift to him from Tat and him and only him was allowed to use his mug.

Patch spooned in some coffee and sugar and furiously stirred in some milk. The drink made, he ambled over to the decks to take his seat beside Tat, who was already fiddling with knobs, adjusting levels on the mixer and telling Patch about his day, which had mostly involved doing very little. He didn't mention anything about his reflections on the events so far throughout October.

'The Old Bill are really putting the blockers on everything now,' said Patch.

This was just what Tat wanted to hear! Tat did his best to look busy as a means to avoid engaging in a conversation about the topic. This of course didn't register with Patch and he continued.

'Did you read all those pages the other night about ravers getting sold aspirin instead of E's and pieces of paper pretending to be LSD? There were loads. It's really gonna start pissing people off. I mean, it would wouldn't it. Can you imagine how you'd feel if you bought an aspirin for a score and what you hoped was a tab for ten quid? I know you'd have the right hump.'

Tat had also heard the tales circulating of people getting mugged off at raves. It hadn't gone unnoticed that raves were starting to attract the wrong type of people; people who were not there to enjoy the music, the event or the occasion, but were there to seek out ways and means to get something out of what was happening and this meant making money off the back of other people's graft and good will.

'I would, you're right. I'd go right off my nut if I got turned over like that,' replied Tat, who had now finished pushing and pulling things on the decks and mixer.

'It's not right is it?' Tat continued, 'Greed, Patch mate...pure greed!'

Patch had to agree. He was also aware that the finger-pointing had begun and that many of the 'good guys' were suspected of being behind some of the unsavoury behaviours. But Patch knew it was bollocks.

'I was talking to The Ozzard in the week too and he told me about the Biology promoters getting threatened by gangsters. Did you hear about it?' said Patch.

'No. So what's that all about then?'asked Tat.

'Well, it was really only a matter of time until the party promoters would get rumbled. I mean how many times have you and me seen bin liners packed full of cash being dragged into vans parked on site. Usually there's only a few people guarding the cash too. It wasn't even like it was trying to be kept discreet, so it was bound to come to the attention of the wrong sort. There's just too much money being made. The promoters are taking risks and, in some cases, getting sloppy. I mean, I've seen promoters getting just as much off of their tits as the next person.'

'Yeah, I know what you mean,' agreed Tat, 'And then there's the dealers. It all got too organised. Organised crime! Once the security controlled the doors, they could control the dealing inside. There are certainly more stories coming through of unauthorised dealersgetting a kickingfrom the security, having their pills taken off of them, and then the security have their own dealers re-dealing those pills that they've nicked. It's all wrong mate! It's getting out of hand.'

Patch could sense the anger in Tat's voice. He'd not heard that sort of anger in his mate for a long time, but he had to agree.

'Yeah, getting a kicking is one thing, but when gangsters start pushing shot guns down promoter's throats, that's a whole different ball game and a scary one at that.'

'And that's just another reason why the Acid House Squad will come down even harder. And they won't take any shit. It'll end in tears,' said Tat lifting the mug of coffee to his lips.

'Tears, so many tears,' Patch started to sing in an attempt to lift the mood. After all, they were only minutes away from starting their show.

'Regretting nothing but the pain,' Tat sang back. It felt good singing his favourite lyric from the Frankie Knuckles track. 'But no, seriously, it's not good and we need to be careful too.'

'What d'ya mean?' asked Patch.

'Well, with Eclipse. Being as the Old Bill have come down on Centreforce, it's only a matter of time until they come down hard on all of us pirates. We need to be careful, that's all that I'm saying.'

'Fuckin' hell. OK. Voice of fucking doom! Don't you worry, we'll be alright, they'll never catch us.'

Optimism was one of Patch's most precious qualities. It was one of the things that Tat admired about his friend. Ever since their school days, Patch had been the one who had made them feel untouchable. And the truth was, somehow he did always manage to get away with things. There'd been countless days out at football were Patch had escaped the clutches of the Old Bill or avoided a good kicking from another firm. There'd been times when he'd pulled off one-night stands with the younger sisters of some of the other firms' top boys and never been caught. He'd been pulled over by the Old Bill numerous times but had always managed to talk himself out of getting a fine. Patch had had his fingers in so many hot pies that most people would have got burnt badly but, again, somehow he'd always walked away with clean fingers and a full belly. Patch had reason to feel bullet proof. Tat just hoped it would stay like this and they needed it more than ever at the moment.

'Yeah, and I'm sure that's what the DJs at Centreforce thought too mate,' replied Tat, 'Come on, it's time, flick the switch.' And with that, Patch took charge of the microphone.

'Here we go London. Let's go, let's go. DJs Tat and Patch are with you for the next two hours. Hope you're locked on Jim 'D' Donovan. Are you ready to ravvvvvvvve?'

Salsa House kicked off the show. It was deep into the track before Tat took a turn on the microphone.

'A big shout going out to Pasha and the other Centreforce DJs. Good luck fellas.'

'And another shout out to Genesis Wayne too. Nice to see you the other week at the Rave in the Cavedown at the Elephant. I bet you needed a good rave up, especially after the day you'd had eh? Yeah good memories of that Genesis party in Aldgate last year.'

Tat put on another record whilst Patch started to check the pager. The messages were coming in fast.

'Hello Keith from Slough, good to see you're locked on mate. We hear things are building nicely down your way,' said Patch with one eye on the pager and one on the microphone.

'Did you also hear that Shoom have announced a date for their last party?' said Patch turning to Tat, rememberingThe Ozzard had also mentioned that to him, 'Yeah, it's gonna be on the 8th. Do you wanna go?

'I did hear that, but no, doubt it. You?'

'Maybe!' replied Patch lifting his shoulders.

The Eclipse show rolled along, notching up another level as each track got spun. But Patch could still sense that not all was OK with Tat.

'You alright mate? You don't seem yourself at all tonight. Come to think of it, you haven't done all week,' Patch had to enquire.

'Just tired mate. It's been a mad few months yeah,' replied Tat not really wanting to expand on anything.

'For sure,' Patch agreed, 'I suppose it does feel that things are getting a bit intense, but intense not in a way that it felt back in the summer.'

'The summer months were mental,' returned Tat, 'Well, it's been mental since the end of '88, and then we started spending every weekend going to some party and then the raves took off and we found ourselves charging around the M25 and through country lanes in the middle of the night. And then we started up Eclipse...'

'And then you met Kim and fell in lurve,' Patch butted in.

Tat hastily changed the subject and checked his watch.

'Time for another record mate. Pass us that one will ya,' said Tat.

Patch was surprised by Tat's choice but, doing as he had been asked, he handed him a copy of Silver Bullet's Bring Forth The Guillotine. The track made perfect sense to Tat. He put the record on and leaned into the microphone.

'Just so you know London, Patch and me won't be rocking London from the Eclipse headquarters next Saturday coz we spent our last £8.50 on tickets to go and see The Stone Roses at the Ally Pally. We're sure to see some of you there too.'

For a moment, Tat felt his spirits lifted as he thought about going to see the Roses play.

'Manchester vibes will be in the area,' whispered Tat into the microphone as the Silver Bullet track shook the show up.

WHAT THE WORLD IS WAITING FOR

Tat's flat had been the den in which he and Patch had been lazing around since breakfast. Patch had stayed over the previous night. There had been no Eclipse show due to a bout of flu which was working its way through all the Eclipse DJs, so Patch had suggested he and Tat just go to the pub and relax. It had seemed a good idea at the time and the first few drinks went down a treat. They had felt well-earned. However, alcohol just didn't seem to satisfy their souls and they craved for something more. This 'more' presented itself in the form of The Ozzard of Whizz. He bowled into the boozer in his usual fashion-one eye on the bar and the other on any potential customers.

Removing his red Berghaus bubble coat - a prized left-over from his terrace days - and plonking himself onto the seat beside Tat in one seamless movement, The Oz settled himself and a grinned at his drunk companions.

As per usual,The Oz retold several stories of recent adventures about bopping around London selling his wares and being creative in the ways he'd manage to evade the law. Tat and Patch politely sipped their lagers as they listened.

Thirty minutes later and two pints swishing around in his gut,The Oz announced he had to head off to make a few deliveries. And that was when he mentioned the Buddhas which he was keeping safe and dry in an envelope. Of course,The Oz clocked Tat and Patch's interest and quickly removed the envelope from his coat.

Before The Oz left, he'd sold two Buddhas and Tat and Patch had swigged them down only moments after The Oz had departed the boozer. Not wanting to start tripping in their local, they'd made a beeline for Tat's flat.

The next eight hours had been spent playing records in-between locking onto Centreforce or Sunrise, slipping into worlds of their own that included hours watching patterns which seemed to come to life on the walls, floors and cushions. And there'd been roars of uncontrollable laughter where tears had run down their faces. And the colours - wonderful, amazing, vibrant, out of this world colours everywhere. The Buddhas had indeed been good, just as The Oz had promised.

As Tat now lay on one of the cushions on the flat's floor, he recalled it had been around 6am when he'd switched off the light. He remembered Patch had already fallen asleep on the cushion where he still lay, wrapped in his coat and wearing one of Tat's bucket hats.

There had been no rush to embrace the day, so Tat and Patch had taken turns to make cups of coffee and share the digestives around. It took a while to shake off the acid and for them to start to feel normal again.

Tat had bought The Stone Rose's debut album when it had come out back in May and it was never far from the decks. Now sat up, with legs crossed and smoking a joint, Tat fed on Waterfall, which was one of his favourite tracks from the album that had been playing for a second time that morning.

The joint that Tat was smoking had been rolled on the album's sleeve. For the hundredth time he studied it again and his thoughts had turned to the meanings contained in the imagery that John Squire had created. Tat knew the artwork was called Bye Bye Bad Man. The red white and blue stripes represented the French flag and this related to the three lemon slices. Tat had read that whilst Ian Brown had been travelling in Europe, he'd met a man who'd been involved in the riots which happened in Paris in 1968. The man had told Brown how the rioters had used lemons as an antidote to the tear gas which the Gendarmerie Nationale had used on them.

'Ere have you seen this? The Stone Roses are featured on the front cover of the NME - Never Mind The Pollocks-Here's The Stone Roses,' said Patchwho was now quite awake, but looking like shit.

Tat picked up the NME that had been tossed in his direction but pushed it to one side. It was evident that something wasn't quite right with him and Patch knew it wasn't just the come down from the LSD.

'What's the matter with you? Someone died? I thought you'd be jumping around with joy, what with the Berlin Wall coming down recently.'

It was true the Berlin Wall had indeed been pulled down, and this historical event had dominated the media for the past week, but Patch was correct in his observations that his mate had hardly been jumping up and down about it- and this was odd because this was exactly the sort of news that Tat would want to celebrate.

'Did you manage to score that hash off of The Ozzard?'askedTat, avoiding Patch's curiosity.

'You nearly run out then?' answered Patch, deciding not to press his mate any further; he didn't feel up to a heart to heart anyway.

Instead, Patch reached for his coat and pulled out a bag containing some hash, which he had scored off of The Oz a few days earlier but had forgotten to hand over to Tat.

'Yeah of course. Do I ever let you down? I met him in that café in Bethnal Green again. He was telling me some story about travelling to some rave with Evil Eddie Richards. He drew Eddie's life story out of him - even down to the part about when Eddie used to run his own mobile discocalled Ministry of Sound. That's a cracking name for a disco innit?'

'Yeah I suppose it is. I bet Evil Eddie was glad to get out of the car though. It's hard work spending more than ten minutes with The Ozzard-especially when he's rushing off his tits.'

'Yeah I know what you mean. His heart's in the right place though and he does get the best gear.So, c'mon, roll that and let's get in the mood to go and see The Stone Roses later.'

The thought of seeing the Roses lifted Tat's spirits and for a moment anything else that was bothering him faded away. He hummed along to Bye Bye Bad Man as he began the process of building the joint.

By the time Tat and Patch had left Eclipse Towers in the safe hands of DJ Lenny Mash, they had started to feel a bit more like themselves, although they were very stoned. Getting stoned had seemed the best way to ride out their come downs.

Tat and Patch had hopped on a bus to get then to the Ally Pally. The journey had been okay and they'd mostly just chatted shit about their wishes for the future of Eclipse. Theyjumped off the bus atMuswell Hill and dived into a pub which was already full of people who were evidently also going to the Roses concert.

Patch and Tat pushed their way through countless pairs of flared jeans and bucket hats until they got to the bar. It was clear there was a right mix of people. London accents mingled with northern and the vibe was friendly. As is often the case, the sense of anticipation prior to a concert hung over the ravers' heads and this mingled with the occasional waft of hash.

Three pints later and feeling quite lively, Tat and Patch left the pub and joined the throng of concert goers who were now also making their way to the venue. As they approached the impressive looking 19th century building, Tat found himself imagining walking towards 'The People's Palace' back in April 1967 for the 14 Hour Technicolour Dream event. He pictured himself with long hair and wearing a tie-dye sweatshirt and flares,which made him chuckle as he thought this was pretty much what he and a multitude of young people were wearing again anyway.

Holding onto that thought, he imagined a pocketful of LSD ready to bedropped to help absorb the experience that included groups such as Pink Floyd and The Pretty Things. Seeing these in their psychedelic prime would have been amazing enough, but then there were the performers such as the Tribe of the Sacred Mushroom and the Exploding Galaxy Dance Troupe and he could only wildly imagine what watching them would have been like whilst under the influence of a trip.

Tat was still thinking about the 14 Hour Technicolour Dream event when he felt Patch nudge him. Tat looked up just as Patch pushed his entry ticket into the palm of his hand along with half an E.

In a swift and yet discreet motion, Tat popped the E into his mouth just as the venue's security waved him forward and pointed to a kiosk where he would need to hand over his ticket. A few moments later, Tat and Patch found themselves standing in the Great Hall surrounded by a large crowd of excited ravers.

By the time The Stone Roses opened with She Bangs The Drum, Tat and Patch's E had come on and it was strong. They watched on as Ian Brown danced around the stage in his red sweatshirt and wobbled his head as he did so. It didn't matter to them or anyone in the audience that he sometimes sang out of tune; it just didn't matter because the band was great. How could they not be with their rhythm master Reni on the kit, white bucket hat on his head, playing some of the best drums of his generation;Mani with his pony tail loving every second; and John Squire, a man who appeared to be tripping in his own creative world, every note played accounted for and performing brilliant songs such as Waterfall, Shoot You Down, Sally Cinnamon and Fools Gold.

The only down side to the concert was that it seemed to go too quickly and before long Tat and Patch found themselves strolling back down Muswell Hill. They felt the cold chill which was uncomfortable against their sweating bodies. Patch was pleased he'd decided to wear his Timberlands and ski coat rather than anything lighter. The further they got from Ally Pally, the more the crowds thinned out. Both seemed happy to take their time as they searched for a bus. The E was still keeping them up anyway.

'The Stone Roses were fuckin' brilliant. I've never been to such a fantastic concert,' said Patch.

'Shame the sound was so shite though,'replied Tat - and he had a point.

'Yeah sure, but just to hear Shoot You Down, Elephant Stone, Waterfall, Sugar Spun Sister, Made Of Stone and then ending with Fools Gold...I loved every second of it,'replied Patch, spotting the bus they needed and pointing it out to Tat.

'Dave Haslam's set was mental too,' said Tat, quickening his pace to keep up with Patch, before adding 'Good job you dropped that E.'

They reached the bus and jumped on, spotting two empty seats near the back where they went and fell onto them.

'They would have still been brilliant,' said Patch looking at Tat, noticing his mood seemed to have altered again. 'Come on, what's the matter? You've not been yourself all night.'

Tat took a few seconds to reply and then, turning to look out of the window, said, 'Me and Kim have broken up. We had a fuckin' big row in the week and that was that.'

'Shit mate. It'll be alright. She's probably waiting for you back at yours now.'

'Not this time Patch mate. We've had a few arguments over the past few weeks. I can't even remember what some of them were even about. It's over mate. Feels like a lot of things are coming to an end.'

'Cheer up mate. It's not all bad. We've still got The Stone Roses eh,' replied Patch, not thinking of any else he could say. He had to admit that although he'd sensed Tat hadn't been himself, he had put two and two together and put it down to woman troubles.

As the bus weaved its way through the streets of London, Tat and Patch didn't talk much more. Tat seemed content to reflect on the recent events in his world and Kim was in the forefront, whilst Patch played over the Roses concert, song by song, buzz by buzz. He was happy enough and now just wanted to get on the ones and twos.

Tat and Patch didn't see one another for the next three days, but when they did it was because Patch picked Tat up outside Eclipse Towers and drove him to Stoke Newington. Patch had been having regular conversations with some of the people behind the event and they'd given him a bunch of tickets for their party called Alive and Kicking which they were running out of a club on the High Street in Stoke Newington. The doors opened at 9.30pm and it was almost ten. Enroute, Patch told Tat that the DJs that night would include some of Centreforce's finest: Mr Pasha, the Corporation and the Run Tings Crew. This meant the rave promised to be literally alive and most certainly kicking.

IT'S ALRIGHT

Patch bounced into Eclipse Towers rubbing his hands vigorously. It was evident to Tat that his mate was freezing his bollocks off and, to be fair, it was 'taters' outside.

Tat was sat in his favourite chair. He'd been awake early and, following a poorattempt to make a full English breakfast, he had plonked himself onto his chair and had watched the East End folk of London unfold from their well-earned slumbers. As each minute passed, the streets below Eclipse Towers swelled with people wrapped in heavy coats, their faces mostly covered with Burberry scarves and their hands tucked deep into their even deeper pockets. But Tat knew those pockets would be pretty empty by the end of the day because they would have spent all their cash on Christmas presents for their families.

The thought of Christmas made Tat shudder. He had never been one to fall into line and get caught up in the festive madness. Tat had managed to keep Christmas present buying simple. He only bought something for his mum and he'd done this back at the start of November after spotting some ornament of a woman holding a small child. It was made of wood, which he had thought was unusual. It had cost twenty pounds-the most he'd ever spent on a present, but of course his mum was worth it. Wrapping it was still on his to-do list.

Patch boiled the kettle and helped himself to some Rich Tea biscuits. He moaned and complained about the weather as he did so. Tat wasn't especially interested and he didn't really know what his mate was going on about because he hadn't been out of the flat for three days and even he was starting to feel like he was becoming a hermit. This thought had made him chuckle because he'd heard that one of the Centreforce DJs got his name Hermit because he rarely ventured out from his flat.

120

With his tea made, Patch went to stand beside Tat and looked out of the window across the city that he knew so well. Familiar rooftops and chimney stacks blended with an army of tall cranes. From the Eclipse Towers' view point, it was clear that London was changing at a rapid pace and Patch sensed that there'd come a time when he would hardly recognise the place. The thought left him feeling sad, so he took a gulp of tea to try and sweeten things up.

'Here look at this?' said Patch handing Tat a flyer.

Tat studied the flyer, absorbing the information about a rally being organised called Freedom To Party. The flyer mentioned that dance party promoters, radio stations and record companies were joining forces to protest against the government's increasingly hostile efforts to stop the raves.

'We're going yeah?' Patch added.

'For sure! We'll start rallying the Eclipse troops on the show tonight.'

The thought of Eclipse Radio helping the cause sent a tingle through Patch's body and he rubbed his hands again, this time not from the cold but from excitement.

Placing his mug of tea on the floor beside a pile of cushions which DJ Smile had left in a tower formation after the previous night's show, Patch made his way towards the decks, found Sterling Void's 'It's Alright' and put it on. The tune had been running around his head since he woke up and he needed to hear the song in its entirety.

Patch couldn't restrain from joining in with the intro, one which he felt was up there with the best. By the time the song reached the second verse, Patch was singing his heart out about 'generations coming and going' and 'the music going to play forever.' Hearing Patch belting out the song to the best of ability lifted Tat's spirit too and all thoughts of Christmas, the cold and Kim faded away.

The next few hours were spent playing record after record from the DJ International Records label. Such was the mood that Tat and Patch felt they needed to hear soulful house tracks from Joe Smooth, Tyree, Fast Eddie and of course Sterling Void.

Come seven o'clock, Tat and Patch had the decks well and truly fired up and they had a stack of records ready to play on their show.

Patch made a few joints and positioned the pagers, and Tat piled some biscuits onto a plate and brewed some coffee.

'Eclipse FM 89.9. Are you ready? Here we go London,' said Patch kicking off the show whilst Tat eased in Fantasy by Z-Factor, a song that he knew was credited as being the first song house song and brought to the world because of the geniuses that were Jesse Saunders and Vince Lawrence and the amazing vocals of Screamin' Rachael.

Z-Factor was followed by Fingers Inc, Phuture and Royal House and Eclipse Towers was really starting to rock. Patch and Tat were in their bubble, their happy place. It was just them, their house music, the Eclipse faithful and the station which they had spent the last few months building. They felt brilliant!

'Thanks for locking on Lorraine from Luton, Can You Party was for you because we know you can-we've seen you!' said Tat.

'And a big shout going out to Spencer and Matt down there in Maidstone. Yeah, see you at the Adamski bash in Brixton on New Year's Eve,' spluttered Tat as he spilled some coffee whilst reading the pager.

'Eclipse FM on 89.9 and send us your messages to 08550 32020. We are here for you London,' Patch shouted out.

The show continued getting deeper into the sounds that had been coming out from Chicago for the last four years or so, and that certainly made up the majority of Tat and Patch's record collections.

A further hour passed and along with dozens of shout outs and mentions of the Freedom To Party rally. The response from the Eclipse listeners was incredible and proved that the raving community were willing to make a stand for their right to party.

Patch was curious why Tat had disappeared for five minutes; it was unusual for him to abandon his station whilst a show was in fullflow. But as he returned clutching a copy of The Beastie Boys' (You Gotta) Fight For Your Right (To Party), his face lit up.

The record was removed from its sleeve and placed onto the deck, the needle lifted and dropped carefully - and bang! Off with the record. Tat and Patch fell about laughing. They knew their listeners would also appreciate the song and see the funny side.

It was just as the third verse began that Tat thought he heard some noise outside the flat's door. It was an unusual noise that left him feeling uneasy. Such was Tat's feeling that he felt compelled to go and investigate but, just as he pushed himself up from his chair, there was an enormous crashing sound as the flat's door burst open and slammed against the wall. Both Tat and Patch froze. That's all they could do as the chaos unfolded.

Half a dozen police officers dressed in full riot gear marched into the flat, shouting out orders and making their intentions and presence known. One of the officers raced towards Tat and violently pushed him back into his chair. As he did, Patch reacted and stood up. However, another officer shot him a glance that basically spelled out to him that if he tried anything he was going to come out of it worse off. Patch had seen that look in the eyes of police officers at football many times and he knew it meant trouble.

As one officer took control of the situation and attempted to explain to Tat and Patch was happening, the other police officers turned Eclipse Towers upside down. They threw cushions around and knocked over chairs. Two officers produced large plastic containers and unceremoniously started to toss Tat and Patch's records into them. Another officer started to dismantle the Eclipse FM equipment and bundle leads and wires and boxes into bags.

The police were still turning over the flat as Tat and Patch were marched out and taken down to the Old Bill station.

FREEDOM TO PARTY AGAIN

The last few days leading up to Christmas had been shit for Tat and Patch. Since the police raid, they had both been pissed off in a way they had never experienced before. The memories of that night haunted them like no nightmare they'd ever had. It was now New Year's Eve and what did they have to look forward to? They didn't even know if they wanted to be at the Sunrise, Biology and Genesis rave that was going to happen at the National Panasonic Building in Slough, or the Adamski event at the Brixton Academy. They had tickets for both events, kindly given to them by the various promoters.

Patch had visited Tat in his flat every day since the raid. They had tried to work out what they had done wrong and how had they allowed it to happen. They knew they talked about getting better locks for the flat's door and they beat themselves up for not actioning this. The flat didn't even look the same anymore. During the raid, the police had broken Tat's favourite chair and the battered remains of that now lay heaped in a pile on the floor. Some of the cushions had been ripped and torn apart too as the police searched for drugs. On the night they had only found some hash, and both Tat and Patch were going to be in trouble for this alongside the charges against them for running an illegal radio station. There was also an empty area where the radio equipment, decks and record collection had once lived. All of which had been confiscated by the Old Bill and it wasn't looking like any of it was likely going to be returned, which left Tat and Patch feeling very sad and very angry.

The only positive that seemed to come out of the situation was that Kim had visited Tat. This had meant a lot to Tat and he had enjoyed talking and being with her. There had been tears too. Kim had stayed for a couple hours on that occasion and, when she left, she'd kissed Tat on the cheek and told him that she may see him at the Freedom To Party rally or rave. As he'd watched her walk away from the flat and along the corridor, he hoped he would see her at the rally or the rave.

Eclipse Towers had also been quiet for reasons other than the decks and records being absent. The other Eclipse DJs had been advised to avoid the flat, but they'd all stayed in contact and met for drinks and a dance in Echos one night. The Ozzard of Whizz had also kept a low profile for obvious reasons. In fact, Tat or Patch hadn't seen or heard from him at all, but they understood this was for the best. After all, they didn't know if the Old Bill still had them under surveillance.

All Tat and Patch could do was wait patiently for their court dates to arrive and see what happens then. They could live without getting their radio equipment and decks back, but the thought of not having their records returned was too painful to consider and they'd drowned out the thoughts of this down the pub nearly every night since the raid.

In the end, Tat and Patch did go to both the Adamski and Genesis, Biology and Sunrise raves and, for that night, they had managed to forget about their troubles. The E's that they took on the night of course helped.

They had also been part of the Freedom To Party rally. It had been important to them that they should go and have their voices heard. They'd bumped into many 'faces' from the rave scene and all had shaken Tat and Patch's hands and told them how great they had thought Eclipse FM had been and that it was missed.

After the rally, Tat and Patch had hooked up with all of the Eclipse DJs and they had travelled to the Freedom To Party rave which had been held in a warehouse on an industrial estate in Radlett. Tat and Patch had gone with DJs Jewels and Smile and, on their arrival, they'd needed to park the car quickly and leg it to the warehouse where the promoters were hastily trying to pull ravers into the building. There was already a strong presence from the police and it was a matter of the promoters getting a certain amount of ravers into the warehouse before the Old Bill could prevent the rave from going off.

Once inside the warehouse, Tat, Patch, DJs Jewels and Smile had foundthe promoters were still busy setting up the equipment. This meant there was no music playing and no lights flashing. They just stood in a big warehouse, waiting.

Eventually the lights did go off and some music started to play. The warehouse also began to fill up at a rapid pace. But, looking around at the people and the faces, Tat felt that something was different. The feeling he'd had the past couple of months of something changing was starting to make itself known to him. This was confirmed that night when Tat witnessed a group of lads in long black leather jackets surround a lone raver who just wanted to dance. The lads searched his pockets and robbed him of his possessions. As they were doing this, one of the raver's friends ventured forward to intervene, but was warned off by one of the lads opening his leather jacket to reveal a gun. This was the first time Tat had seen a real gun and the image of it had sickened him. He couldn't believe that anyone would bring a gun to rave. Seeing the gun that night confirmed for Tat that the Summer of Love was well and truly over, at least for him.

Despite what Tat had seen, he'd stayed at the rave, taken an E and had danced the night away. He'd also bumped into Kim and they had talked and danced together. They'd also agreed to meet up for a coffee in the week and talk about them. This left Tat feeling hopeful that there may be a chance of them getting back together and this was what he wanted. It's what he knew he needed.

It was around 4am when Tat and Patch left the rave and they did so cooking up a plan. It was DJ Buzzlines who had come up with the idea of doing one last Eclipse show and it had been agreed by all that it was worth taking the risk. However, the only problem they had was that they had no equipment.

DJ Spank E had stepped up to take responsibility for getting hold of the equipment they'd need and during the day he'd contacted Centreforce Radio and they had loaned him all that he needed.

It was approaching nine o'clock when Patch flicked a switch and Eclipse FM 89.9 went live again for one more show. Tat sat beside his best mate and Kim sat beside him. Looking over their shoulders were DJs Smile and Jewels, DJs Spank E and Sensible Simon, DJ Buzzlines, DJ Need All, DJ R E White and DJ Lenny Mash and, in amongst them, was squeezed The Ozzard of Whizz.

Everyone had the biggest grins spread across their faces. They were a family and they knew they would always be so. And, with that, the last Eclipse show kicked off with Frankie Knuckles' Your Love. Of course!

CENTREFORCE WAREHOUSE REVIVAL
PART ONE

Patch was the first to finish off his lager. He did so with a huge gulp, which he followed with an even huger smile. It was his smile that signalled to Tat and Kim that it was time to leave the Dovecote and jump on the coach which Andy had laid on to get the pub's faithful to the Hackney Wick.

Grabbing their coats and falling in line behind others also keen to get a seat on the coach, it was Kim who noticed Jack Bass first. He was already climbing the steps onto the coach. She elbowed Tat and pointed Jack out.

'Jack!' yelled Tat which made everyone look around, a mix of friendly and confused expressions on their faces. It was because of his Manc accent.

Jack glanced over his shoulder and smiled. He then shouted something back which sounded like 'Talk to you in a minute.'

The coach quickly filled up and, in no time at all, it was speeding through the streets of Chingford. The travellers were keen to get to the party. Expectations were high. It was the 17th November, the night of the Centreforce Warehouse Revival rave-the first rave the station had put on in years. It was common knowledge that over five hundred tickets for the event had sold out in just a few hours. There had been a massive response. The rave promised much and people knew that the Centreforce team would deliver.

Kim pushed her way to where Jack was sitting and plonked herself down beside him. Tat and Patch were not far behind, but they had plenty of hands to shake. There were old ravers on the coach who they hadn't clapped eyes on for years.

The mood was good, the chatter lively and the spirits high by the time the coach pulled into Autumn Street. The road was narrow and dark and there were a few ravers strolling down it. They looked cold. It was cold!

The coach stopped and people hastily piled out. The bar was open and they could hear the music booming out from inside. DJ Lust was taking care of business. Patch, Tat and Kim didn't delay in getting into the venue. Passing through security without any bother, they handed over their tickets to the woman who stood behind the hatch and, turning right, made their way towards the music.

It was only 10.30pm and there were already about fifty people dancing and many others crowded around the bar area. Patch made a bee-line for the bar, whilst Tat and Kim found a space and chatted with Andy and Jonny C. They appeared to be happy with the venue and the ever-swelling crowd.

By the time Patch found Tat and Kim holding cans of Red Stripe, Andy had been pulled away to meet and greet people and Jonny C was sorting something out of a technical nature.

Still holding their cans of lager, Tat, Kim and Patch made their way into the main room which was full of dry ice. They scanned the room noticing the backdrops of rave flyersfrom back in the days when Eclipse Radio was alive and kicking. Moments later, all three had discarded their beer cans and were dancing to Jim EP's set. The dancefloor was crowded and there were a lot of smiles and happy people.

The next three hours passed quickly as they danced and caught up with people. The Centreforce DJs kept the party going and Patch and Tat had caught up with Jumping Jack Frost, Keith Mac and Nicky Brown. Between them, they had pieced together some recollections of the heady rave days of the Second Summer of Love, Centreforce, Eclipse, Energy, Biology, Sunrise, the convoys and the amazing and brilliant music that had come out from that period.

Kim kissed Tat on the cheek and pointed to the female toilets. He understood and nodded. Patch sidled up to Tat and clinked his beer can against Tat's. They looked at the people dancing around them: Danny S and his generation, Andy S and his - of which they'd been a part and had had the time of their lives. They grinned at one another and it felt good knowing that Centreforce was back in fullforce and they, like the people that surrounded them, were still raving. Tat and Patch gulped down their lagers, dropped their cans and headed for the dancefloor just as Joe Smooth's Promised Land started to play - and they knew they'd still be dancing at 5am.

100 ECLIPSE RADIO 89.9 FAVE RAVES
(in no particular order):

1. Your Love - Frankie Knuckles
2. French Kiss - Lil Louis
3. Pacific State - 808 State
4. Voodoo Ray – A Guy Called Gerald
5. Sun Rising -The Beloved
6. Ride On Time - Black Box
7. Can You Feel It - Fingers Inc
8. Break For Love - Raze
9. Bomb The Bass - Beat Dis
10. The Theme-Unique 3
11. Let's Get Brutal-Nitro Deluxe
12. Let Me Love You For Tonight-Kariya
13. Right Before Your Eyes-Patti Day
14. Rich In Paradise-FPI Project
15. Weekend-Todd Terry Project
16. This Is Acid - Maurice
17. Acid Tracks-Phuture
18. Someday-Ce Ce Rogers
19. Promised Land-Joe Smooth
20. Rescue Me-Debbie Malone
21. It's Alright-Sterling Void
22. NRG-Adamski
23. Tell Me When The Fever Ended-Electribe 101
24. Wishing On A Star-Fresh 4
25. Motherland-Tribal House
26. The Eve of the War- Ben Liebrand
27. Acid Man-Jolly Roger
28. You Used To Hold Me-Ralphi Rosario
29. Can You Party-Royal House
30. Come Get My Loving - Dionne
31. I Gotta Big Dick – Maurice Joshua with Hot Hands Hula

32. Runaway-Sterling Void
33. Reachin' - Phase II
34. Good Life-Inner City
35. Bad Boy-Frankie Knuckles
36. Fools Gold-Stone Roses
37. Hallelujah- Happy Mondays
38. Sueno Latino-Sueno Latino
39. Rhythim Is Rhythim-Strings Of Life
40. That's the Way Love Is- Ten City
41. Bango (To The Batmobile) - Todd Terry Project
42. Give Me A Sign-Index
43. Tears-Frankie Knuckles
44. Wrote For Luck-Happy Mondays
45. Bring Forth The Guillotine-Silver Bullet
46. 20 Seconds To Comply-Silver Bullet
47. Air Port 89- Wood Allen
48. Humanoid- Stakker Humanoid
49. House Nation-House Master Boyz
50. Jack Your Body-Steve 'Silk' Hurley
51. House Arrest-Krush
52. Jack To The Sound Of The Underground- Hit House
53. Jack n Chill- The Jack That House Built
54. The Party-Kraze
55. Everything Starts with An E- Zee Posse
56. Big Fun-Inner City
57. Fantasy-Z-Factor
58. Salsa House-Richie Rich
59. Time To Jack-Chip E
60. Elephant Stone-The Stone Roses
61. The Real Life-Corporation of One
62. Electra-Jibaro
63. Rock To The Beat-Reese and Santonio
64. Children Of The Night-Kevin Irving
65. Waiting On My Angel-Jamie Principle
66. Dream Girl-Pierres Pfantasy Club
67. Lack Of Love-Charles B and Adonis
68. Wanna Dance-Le Noiz

69. Shut Up And Dance-Twenty Pounds To Get In. (use the intro)
70. Meltdown-Quartz
71. Theme From S Express-S Express
72. Jesus Loves The Acid-Ekstasy Club
73. Do The Dance-SL2
74. Lack Of Love-Charles B/Adonis
75. We Call It Acieed-D-Mob Featuring Gary Haisman.
76. Jack Your Body-Steve 'Silk' Hurley
77. Love Can't Turn Around-Farley 'Jackmaster' Funk and Jesse Saunders featuring Darryl Pandy
78. Pump Up Chicago-Mr Lee
79. Emotions Electric-Guy Called Gerald
80. Magical Dream-808 State
81. Bring Down the Walls-Robert Owens
82. We're Rockin' Down the House-Adonis
83. Carino-T. Coy
84. Useless (I Don't Need To Know)-Kym Mazelle
85. If Only I Could-Sydney Young Blood
86. Pump Up The Volume-MAARS
87. Killer-Adamski
88. Dreams of Santa Anna-Orange Lemon
89. Amnesia-Mr Fingers
90. Do It To The Crowd-Twin Hype
91. Afro Dizzi Act-Cry Sisco
92. Welcome-Gino Latino
93. Jack To The Sound of the Underground-Hit House
94. Don't Miss The Party Line-Bizz Nizz
95. On and On-Jesse Saunders
96. Work The Box-Santos
97. Just As Long As I Got You-101
98. Knocking At My Door-Donell Rush
99. A Day In The Life-Black Riot
100. Turn Up The Bass-Tyree Cooper

EXLUSIVE INTERVIEWS

Andy Swallow (Pasha)

'It was around March/April time in 1989 when we were approached by Roger the Dodge. Roger was with a fella called Jim the Music Man. They were both with Sunrise Radio. It was in Echos one night when they made their approach, saying they wanted to set up their own radio station and did we want to be part of it and it's going to be called Centreforce. So, me and my partner, Jonny Eames, sat around a table with them and they explained that what they had was a box, and that this box was going to cost £200 - and that was a lot of money back then. They then told us that we'd need a rig and some other things. We thought about it and told them that we'd do it. This was how Centreforce came about.

Roger and Jim had a flat on the third floor ready for us in Kingsland Road (Stoke Newington) and we started there. We had the equipment set up-the box/transmitter and we told Roger and Jim that we'd start the station after an all-dayer that was happening at Echos. I left Echos a little bit early on the day so I could get to the studio but, just before I left, we told everyone to tune into 88.3 after Echos had finished. Those people who left Echos that day became the origins of the fan base that then quickly grew.

When I left Echos that day and went to the studio, there was me, Keith Mac, Gary Dickel and DJ One. Gary was the first person to play a record on Centreforce to the people that were tuning in after the all-dayer. This was 8th May 1989.

A lot of my mates had started going to Ibiza in '87. In February 1988, I went there. Around this time my mate was having a stag do. A lot of my mates were going to Futures, which was run by Paul Oakenfold. It was a Tuesday night, I walked into the club and someone put a pill into my mouth and said try this. I came out of Futures that night and couldn't wait to get back in there on the Thursday. This was my introduction into the acid house scene. Two weeks later, I put my first party on and this was in a warehouse just off of Carpenters Road in Stratford. I had broken into that warehouse so that we could use it for the party. I designed a crude little flyer and went around the clubs handing them out. That flyer had smiley faces in rows going over a bridge. We charged a fiver a ticket and, on the night, Tony Wilson was one of the deejays. There were big cages all around the warehouse. On the night of the party, the Old Bill showed up and told us to get out. We said no. They then told us that whoever leaves the warehouse wouldn't be allowed back in. We said alright, shut the doors and didn't leave there until 11am in the morning. There was about two and half thousand people there for that first party.

It was a year after I had been to Ibiza that we did the Centreforce tour there. This was quite soon after Centreforce had gone live. When Centreforce was in Ibiza we played in Space, Amnesia, Koo Club and Es Paradis. We were one of the first to play in Space too because it opened around the time that we went there.

I have many fond memories from those early days. I did a lot of warehouse parties and events but one of my fondest memories was of Shinola's in Hackney. This was the first time we did a warehouse party under the Centreforce name. You went through the doors of the place into a small reggae blues club and there were some doors which, when you pushed open, led to a big warehouse. Centreforce put on an all-dayer and I remember walking in and seeing green lasers moving across the smoke and I thought that's it, we've finally cracked it.

Even before Shinola's I'd done bigger warehouse parties, but there something about that party with all the new lasers that made it different and took it to another level.

What Centreforce did was bring forward a lot of new deejays and this happened during a short period of time. The station only had a short lifespan really because we got shut down. We didn't know where it would go, or that people would be talking about Centreforce thirty years later.

At the time we just wanted to be deejays. I wanted to be a deejay but I probably wasn't very good. I couldn't mix then and I can't mix now. But I was busy owning a radio station and putting on parties. Whatever I did or whatever Centreforce did, we did it for ourselves but, because of what we did, we gained a following. What it came down to, was putting on a party on our own, for our own. We never set out to go and play sets and get thousands of pounds. We set out because we loved the music and we loved to party.

We were ravers before Centreforce came along and, even when the station was running we'd do shows, put on parties and then go to other peoples. We were party people and what we wanted to do was party. We went to lots of the raves that other stations and promoters were putting on. The only night I didn't party was a Wednesday night but I partied on the other six nights.

I wasn't part of what happened in 2007 with Time. I went along with Jimmy (my partner in Public Demand Records) on one of the first nights and deejayed, but it was all bit 'don't touch this button and don't press that' and it wasn't for me and I never went back.

I didn't realise the impact that Centreforce had on people's lives until we came back on as Centreforce in the summer of 2017. We started doing the live streams and got our first million views in a month. I now understand the impact that Centreforce had which is really something else for a station that was really only on for just over a year.

In 1990, Centreforce was forced out. It had got to a point where as soon as we went on they'd take us off. There were times when we'd set up three rigs in different locations so that we could switch from one to the next as they got shut down.

I actually think that KISS had a lot to do with the death of a lot of pirates. I think the authority's aim was to give us ravers a station to keep us quiet but at a cost of cutting everyone else out. But good luck to KISS because they went on to a marvellous job and they are now massive. There was a time when I came on the air as Space 100 and this meant that I was using their frequency (before they had it). We used that frequency because we knew it reached right across London.

In 2017 I went to a Rave seminar put on by Raindance. I was asked to speak on behalf of Centreforce Radio. It was after that I thought about bringing back Centreforce but I knew it couldn't be brought back on the FM and it being illegal again. It just wouldn't work. It was Jimmy who told me about Facebook and how it works and we decided to give it a go. We did our first show and it went through the roof. We started to do more shows and it just got bigger. I do thank Facebook for that because without them we wouldn't have been coming back on.

It's been a natural evolution to go for the DAB licence. We all know technology is changing and we've looked at ways to make the station work. DAB is the way forward because it's the way to reach a lot of people and a lot people access DAB in their cars and on their phones.

What people have to remember is that if Centreforce had stayed on over the years, we'd be playing the big tunes of today. We were a house station in the start and that's our core but we need to expand now. Our aim is to be current and to play the best music. The key is to put on designated shows that concentrates on the music of 88/89 and play all the classic house tunes that people want to hear and then there'll be the sets that bring the station into today and play the new breed. If we don't play the new breed the station will eventually die. It's not going to hurt us to evolve and the future is unknown.

Being a good radio deejay is different to being a good club deejay. They're two different animals. Centreforce has always been about people who want to play music and what the station wants is people that can play good music. We know the two can cross over because we've seen it with the likes of Pete Tong and Andy Weatherall. What we want Centreforce radio to be about is you get in your car and what we're playing makes you feel good. That's what we've always tried to do. It's always been about the music and that's all.'

Keith Mac

'I knew Andy from Echo's. I was only young, a lot younger than most of them. Andy gave me my chance to DJ and on the day of the Echos all-dayer he said 'come on' and we drove off to some block of flats near Bow. He told me he was doing a pirate radio station and that I'd be deejaying on it. I was like, but I've never done any radio in my life. That didn't bother Andy.

In this flat there was record player and a crappy old mixer. A few weeks later we moved to a different location and then onto another.

It was brilliant to do because it was all new. We just got on with it. We were in it. It didn't bother us that what we doing was illegal. We were caught up in it and were living doing it. After the shows we'd go to some party and we never had to pay to get in, which was good.

Whilst Centreforce lasted it was great and we played a lot of brilliant records. We broke Numero Uno on Centreforce, which we were proud about. I have absolutely no regrets about being involved with Centreforce. And it was the first twenty four pirate radio station. I loved it!

Centreforce was also putting on parties at the same time that the station was running. Woodstock was one of them but I didn't play at that because Andy had sacked me. I was probably the most sacked deejay on Centreforce. What happened was that Andy gave me a pager so that I could look after station whilst they all went to Ibiza. But the pager was meant to be for my personal use only and I was told not to use it on the radio. But when I was doing one of my shows the studio pagers went down so I used my pager. Andy found about this and sacked me. This was a couple of weeks before Woodstock weekender. Although I was sacked I still went to the weekender. It was held in a field near Brands Hatch. There was an artic lorry with speakers all over it and the decks set up. There were a load of vans parked up that sold drinks and food. I didn't actually get there until about 4am because I had been deejaying in the Camden Head in Bethnal Green. Now Andy had already told me not to turn up telling me that if I did he wouldn't let me in but when I got there Matthew Thomas, who did the security for Andy's parties let me in.

When Centreforce was running there were lots of parties being put on by Andy. There was Echos, there were parties in warehouses, all sorts of venues. There was one warehouse party where the generator caught fire. Andy had secured a warehouse over in docklands. We spent the day getting the venue sorted and setting everything up, but there was no power so Andy had to sort out a generator. This generator was positioned next to the decks. There were about a thousand people in the party when all of a sudden the generator starts to slow down. We realised it was running out petrol so I grabbed the petrol and poured it into the generator whilst it was still running and all this fire came out of it. Next thing there's Andy and me trying to putting this fire out, which thankfully we did and the party was able to carry on.

There was another time when Andy found a warehouse and we spent the day trying to get through the door. We had been out all Friday night and it was a late one as usual. Andy then phones me about 10am telling me that he's found a venue to hold a party in. This place he found was in Harold Hill in Romford. We get to the place and there's this big wooden door. It was a tongue and groove door. Andy spoke to someone and found out how to break in and this involved cutting out these tongue and grooves. We spent all fucking day cutting into this door until it got to 5pm. We got into this warehouse and it had toys lying around. I remember finding this telephone, which Andy took and used in his home. I think the plan had been to do the party with Genesis but by the time we'd broken into the warehouse it was too late to start trying to get the equipment in and get people out for it.

A lot went on in Echos. It was a brand new club at the time, very Sharon and Tracey and very 80's. You used to walk in and there'd be a cloakroom on your right and on the left was where you paid and inside there was a bar on the left. There was weird coloured 80's style carpet everywhere, the music was pumping out through a shit sounding system and there was the dancefloor. One wall was all covered in mirrors too. There club had two floors too which meant you could go upstairs and look down onto the dancefloor and the deejay booth. There was an office out the back of the club too. I was there the day Centreforce put on their first event there and that was where my connection really started.'

Todd Terry

1. **What turned you on to house music?**
I started out playing hip hop as a live DJ at parties, street festivals whoever would let me play. I was into Hip Hop and starting to produce tracks, then I heard Freestyle and House Music at clubs like Roseland and The Garage in New York City and said "I can do that". That is how it started.

2. How did you get into making your own tracks?

Somebody told me I could get paid for House beats, so I got busy. I started making House beats on my Yamaha drum machine and took what I learned from sampling in the the Hip Hop world and started to grab parts from records, that's how my sound came together. I approached House like a Hip Hop production in the beginning, really I still do even today. Then I got a reel to reel Tascam 4 track and really started work on my production, recording and bouncing tracks together, turning my 4 track in to a 24 track. Eventually I got SP-12 and it all came together.

3. Can you describe what was happening in New York regards the house scene in the mid/late 80's and was it different to say Chicago?

First it was late 80s', I'm not that old. I was aware through the records people were making that there were different sounds coming from different cities. I never went to or played in Chicago back then so I didn't see the club side of it. When I started to travel is was to the UK not Chicago.

4. Did you have any idea how influential and what impact your music was having on the UK acid house/rave culture back in 88/89?

I'm told, but at that moment I had my head down and was too busy creating to listen. Yes, years latter people tell me, hey the fans tell me every gig, so it's good to feel like what your worked so hard on had an impact and lasted, not only with the press and the music industry, but with the fans that came to the gigs and supported the music then and now.

5. You're still touring the UK. What are some of the fave places you play here?

I love the UK, I got my first big breaks there and it's special to keep going back. There are great clubs in London and the last few years some great festivals I played like 51st State Festival, but I think M.O.S. will always be a special place to play for me. So many memories of playing at The FAC 51 Hacienda, now it's more of brand that moves around venues but still a top gig. The last few years The Warehouse in Manchester has thrown some great events. I can't leave out all the great festival like playing Glastonbury (finally) was unbelievable and the last few years at We Are FSTVL has been a great crowd.

Marshall Jefferson

'When I was growing up I listened to rock music. I remember seeing The Beatles on the Ed Sullivan Show and I thought it was incredible. But by 1979 I realised that I really liked girls and when I listened to rock there were no women around so I started to go out dancing instead. So, I started going to clubs because I knew that's where the girls would be.

We had the Mendel High School in Chicago and there would be parties there. I went to some to some to some of those. The parties were held in a big gym an there'd be no furniture just speakers and the DJ. It was a real cash-cow too because it was always packed.

I'm a little fuzzy on whether we called house music at the time of those parties but I think at that point it was more what we called New Wave and European style of music. Basically, what got played was anything that gangsters didn't like. Gangsters liked funk-Parliament and Funkadelic and James Brown and when that music got played all the gangsters would show up and start shooting each other. But we didn't want that at our parties so we didn't play that music. We didn't want gangsters around so we called our parties fashion parties and they wouldn't show up. We also wore clothes that gangsters didn't wear. Some people called us elitist but we weren't being elitist we were just scared of guns and we didn't want them around us.

We started to wear certain styles of jeans and polo shirts. We wore Calvin Klein and designer jeans and Izod Lacoste shirts and deck shoes. We actually embraced the nerdy look way before it became fashionable and way before the movie 'Revenge of the Nerds'. By 1981 we were bugging 'nerdy' and it scared off the gangsters. This was our mentality in Chicago at the time of the birth of house.

I went to a club called the Nimbus and I heard a DJ there use this amazing flanging sound. It reminded me a little bit if rock and roll.

And it made me want to also be able to make that sound. After this I started deejaying. At this same time I was working at the post office so I had money to buy the things that I wanted. There was another guy at the post office and his name was Curtis McClaine. Curtis was the guy who sang on Move Your Body but what a lot of people do not know is that Curtis was a brilliant DJ. I mean he could have been one of the Hot Mix Five. He knew how to do all the deejaying tricks and he showed me how to do them. We would then make tapes for each other.

I got to know Chip E because he was working at a record store and he'd tell us that he loved to see us 'post office mother fuckers' coming into the store with their fat wallets. I mean Curtis and me would spend two hundred dollars a week on records and that was a lot of money back then. I still have about 80,000 12 inch records in storage back in Chicago. There's just about every dance music record you can think of in that collection and then there's records like Frequency 7 by Visage and Rock Lobster by the B 52's.

We didn't have samplers back then so Curtis and me use to buy two copies of all the records that he bought. But if we really liked the record we'd buy four copies. We had to factor in that records could get scratched. Nowadays when I buy a vinyl record I digitise it and it never gets played again.

I composed Move Your Body in my basement but for the most part I would take my music to a studio. The studio I used had a small eight track in it. No Way Back by Adonis was also recorded in that same studio and I've Lost Control Sleezy D. I also did the Virgo EP in there too.

When I did Move Your Body I knew it was a great record. If there was ever going to be a House Music Hall of Fame I would get in it because of that song. When I did it I was just a kid making music in my basement and I had dreams.

After Move Your Body I came to the UK to do a tour so I knew what was going on in the UK around '87. I witnessed a six month gap where at first the people in the clubs like the Hacienda were wearing suits and ties but when I played a second time, around the time of working on Acid Tracks by Phuture they were wearing smiley tee shirts and screaming 'acieed'.

It had gone acid house and I was like 'what the fuck'. We didn't call the music acid house. My TB-303 that I paid one hundred and fifty dollars for I then sold for one thousand dollars a few months later.

I got involved with Trax Records after I saw Jesse Saunders getting his records out there. There was Precision Record around at the time and I saw the address that was on the records. I went to the address and I paid to have my first record Virgo Go Wild Rhythm Track pressed up. For a few months after this I stopped making music and this where all the confusion starts with the Virgo name. Vince Lawrence decided to put out Virgo Tracks again because he and everybody thought that I was out of the music business. But Ron Hardy started to play my music and I saw people dancing to them and this motivated me to start making music again.

One guy I got involved with was Mighty Mike. He later changed his name to Adonis. Adonis and I started to make some music together and we stated to record an EP. I was putting up the money to get the records pressed up. Adonis said he wanted to make a record like I've Lost Control and he came with No Way Back. It used the TB-303 and 808 drums and he understood how to do the programming whereas I didn't. So No Way Back became a blazing hot song.

The song got played at a club and Larry Sherman was there and everybody in the club went wild. He took Adonis to one side and told him that he wanted to put it out on Trax as a single. It was Adonis's first taste of stardom and something changed and we didn't do the EP and I had to replace No Way Back with something else.

At this time, I had Move Your Body and there was I've Lost Control but at first Larry didn't want to press them up. He didn't know what was happening in the clubs so although the records were recorded in '85 both didn't come out until '86. But I had reporters ringing me from the UK asking me about house music and I also had a guy call Jazzie B calling me and we'd talk for hours on the phone about house music and he helped spread the word about my music. A bunch of reporters from the UK flew out to Chicago and they came to the studio to watch me record a version of Move Your Body and after this Larry Sherman really got involved and started to put out house records. By this time Move Your Body had been played in the clubs for seven months but Larry saw the response in the clubs and he pressed the record up the next day on Trax Records. From there on it was wild.'

Jumping Jack Frost

'I started out in sound systems and hanging out with people like Jazzie B and Soul 11 Soul and I was going to the Africa Centre every week. That was the school that I came through along with Trevor Nelson and Paul 'Trouble' Anderson. And then I went to Clinks one night where there was an acid house party happening and Evil Eddie Richards was there and my life changed that night and after that I also started playing acid house music. I then started playing at Sunrise and Energy raves and it went from there.

Around 88/89 I had a night going on called The Gallery which was near Bow. In the venue we went to a lot of trouble with the décor and we had these big heads hanging around the place. We then heard that some people were using our venue and they were using the heads that we'd put up. I didn't like this and I lost my nut over it. I was doing the Gallery with my two partners and I was angry and told them that I wanted some money off the other people for using what we had.

We went to one of their nights and I was asking around who was in charge and telling them that they were taking the piss. So there I was shouting the odds and making some noise and then Andy (Swallow) comes out. Andy was like 'now calm down' and telling me that they didn't know anything about my nights. But I was still shouting and telling him to fuck off but fair play to Andy he still kept telling me to calm down and take it easy. But I kept on and started telling them that I was going to come back and start throwing bricks around. As soon as I said that one of Andy's lot went bang and laid into me. It wasn't over the top but it was enough.

Then something happened and Andy found out what I had been going on about and realised that I had a point. We talked, sorted it out and me and Andy shook hands. After this we started working together and we've been sweet ever since.

That Centreforce lot are as good as gold and I love what they are doing at the moment. I've done shows for them and I done the party they had in the Bloc, which was a really good place to have their first party in. It was good and I really enjoyed it. They had the right crowd on the night.

Back in 89 Centreforce was very important. Back then it was a revolution time and Centreforce was banging it out. Andy and the deejays believed in what they were doing. They had loads of passion for what they were doing and they done a lot for a lot of people. People calmed down and people started to see people differently. A lot of people wouldn't even know each other if it wasn't for happened back then. The rave scene was so important an Centreforce was integral to helping to change culture and the way we live our lives.

Lisa Loud

My story with house music starts after I went to Ibiza in 1986 and seeing what was going on out there. Whilst there I got to meet people that went on to become the 'superstar DJ's' like Paul Oakenfold and Carl Cox and Alfredo. They became the leaders in electronic music and they paved the way for came after. I was only young, still a teenager but I was hanging out with those people and going to all the original clubs like Amnesia.

Everything about Ibiza was great. Musically it was the biggest turn-on and we were in the sun and loving it. There was also a coming together of lots of different people from different backgrounds. There were people from all parts of London, Essex and from up North and they brought what was happening back to London. What was inspired by Alfredo got regenerated by Paul Oakenfold and it just exploded. I was one of the few people that experienced it in its original form in Ibiza and I saw what happened back in the UK.

It's hard to describe what the original thing was because it was much more than just house music, It was a sound. A feel. People call it Balearic but what does Balearic mean? Does it mean music that is influenced by percussion and guitars with a Spanish feel? For me, what Balearic meant was having no rules. It was also an eclectic mix of so many different musical styles: Bowie, Beatles, Cure, Mr Fingers-everything and anything really that created an over-worldly feel.

When the Ibiza thing came to the UK I saw it grow. For my part I got very interested in the mechanics of how things worked in the dance music industry and I went on to work with people like Soul 11 Soul and Sydney Young Blood and promote their records. I also got involved with labels like the Junior Boys Own and Talking Loud.

I also worked with the people that were reaching out to those interested in dance music and that included the pirate radio stations like Centreforce. Pretty much every campaign I ran to promote a record included me working with the pirates. They were our voice and they could let thousands of people know about a new record.

Even today there are pirates and digital radio stations that are smashing it every week and they still have that underground feel. And they are still out there breaking records and giving the artists a voice and Centreforce are doing it again and serving a greater purpose.

Keith Davis, Menace...various recollections from early rave days

First exposure to clubbing as we know it was visits by me and my mates to clubs such as The Purple Pit and then The Purple Pussycat which were held at The Electric Ballroom and a place in the basement of a church in Deptford (may have been The Crypt) and also odd nights at The Wag etc around about 1985 these places played rare groove, soul, disco and the first house orientated tracks that had found their way over to the UK. The DJs I am not sure of apart from one who was called Paul Anderson although I am sure this was not Paul "trouble" Anderson.

The first time I heard acid was on a trip to Ibiza in 1987 where I stayed in Playa Den Bossa, I remember being in a club that was playing stuff I had never heard before, we had met up with some lads from East London who had obviously heard the music before as every time an acid/house track was played they would all chant "Acid! Acid" and would start to wave their arms in the air...of course we joined in and loved what we was hearing, we was hooked.

One particular mad night out was at a warehouse rave we had heard about on Centreforce, totally unsure of the exact location but it was a total roadblock and the police were there and just had no idea as to the lengths people were prepared to go to get into the party, we managed to get in without any problems as we had got there early.

The main memory of the night was being in the middle of the dancefloor totally lost in the moment and looking up only to see people ripping open the skylights and dropping down into the crowd below, as the police had blocked the doors they had resorted to climbing on the roof in their desperation to find a way in.

Another mad night was Energy in Heston during 1989, again the police were on the scene but were totally unprepared for peoples determination to get into the party at all costs, they thought that blocking the motorway exits would be enough to stop anyone getting to the location...little did they know that people were more than prepared to dump their cars on the hard shoulder and run across 6 lanes of traffic to get to the warehouse.

Again, we were there early as this was a local one for us.

We got to the approach road to the warehouse and found two policemen standing there turning people away. The crowd of 5 or 6 people soon grew to a crowd of 100+ the police just stood there confident that their presence was enough to stop anyone from going any further. After a few minutes the cry went up to just "steam the old bill" no one had any intentions to attack the police it was just an attempt to get past them and get through the gates to the warehouse that were so temptingly in our view.

As soon as the cry went up the crowd charged towards the police who made half-hearted attempts to grab hold of randomly selected people as we charged past them, I personally think they didn't actually want to catch anyone as they didn't know if the crowd would turn on them if they had actually caught someone.

As we reached the gates the doormen swung them open and let us through, one of the girls who was with us was a bit slower and the gates had been shut again and by the time she had reached them the police were there and blocking her way.

Come on through said one of the bouncers to which she replied "I can't, the policeman will get me" the bouncer replied "if he gets you, I will get him" and she calmly walked by while the police just stared at their shoes.

We entered the huge warehouse which only had about 2-300 people in it and soon started to enjoy the evening, during the next half hour or so the place filled up with a few hundred more people all buzzing off the fact we had all managed to outwit the police, then the announcement came over the PA that the police were allowing the rave to go ahead as they wanted the thousands of people gathered off the streets... within minutes the place was rammed with 1000s of people and the night went right off.

The highlight of this one for me was Adamski playing, I was up on a dance platform when he launched into NRG and I looked around as 10000 like-minded ravers lost their minds... again this one made the mainstream press and this only reinforced our beliefs that we were a part of one of the greatest youth movements in history.

I had been involved in music before having played in punk bands and helping to organize a few gigs so it was a logical progression for me to get involved, I first bought a set of decks at the end of 1988 and began buying vinyl and practicing in my flat, my sound collection soon grew into a few thousand watts so I started putting on house parties wherever we could, one particular night was a house party in Furnival Avenue in Slough.

Lack of DJs at this point meant I had to play for 8-9 hours straight, I wasn't complaining as I was doing what I loved and really getting off on the fact that the few hundred people in attendance were going even more mental every time I played another track to beat the previous one... I have been told by various people in attendance that for them it was one of the highlights of the year for them.

The sound system grew into a professional set up of 30 thousand watts that we would haul all over the country both hiring it out and putting on our own events and eventually taking the Menace name to Amsterdam to perform a support slot for The Prodigy at The Vries House Amerika festival.

These were the days of my life and me and my mates just felt like every weekend was like experiencing our very own Woodstock.

Screamin' Rachael (Cain)

'I got my name Screamin' Rachael because it's all about the attitude. I walk into a room and I don't have to say anything. It's all about the way that I carry myself and use my voice. I have a big presence and this is why my name came about.

When it comes to the origins of Trax Records, people from around the world don't really know how it was. There have been lots of people writing about it but they weren't there, so they don't really know or understand what it was like for us.

What was going on in Chicago and with Trax Records was a youth culture explosion. It really was. I mean, you don't see it now, but back then what was happening - the music - was taking over the streets. When house music started in our town it took over the streets and the radios. And, one of the reasons why Trax was able to make that happen, was because we had a vinyl pressing plant. We also had Larry (Sherman), who was the designated adult at the time. We had the ability to make our music in one day and, on that day, we could have a reference disc and take it down to a DJ, and it would get played and we could see how it worked in the club. This meant we'd know immediately if it would work in the clubs and, being able to do what we could, also meant that me, Jesse (Saunders) and Vince (Lawrence) made everyone else in Chicago want to be like us and so other people wanted to get records made and played really quickly too.

Trax was a miracle and it's been able to stand the tests of time. The music that we did many years ago still stands up today. There are also a lot of kids hearing those Trax records today and they think it's new. Many of them just don't realise that those records were made thirty years ago.

Another important thing about Trax was where it came from. In some ways London reminds me of Chicago, in that there are a lot of working class people. At the time, Chicago wasn't a music industry town like LA or New York, so when we were making the music we weren't really making it in the way that many people do, where they are wanting to be part of one of the major record labels and have the big money. This wasn't our motive for what we were doing. We were just doing what we were doing and we were excited by it and I can't say that I've seen anything like it since.

There's been some excitement lately for Trax Records and I think this has been because there's been some documentaries which have come out that have heavily featured Trax music. People see Trax as being the original home for house music so it gets that attention. I'm also seeing a tremendous amount of love for Trax and this is a little scary actually, because I have all these people trying to push their way into this little label. But we've always managed to maintain our independence and it was this independent spirit that started us up at the beginning when it was just a small group of friends who, by doing what we did, became the backbone of a movement that has since become a genre of music.

It's still exciting to hear on the radio one of the first tracks that me, Vincent and Jesse did, like Fantasy. This was a track that we actually recorded before Jesse did On And On. Fantasy was really the first song of the house thing here in Chicago and it just exploded and got so big on Chicago local radio. At the time, we didn't even have anything like radio promotion or publicists, but somehow we created something that just couldn't be stopped.

I think when the rave thing was starting up in the UK, we did have a small sense of what was happening. There had been something written about us in a couple of books and there'd been a big article about us in The Face. There'd also been several journalists sent to Chicago to interview all of us and, it was because of all this that we had a sense that something was going on in the UK.

I fought very hard for what I've done and that includes my story alongside the Trax Records story. I've now written a screen play based on this, and this is being shopped around at the moment. And for this I will keep control over what happens because I'm very fussy about my story and the Trax story-which is one of the reasons why we've never sold out to a major record company. I feel that we still run Trax as a little company, but one that has a big heart. We still follow our own beat and we do things the way we want to do things.

Sometimes people ask me about the Trax sound. I tell them that each track is different and each has its own sound. I mean, how can you compare Acid Trax to Love Can't Turn Around or Move Your Body. You really can't. And then there's the hip house and cool rocksteady stuff and this again is completely different. In some ways, I feel we at Trax are the beat of this generation. People want to dance and house music does that for people and this is funny because I was there at the beginning when some people used to laugh about house music.

The future for Trax is looking very positive. We've never stopped and we continue to put out new artists and new music. We recently released 'Acid Trax 30' because this is the thirtieth year anniversary. We have new and old classics on this album. We also have a product coming out that has a tongue in cheek title of 'Now That's What I Call Trax' and this is us showing people what we've been doing the last ten years. We've also got into movie soundtracks too and one of these is for a movie called Vamp Bikers. Yeah, I think the future for Trax looks very bright and we are moving forward whilst we continue to honour the past. For example, I'm still working with people like Joe Smooth and touring with Marshall (Jefferson) and there's going to be a Trax Tour (if anyone is interested in the Trax Tour contact MN2S).

In the beginning, my dream was that our music would be known throughout the world and that people would have respect for it and that is exactly what has happened - andI'd like to thank Jorge Cruz for being my righthand person these last 10 years and Mark Suchocki for being the designated adult helping with all of our business concerns.'

Virgo
'I got into house music after going to Mendel Catholic High School in Chicago. This was around the early to mid-80s. At the time this place was the hub of house music. I heard what was going on and thought I could do this and went out and bought some equipment that included a four track portable studio and a 505 and a Juno. After a while we learned the ins and outs of the Juno and the 505 and we started going from there. Before all this I had been

playing bass guitar. That is my main instrument. The keyboards was kinda like the third instrument that I started playing.

In Chicago at the time you had the Hot Mix Five and there was Ron Hardy. He was the big deejay at the time. There was also Frankie Knuckles. There was also the Power Plant and the Underground Club. We used to go down town and go to see these people at these places. There was another place we'd go to also called Sawyer's. There was a big scene in Chicago, it wasn't just the music. It was a culture that had the music and also there was a way of dressing too.

We were doing what we were doing but we didn't have any idea what was happening in the UK at the same time. I had no idea whatsoever. The thing is we were not deejays. A lot of people at the time who were making house music were also deejays.

Being part of Trax is an adventure all by itself. We had an up and down relationship with Larry Sherman. Overall it was pretty positive though for me and at the time I was in college and he (the music) helped pay for college for me. But getting money out of Larry was legendary. If you got a cheque you had to go and cash it straight away because if you didn't they would bounce. I mean you could play basketball with Larry's cheques.

Larry and I actually became pretty good friends. I would go to his house and hang out with him, talk to his wife and play with his dog, play video games. The relationship was pretty good.

Thirty years on and we are still here. I'm out touring with Virgo Four. There's plans to come to the UK again. We were there in spring 2017 and then we went and spent the summer in Italy. We also played in Spain and Switzerland. We do a lot of touring and we expect to do more because we have some new releases coming out in 2018.'

Dean Lambert
'I started deejaying back in the rave days and played out in places like the Astoria and Busby's. This was '89 and I knew Andy and the Centreforce boys because I was a West Ham. I didn't get involved with the station in '89. I came on board later on. In '89 I was busy doing different things. I would often play in what was

called back then the chill out room, which was more of a US house room. This was before garage came in. In 1989 I listened to Centreforce and I was aware of how important it was on the rave scene.

I had the Gas Club in Leicester Square for a while and this was around the same time that Andy also used it. This was the break of the garage scene-the real garage scene. The Gas Club was one of the most darkest and dangerous clubs around at the time. Me and Brandon Block then went to Thailand and I fell in love with the place. It was when I came back that I saw Andy and he said to me that I should come down his pub and see what was happening with the Centreforce shows. After that I ended up doing a show, which got something like 25.000 hits, which I was over the moon with. I couldn't believe the power of what Centreforce was doing with those live stream shows.

I then deejayed at the Centreforce Boxing Day party at the George 11 in Hornchurch. It was a good night and a lot of old skool got played. My next show was with Andy at the Dovecote on New Year's Eve.

Getting the DAB is perfect for Centreforce for where they are now. Other stations like KISS have gone very commercial which means there's a big call for a station like Centreforce which doesn't play the commercial stuff. It'll work and it'll be good.'

DJ Seeker

'From an early age I was into music, I was listening to hip hop and RnB and when I was thirteen I bought three turntables. So when the house music started to come through I got into that too and really started to concentrate on the acid house scene. What I really liked about house music was the tempo. I liked that it was upbeat and enjoyable to listen to.

My connection with Centreforce came about through some friends of mine that knew them from going to football and they recommended me. I was part of a group of deejays called the Corporation, which was Corporation Dave, MC Scotty, DJ Hugs and me. I knew two of them from school and I played football against the other two. We had similar interests in music and started something up. The name came about because me and Dave was driving through London and saw a sign which said the Corporation of London. I nudged Dave and pointed it out to him and suggested I would be a good name for us. We all agreed and that's what we started to use.

Centreforce saw us play and after that we got invited to do our first show.

During my time with Centreforce I went to lots of places where they had their studios set up. They'd be changing locations every few weeks. They were basically flats that Centreforce were able to use.

Back in them days I didn't use to talk much when we were doing a show. I was quite mic shy and was happy just to let my fingers take care of the entertainment. I'd just say something short like 'this is DJ Seeker, let's go'.

As I got more involved with the station I left my job as an estate agent. I just wanted to play music. I was eighteen at the time but I wanted to go and do what I loved.

At the time I didn't really know how important Centreforce was to people. I was just running on pure excitement. I lived Centreforce at the time. It was in my veins every day and I would be buzzing to get back on the station and do another show. Sometimes we'd play all through the night. It was that good to do.'

Derek 'Smokin' Joe

'I started listening to house music in my basement really. I would listen to the Hot Mix Five and at that time they'd only been going for about a year. I remember a friend phoned me and said 'are you listening to the mixes' and I replied 'I don't know what he mixes are'. But I tuned into WBMX Radio and listened to the Hot Mix Five. This was around 1985 and me and house music kinda went on from there.

I went to the Mendel High School too and participated in those events. At that time I wasn't a DJ but I was in a dance troupe called Straight Up and Down. There were a lot of dance crews back then and we'd go to the Mendel High School and dance there. I really

153

fell in love with house music by going to Mendel. I frequented there a lot. It was our age group and I met people there.

I started dealing with some of the guys from Wall to Wall Sounds. Before they started doing house parties they were doing regular R&B parties. I got involved with a promotional company called Park Avenue. Park Avenue productions had a crew of deejays and we'd g out and do a lot of parties. There was a lot happening in Chicago at that time.

I loved house music and being a house deejay. But before this I was into rock and roll. I listened to Journey, Kiss, The Police and Phil Collins. I didn't know anything about the R&B and disco really. I was a late bloomer to in some ways but I remember lying in bed and dreaming about someday being a deejay on stage and travelling. I would hear music in my sleep but I never had a clear view of what I would end up doing but I just knew I would end up doing something with music.

As house started to progress more in my life I started hanging out with guys like Steve Hurley and Farley Keith. Farley was my first mentor and he showed me how to make my first record. My first drum machine was a Linn Drum and I did a track called Home Boy, which has gone down as a cult classic and it's really big in Japan right now. Home Boy was made using a home studio because back then that's how a lot of made our music. I used the drum machine to come up with different tom and conga sounds and I would bend those sounds until I came up with what I wanted. I go to work with a famous studio musician too called Keith Henderson and another guy called Marvin Sparkes and they paid down some keyboards on Home Boy.

We were making house music in Chicago but we didn't really know how we was influencing what was going on in the UK. Back in 85/86 we were just doing the music for fun. We wanted to see how the crowd reacted to our music. That was our high. It wasn't about making money. It wasn't until people like Larry Sherman and Rocky Jones started talking about touring guys that we found out how huge house music was. We just thought it was a Chicago thing.

What we had in Chicago was a house culture. It's changed now and what we now is a term I have coined called House Millennials this is about the young guys that love house music. People are saying this now.

Back in the 80's we dressed to go to parties. We dressed in certain clothes because we knew we were going to sweat out. It made no sense to wear a lot of dramatic stuff. This was the 80's though so there was a lot of yuppy and preppy styles of dressing going on. Penny loafers and boat shoes worn with no socks, blue jeans which we would sew the ends of to make them a little tighter around the ankles, there'd be Izod Lacoste and Polo shirts too. This was the look that identified us as being part of the house culture. Some people would put a sweat rag in their pockets too because they knew once they started dancing they wouldn't stop and they would sweat.

When we went to the clubs we went there to dance and to listen to the latest tracks. That's all we wanted. There were so many clubs in Chicago at the time and I hate that now so many have gone and now there are lounges. Back then going to the clubs was kind of like a rite of passage. Every club had its own feel too. Take a club like Sawyers which had Ron Hardy. This was more of a free-flowing club that had a mixture of black white gay and straight people who were closer to high school age. The Warehouse had Frankie Knuckles and this was a more mature crowd with its mixture of black white gay and straights.

It was Ron Hardy who taught me how to play disco. He took the fear of playing disco away from me. There's a scene in the Matrix where there's all these people dancing in a cave. It was kind of like that for me. I'd stand on stage and I would watch the crowd dancing in one melodic movement that was almost trance like. This was awesome for me and it was different to being at Mendel because at Mendel there was more of a free-style thing going on where you had dance troupes and people competing against each other.

What people in Chicago prefer is dark and dingy places to dance in as opposed to a club that had beautiful stages and lighting and an interactive cool bar. The older house shy away from these sort of places. We want to be in places where we think 'oh my God we might fall through the floor but I don't care and this was our house music culture in the 80's.

Tony Grimley

'I got into house music when I was about sixteen. My first club was Twilights and that was where Darren Emerson was playing. It was all new to us at the time but it was a big thing. Then we started going to the big warehouse parties put on by Sunrise and Centreforce. Around 89 I was drinking in a pub called the Spencer's Arms and there was a deejay in there called Mark Williams. He'd play house and the place would get absolutely rammed. I went up to Mark and asked him if I could play a few records. He said yes. I then went to Woolworths and bought one of those little plastic record boxes and some records. The first record I bought was The Real Life by Corporation of One.

I went to college at Havering Tec and there was quite a few of us that went to parties all dressed in our smiley faces tee shirts and dungarees and Kickers. We then started to put our events on and these went really well and we got a bit of a following. I did a party with a friend called Keith McCarthy and we got to know Keith Mac and then we started to go to Echos and that's how I got to know Andy and that lot.

I think what Centreforce are doing is a natural evolution for them. There's loads of people from the original days where the kids are older and some have flown the roost and this is allowing us to go to the places that play that original house music. I played at the Centreforce party at the Bloc in Hackney Wick. I thought it was a fantastic night. It felt like going back to the early warehouse rave days. It was in an old shitty warehouse and this was what it was like back then. Andy couldn't have chosen a better venue to hold the first Centreforce come-back party.

So you have Centreforce, Clock Work Orange and Culture Shock all doing it again and people are turning out for it. People of our age group want to go out and enjoy themselves again like they did back in 89. Whatever Centreforce are doing they are making it work and it'll only go from strength to strength.'

Jonny Eames

'We had a night club in Bow called Echos which was one of the first rave clubs in East London. We'd get over a thousand people every Friday and Saturday night. Echos got very big and because of this we had a lot of deejays coming through it. We had people like Carl Cox and Judge Jules play there. We recruited some of the Centreforce deejays via Echos. At its peak Echos had about fifty to sixty deejays on its list.

Andy had been doing Faces which was in Hackney. We already knew each other through football. I was in the Mile End and he was in the ICF. Then some fella who was on Sunrise called Roger (the dodge) came to us and asked us if we'd be interested in starting up the radio station. It turned out that Roger had also said the same thing to Andy. So, we linked up together to do it and that was how Centreforce took off.

There was an all-dayer at Echos and it was after that when the first Centreforce show happened. It took off really quickly. I mean it was unbelievable. In the end there wasn't a shop or market stall that didn't know about Centreforce. And let's have it right, most of us weren't even deejays but we got to play at those of places.

Some of us went out to Ibiza to play there. This was the Centreforce tour and we had four clubs. I don't remember much more other than getting on the plane to get out there then getting on it to come home.

Between us we found the flats where we ran the stations from. We knew a caretaker and he'd tell us where the empty flats were. There was one time he told us where this empty flat in one of the tower blocks on Carpenters Road was and we went to it. We got there and kicked the door in but once we got inside there were people sitting around a table eating their dinner. We'd gone to the wrong flat.

My fondest memories of the Centreforce days would have to be Ibiza and Woodstock. I remember that I got nicked coming through the airport. Andy and me and had been on holiday in Portugal but he had come back early because we had Woodstock starting on the Friday. Before I left the hotel, I had put a little bit of puff in the back of radio but it got found and I got arrested. They kept me overnight at Gatwick airport then let me go and I went straight to Woodstock.

Shinola's was another good event. The place had two rooms, a front area then a back area which was bigger. Some Turkish guys had it and it would get used for Turkish weddings. It was mobbed when we had it.

Echos and Centreforce raided at the same time. We had been tipped off though by some Sun journalist. We knew it would only be a matter of time. Net to Echos was a warehouse where the police kept all the cars and vans that had been used in arm robberies and what have you. The police would watch us from their windows and film us. We knew they were watching us and we'd drop our trousers and show them our arses. After the raid and the investigation, the case got thrown out so we didn't get done for anything. I remember the celebrations back at my pub that night and what a night that was.

What Centreforce are doing now by getting the DAB licence and going legal is a good thing, and all these years after we had the chance too. When we were a pirate Richard Branson sent someone down to see us. Someone from Virgin contacted Gary Dickel because they'd seen the poll about the top radio stations in London and Centreforce had come top. At that time you even had people like Paul Weller saying he listened to us.

What Branson told us to do was come off the air and stop being a pirate and Virgin would back Centreforce. But we were getting three or four grand a week at the time so we told him to fuck off. That was the biggest mistake I've ever made I think. But that was us then. That was our attitude. We thought who needs Branson we can do it on our own.

We didn't really know how big Centreforce was at the time. I would do the late Saturday show and then on Sundays I take the family over to Clapham Common. There'd be hundreds of people turning up because they'd heard that I was there and they thought there was going to be a rave. The police would turn up and I would be having a kick about with my kid. Centreforce did get really powerful and it was something that we could never had dreamed of in a million years and I was really disappointed when the station did get shut down.'

Hermit

'My connection started with Centreforce when they were set up in one of the fats in my block in James Riley Point in Carpenters Road. I was living on the eighteenth floor and they were below me. This was how I got my name Hermit. Some days it would take me twenty minutes to get out of my own house. I would literally stop and talk to people on the sixteenth floor, then the fourteenth and seventh. I then had people coming around to my place all the time and I wouldn't leave the house for a couple of weeks, so people started calling me hermit.

I noticed the Centreforce people coming and going and I asked a friend who they were and it turned out that he knew them. At this time, I was playing music and had a set up in my bedroom. My friend told me he could get me on the station and he got something set up.

The station then moved from James Riley Point to Lund Point and then onto Dennison Point. This was in 1989 and I was deejaying for them. I was only fifteen. I think I was the youngest Centreforce DJ.

I had got into house music after going to a party with my mate David. This was one of Andy's warehouse parties. I didn't know this at the time and only found out years after. It was a proper dirty old warehouse and it was the nuts-everyone was proper 'avin it! After that I was hooked on the music and started buying up the music from places like Red Records in Brixton.

At the time it was a buzz and it was all new to me. I remember being in the studio and the pagers would be going off and people would be throwing onto the floor in frustration because they couldn't keep up with the amount of messages that were coming through. There'd be two pagers beep beeping constantly. It was mental! I loved those days!

I can still remember the day I first met Andy. I was in the studio and he came straight up to me and said 'hello Hermit'. It blew me away that he knew me and ever since then he's always looked after me. I believe that some of my personality has come out from being around those Centreforce days and being around someone like Andy and seeing the way that he did things.

Chris Lavish

'I have been with Centreforce twice. I got involved in 2007 and it was sort of like a dream come true really. I had been with the station Unknown FM. But I remember listening to Centreforce back in 1989. I was only young but I liked acid house and listening to DJ's like Randall. During my time I've played on other stations like House FM and Chilling FM and I was on Time FM when it was called Active FM.

What Centreforce are doing now with getting the DAB is a wicked thing. It works for stations like Rinse FM and they used to be a pirate but have now gone legal. DAB is definitely the way forward. I mean you pick it up virtually anywhere, online, on the TV, in the car. I think it's a big move for Centreforce and the right move too. They are already established too so getting the DAB just takes it forward. Things also need to get that underground feel back and Centreforce are able to do that.

I loved doing the Centreforce live streams. I hadn't done it before so it was something new to do. I felt like I was in my element when I was doing it. It was good experience and the show got good reviews.

Jim EP

'I used to listen to Centreforce and page in when I was younger. It was Jimmy Lowe who got me involved with the station when they came back on the air around 2007.

I first started listening to house music when I was sitting on the back of the bus on the way to football matches. I used to get tapes and listen to them. I was only about thirteen at the time. It was around 1991 that I went to my first rave and that was in Plumstead and people like Micky Finn was there. I loved it, the atmosphere and the music and coming out of the venue at 6 in the morning. It really moved me from there.

I started deejaying when I was fifteen and bought my first set of decks with a mate. I then started house music and got really into it. And then around 1995 I started deejaying on the radio station called Déjà vu. I got to know a lot of people through doing that and then I got with Centreforce and found my home, so to speak.

I'm used to radio but I found the live stream initially difficult to get into. When you're on the radio no-one can see you, but on the live stream everyone can see what you're doing. But getting the DAB and going forward that way is a good thing for Centreforce. The pirate days are long gone now. People don't want to have go running up and down stairs and be locking loads of doors behind you. I think Centreforce have got a good opportunity to get really big and become the biggest underground house radio station around.

Rooney the Roonsta

'My connection to Centreforce came about because my sister was seeing one of the DJ's. I started going up to where the station was and hanging about. This was when Centreforce were based in Dennison Point and I can only describe it as being rough and ready. It was basic. I have a memory of that time that has stuck in my head and it's off seeing DJ Kirky D sitting with a hoody up with headphones on.

The station then used my sister's flat for a short period of time too. This was a nice set up because there were some decks set up in the bedroom and they got used to have a little practice before starting the show.

I then started doing sets with people like Scratch Master Steve and DJ Seeker. I remember there was one day when they hooked up all the decks and Seeker was on them and you had me and my sister handing him records that we thought would be impossible to mix but he did mix them and he made it look easy. He was shit hot! Seeker knew what he was doing.

Centreforce was the nuts at the time. It was all about getting the music out and the music was important to us. I had got into acid house early and it meant everything. It was my mate Simon James who got me into it. We used to get cheap tee shorts and spray smiley faces on them and take them to the clubs and sell them on. Those days were brilliant.

I was on Time FM when there were the Centreforce sessions and I was part of Chillin FM but now its brilliant because we don't have any worries. Back in the days of the pirates we worried that we'd have our records taken away from us. Mixing and deejaying was what I knew I wanted to do from an early age-its been a passion. And then it happened and it was my mum who gave me my DJ name and I with it and I stuck with it even when back in the Centreforce days they called me Hot Rod.'

Sterling Void

'I used to be a neighbourhood DJ and would go to a house music club place called The Playground on 1345 South Michigan. Now there was a deejay in there called Jesse Saunders and another called Farley Keith-who became Farley Jackmaster. This was how I brought to the sound and the whole life-style of house music. There was also Steve 'Silk' Harley around and he was doing parties too. After this I was introduced to the Power Plant where Frankie Knuckles and Mike Winston were playing and my involvement with house music really started to pick up.

I then met a couple of friends and their father was a musician. He played keyboards and his name was Ken Chaney also known as Finger Man and I give respect to this man. Ken loaned us all this equipment which meant we could start to make our own tracks and I started to take this further.

I then got to know Ron Hardy-rest in peace, and I got to know the Music Box and I was making tracks and one thing led to another. And then I met Marshall Jefferson. Right away I saw how talented Marshall was. I moved in with Marshall, he had an empty room and I stayed there.

I was at Marshall's one time and Kym Mazelle was there. They were just getting ready to make Taste My Love. At this time, I was actually called Sterling. Sterling is my AKA my real name is Dwaine. I had started a little group called Void, with my first wife-she took the name Sybil Void. The group didn't really work out because people weren't really into it, but I was and I kept the dream and I kept pushing. And it whilst I was sitting in the kitchen in Marshall's house that I looked up and on top of the refrigerator and there was a box of nails and on the box was written sterling. I said to myself 'Sterling' 'Void', 'Sterling Void' and that was how I came up with my name.

I went to the studio one night with Marshall and my first wife. Marshall told us that he had a session another session and did we want to hang around. Curtis McClain was with him and a few other guys. We listened to what they were doing and that was the first time that I ever heard Move Your Body. I said to Marshall 'you got something there man-you're gonna start a revolution' and the rest is history.

The house music thing was just starting to really happen. You had guys like Jesse Saunders making On and On. I think he was the first person to have a house record out of Chicago to go onto vinyl.

At the start there wasn't what I would say was resistance to house music but there was ridicule. This was really because house music got played in the gay clubs. In Chicago there was a strong gay music scene in the clubs. So as far as there were people like me going to these clubs, like the Power Plant, there'd be people saying things like 'why are you hanging out down there with those faggots'. But they didn't know that it wasn't just gay people going to these clubs, there were also a lot of straight people too. We went to these places because this was where the house music was. But yes, it was the gay scene that started off the house scene.

I was on the DJ International label and a guy called Rocky Jones had that label but he didn't always tell us about the success that guys like me were having in the UK. For a long time, I never found out that It's Alright was doing so well until about a year after of being out in the UK. I was just a neighbourhood kid and people like me didn't go overseas so we didn't know what was going. Rocky did though and he'd come back and tell us what he thought we needed to do but not what we needed to hear. I didn't even find out that the Pet Shop Boys covered my song until two years after they released it.

Things are different now and I can talk to people all around the world. It just wasn't like that back in the days when I was recording tracks like Its Alright. I have to give credit to a guy called Mike Morrison. It was Mike who introduced me to the real business of house music. Back in the day when we were just kids we'd just be walking around Chicago carrying our records. We didn't really know or understand much about the business part of it all. We needed to understand though to stop people taking us for a lot of money-which happened to us back in those days.

At the time DJ International was putting out good house music and Trax was putting out good house music. I don't think there was competition between the artists on the labels. I mean Trax had Mr. Lee, Marshall Jefferson and DJ International had Joe Smooth, Fast Eddie and me. We didn't look at it as competition. It didn't matter to us what label we were on-we were still buddies. It just meant that we'd got different deals at different times with different record labels. And even when we had different labels we still did stuff together. I mean I did stuff with Marshall Jefferson. At the time we all just saw it as us all making good house music. Back then there were only two places to look for good house music and that was DJ International and Trax Records-period!

Looking back now I'm really proud of the legacy that guys like us made. I love what I set out. It tickles me to death when I hear young guys say to me 'hey man, you were one of the pioneers, it was you guys that first put this stuff down'. Now these cats are the future and I love it and I love that I was part of it back in those days. They were some really great times.

Moving forward I'm going to be working with a guy called Andy Daniels from Defected Records and this means there'll be some Sterling Void music coming out. I've also got a couple of tracks coming out on Spinning Records and I'm messing around with the idea of bringing back my label too, which is called Void Digital Music. There's also a European Tour coming in 2018 so look out for that.'

Jon 'Mr Music' Fleet

'I was seventeen years old, growing up in Hackney and East Ham and was setting up sound systems and we did work with Soul 11 Soul at some of their parties, we also Notting Hill Carnival and a few warehouse parties, and then one night we were driving along some road in East London in our van and Andy Swallow stepped out into the middle of the road waving his arms in the air.

At that time, I was a DJ on some hip hop pirate station and so I had hip hop records but very little house music, but I ended up doing a show on Centreforce. I was one of the early DJ's to be on Centreforce-one of the originals. I was one of the youngest, Keithy Mac being the youngest. The very first tune I played on Centreforce was No Way Back by Adonis, that was the track had had switched on to acid house music a couple years before.

At the time, for me, I was all so new, even though I had had a bit of experience with the hip hop station. I mean I had played records in some guys flat, whilst another guy slept in the bed behind me. But Centreforce was more structured. The studios we used were better and we had a few of them, Andy was always moving us around. He was always telling us that we'd be in this flat next week or that premise. Of course we used that flat in the block of flats in Canning Town and that's still there now.

I remember one studio being on the top floor of the tower block and that there was no lift so we had to walk up the stairs, twent-nine flights or something, carrying our record bags. The studio was very basic. It was literally an empty flat that Andy had managed to secure somehow. Then there was a table with the decks on it, no carpet and the antennae was on the roof somewhere-Andy would have climbed up there and stuck that up. I would be there, playing records and trying to manage the messages that were being paged in at the same time. So I'd read the message and put the shout out. Yeah, that one sticks in my mind.

It all felt so normal to us. We didn't care that it was illegal. That never crossed our minds. We had to hide what we were doing and be careful. I used to carry my records in a shoulder bag and a couple of sports carrier bags and at that time I still didn't even have that many house records. It was only as my show progressed and I had to get more records that my bags got bigger.

For some shows we'd double up. I did some shows with Danielle which was always good. Back then there wouldn't be too much talking, we just be trying to manage the requests and shouts and play our records. It's funny seeing the Centreforce sessions now because its still happening, except without the pagers.

I would do shows and still go raving. I spent my eighteenth birthday at an Energy party. I also deejayed at places like Echos and place called Galleries that had all these papier-mache heads all around the place. But there were times when we'd be kept in the dark and wouldn't know about the location of some party until the last minute. There was only me a few mates who were doing the rave thing at the time. It was a very tight-knit thing.

I was fortunate to have not been in the studio when the station got raided, but in the end Centreforce did get raided. I remember there were some close calls and getting told that we had to move out quickly, but I was one of the lucky ones and never got caught.

I don't think at the time we knew how big Centreforce was. It's only now looking back do we get an idea. For me it's a phenomenal opportunity to come back and DJ again on the station and to see how happy people are. And its also good to see kids saying they like the records that their parents play Its good to see the new generation coming through.

DJ Connie

'I went to a Genesis rave and I remember coming out and thinking 'yeah' I like this. This was around the time when I was going to Camden Palace and listening to tracks like Adeva's Respect Me and I liked the vibes that I got from that as well and this sort of helped get me interest in house music. I was already deejaying by this time and I was playing soul funk rare groove, so mixing with house music for me just came easy.

After that Genesis party I went out and acquired more house records. I then started playing at Dungeons and this was when Paul 'Trouble' Anderson was there. My first nights were playing upstairs and people just got on it-dancing and enjoying themselves. And so because of that I was asked to come and play downstairs. At this time people called Mister Mix-it-up Connie.

It was through the Dungeons connection that I got hooked up with the Run-Tings Crew and they were putting on raves. Me, Baby Face, Mr C and Rhythm Doctor were main DJ's who were the Run-Tings Crew.

It was then through my connection with the Run-Tings Crew that I got to know the Centreforce people. I spoke with DJ One and it was arranged that I would go up to the station which was in some tower block in Carpenter's Road, Bow area. When I got there, I was introduced to some guys and it just started. I remember walking into the flat and straight into the room where the studio part was. I never went into any of the other rooms. It was all very basic. The decks were placed in front of the window and this meant you looked out over Stratford. There were just two decks a phonic mixer and the pagers. We had lots of music. I was buying all the latest stuff and also people and producers were sending us stuff-we had loads of white labels.

The Centreforce listeners were driving around in their cars and feeling the music. Centreforce was also like a central point of information for them. People tuned in to find out where the next rave was going to be, listen to the latest music and the other thing that everybody used to love was the shout outs. For people driving around in their cars suddenly hearing their names being called out was a big deal. I mean it wasn't like people were going to get their names called out on Radio One or Capital. This was a huge buzz for people and for us deejays too because there'd be times when I'd finish a show, go and get in mu car and another Centreforce DJ would say something like 'big shout out to Connie who ripped it up tonight'.

There were times too when another deejay didn't show up and so you'd end up playing for another two hours, but you did it because you didn't want to let the station down. We needed to keep the music going and as far as I was concerned Centreforce was the main house station at the time. I look back on those days with fond memories.

It was around that time that everything started to happen. Centreforce really started to take off and people got to know about Run-Tings, we all went to Ibiza too, we all stayed in a villa and it was a good time. The scene got really good and it felt like everyone knew everyone. I got to know a lot of DJ's because of that time and a lot of them are still deejaying.

What Centreforce are doing now is keeping it all alive. You have the nostalgia thing mixed with the new thing and this is a good thing. Andy and Danny are supporting deejays and helping new people come through and this is good too.'

Matt Early

'I've been involved with producing for about the last fifteen years. This has included writing and producing and remixing for people like Gloria Gaynor, Barbara Tucker, Kenny Thomas and Frankie Knuckles and even Peter Andre. I've loved it and this led up to me eventually starting up my own record label called Far Horizon Records.

House music has been in my life for a long time and over the years I have played places like Ministry of Sound and range of clubs around Essex. Doing this meant I met a load of people. I then got into playing percussion (I had been playing drums since the age of thirteen) and this came around due to a connection with Secrets nightclub in Romford. This was my entry into playing percussion in the clubs.

The percussion side started to take off and I started to get invites from people who wanted to work with me and one of those was Paul Hardcastle jnr. He is a sax player and we have some stuff coming out soon.

And then my story begins with Centreforce. Danny's mum saw a video of me playing percussion and she said to Danny that he should get me involved with the station. I then went and had a meet with Andy and we talked about a lot things-including a possible Centreforce Record label.

Doing the first Centreforce live stream show with my girlfriend Carly was amazing. Carly plays some really good stuff and it gives me a buzz. She plays me stuff and it gives me shivers down my spine.

What I really like about what Centreforce are doing is that its bringing together a community of deejays. Many of these have worked together or crossed paths over many years. For me I love it that Centreforce are pulling together deejays that have credibility and knowledge and who really know what they are doing and Centreforce is pushing this forward and reaching new people that love the music and who want to come through as deejays in their own right. I hope the station goes from strength to strength and that it helps to bring in a new movement that gets people up and dancing in clubs again because I think the club scene is dying a bit because of it being all about R&B-and you can't rave to that all night and raving is what many of us want to do.'

Jonny C

'I've been involved in radio stations for over thirty years. I've been on station that have had first five listeners on the first show but then the next show there's two hundred, it can go that quickly and that's what's happened with Centreforce again.

I wasn't involved with Andy and Centreforce back in '89, but I came into it when it came back on around 2010. But it wasn't able to last long because we were getting hassle from Ofcom and that were on our case twenty four hours seven days a week, so it became a no brainer to just stop what we were doing. Ofcom just didn't want us. It was just like 1989 all over again.

So being back on now we have applied for a DAB (Digital Audio Broadcasting) licence and so we have to be good. This will mean things will change for us. When we were a pirate we couldn't have the big named DJ's on the station because it was a risk to them and they couldn't take the risk of being linked with something illegal. I mean you couldn't have some well-known DJ doing a show and the studio gets raided by the DTI (Department of Trade and Industry). There was a time when we had Artful Dodger on and we knew it wasn't going down well with the likes of Kiss FM. Back in 2010 Centreforce was getting lots of interest and one day a letter for Andy turned up from Ofcom basically saying Centreforce couldn't have the Artful Dodger on and they threatened legal action and all sorts. It's was a battle we wasn't going to win.

Going forward now it's different. We sat around and talked about the idea of making Centreforce work again, but were all unsure. Then Andy had a charity do at the Dovecote and we set up a basic studio, which we kept running for a few days, pulled in a couple of DJ's and after the first week we couldn't believe the figures that we were getting. We realized that with things like social media we could access people on a larger scale. It opened our eyes so we had another meeting and decided to give Centreforce another go. My feet haven't touched the ground since.

Ashley Beedle

'My history with house music began when I was involved with a sound system called the Shock Sound System. The guys involved in this introduced me to house music. I also started going down to Jazzy M's record shop in Croydon which was called Mi Price. We'd go down there and buy house records. I was aware of house music and knew that the Watson brothers were playing it at places like Delirium but even at that time house was still being mixed up with other stuff.

The first warehouse party that I went to was in 1988 in a venue near Hanger Lane (Hedonism). DJ's like Colin Favor and Jazzie B were there. It was amazing and a real mix up.

We were then invited to provide the sound system for the RIP raves that started up in Clink Street. They let us use one of the spare rooms that they had going in the venue so we were allowed to play, which was a lot of mad house music and some quite intense fast stuff.

And, of course, whilst RIP was going on, just across there was Shoom. Now Shoom finished before RIP which meant that a lot of the Shoomers would come across to RIP. We got to meet people like Mark Moore because of that and we would tell each other about what we were doing.

It was in Clinks one time when we were playing Robert Owens Bring Down the Walls. I jumped on the mic and kind of insisted that everyone started doing that and they did. You actually had people pulling down the camouflage netting that was up and bits of the wall.

The pirates were getting big at that time. During my career I got involved with some pirates. I got sacked from one of them because I had a guest on the show and I hadn't cleared it with them and that annoyed them. The guest had been Paul Denton who was one of the Shock Sound System crew.

Stations like Centreforce were very important. It was station underground news. You had to listen to the station to find out what was going on. It was very much needed. A pirate like Centreforce helped people keep up with the changes and things start to change quite a lot as 1989 went on. The whole rave thing had been going at a super speed. There were characters jumping onto the scene too who kind of hijacked it a bit and it went from that initial raw energy thing into some different. It was basically people who wanted to make money off the kids. I think things started to get quite chaotic towards the end of 1989.

Looking back at those days I think at the time I started to feel more and more negative about what was happening, but now, at the age that I'm at I look back on it as being quite an incredible time. I think we were shaking it up and I think acid house was the last big thing to happen since punk rock. And I think that because of acid house society changed-it became day-glow. Also people got jobs out of it, made careers out of it and companies got formed and I think what happened with acid house still resonates nowadays.'

Slipmatt
'I wasn't part of Centreforce back in the day but I'd cross paths with Andy and some of the others that were involved with Centreforce. My history was really with Raindance and that was from the same manner as Centreforce and those boys.

I had my own pirate station called Raw FM and that started in '89. We ran out of a tower block in Hackney Wick. We weren't that clued up and had our aerial sticking out of the flats balcony and we got done by the DTI straight away. After that we moved up to the twentieth floor and had good security and we ran shows at the weekends. Things moved along and my brother Paul started up Raindance. I deejayed at Raindance parties and that's where I started to make my name.

A few years on those involved with Centreforce started doing something over Romford way and started to do a few shows with them. That was pretty cool because Centreforce had been a huge part of my own rave history.

Seeing Centreforce back doing stuff is really good. That Facebook live stuff is massive.

Carly Denham
'I was only about nine or ten when I first heard house music and this was because I discovered pirate radio stations. I had a little

ghetto blaster in my bedroom and I would spend hours listening to the pirates and thinking wow what is this and I didn't really understand it. This was around 1989. From that time on I just had a fascination with pirate radio and house music. I loved the way the DJs talked to the listeners.

Music is me, I just absolutely love it and for me its always been the more underground type of stuff. From an early age I dreamt about becoming a DJ but for a long time I thought it was out of reach because being a girl. There just wasn't many female DJs around at the time.

I did start deejaying though when I was about nineteen. I had had collected quite a bit of vinyl by then. I also got my own decks and along with a friend we would nut about around the bedroom. And then I started getting on some stations and this led to me getting a regular slot on Force FM. I hosted a show on Force for about three years. I ended up doing the drive time show on Saturdays. This was around 2008.

There's a similar feeling I get doing the shows with Centreforce as I did back with Force. My partner Matt (Early) and me have been performing for years and we have the residency at the Brick Yard. At one of the parties someone filmed it and it went onto Youtube and went viral and Danny (Swallow's) mum saw it and we got contacted about going onto Centreforce to do a show.

We did the show and I loved it. But, at first, I felt really nervous. Being videoed live was really quite nerve-racking. I have had radio experience and played out live but having people watch live and contacting you at the time is a bit strange at first. It's an added pressure.

But since the show I have been absolutely buzzing because I think what is happening at Centerforce is such a great thing to be part of. The DJ's and the management are such a great bunch of people and so supportive. This is quite unheard of nowadays I think. So being involved with Centreforce is very refreshing.'

Mickey 'Star' Lewis

'I used to go to a club in Shaftsbury Avenue and there'd be people there like Randal and Paul 'Trouble' Anderson and then there'd be raves put on by Sunrise and then I'd go to places like the Astoria. And then a couple of years on I decided to get some decks of my own and I started to get gigs and it grew from there.

I got involved with radio stations like Shine and Pleasure and was with them for ages, which was something I wanted to get involved with because I had listened Centreforce all the time back in the day. We'd have Centreforce in the car as we drove to parties. They were good days.

It was my missus who caught one of the new Centreforce live sessions and she showed me. I could see Andy so I thought I'd give him a call. We spoke on the phone and I got invited to do a session.

It was really good fun and they were the nicest people, they really were. They were welcoming and it was like I'd known them since forever. I think it's fabulous that what they are doing now and the response they are getting. The feeling I get is what it was like back in the day. Everyone is having a good time and dancing and it's about the dancing.

I look at Centreforce and what they're doing and I think it's like a massive family. They have been really supportive of the stuff I'm doing. There's no jealousy, just a lot of humility and positivity. What the world needs is that bit of togetherness and Centreforce are managing to do that again.

Nicky Black Market
'The Centreforce studio was our safe house. We'd never turn up at the location with record boxes. We used bags to conceal what we were carrying. We were also part of the cycle. There were the pirates, then flyers, then the parties and they all needed each other to work'.

Danielle Montana
'To see the responses that Centreforce are getting again just after a few months is amazing. It says a lot about what people think about Centreforce, which is good because there have been people who don't want to admit that Andy and Centreforce had the first house radio station-and you can't take that away. One of the reasons why

people don't want to talk about it is because they came along after the scene, but did well in the scene. But they can't say that they were with the first house radio station, so they tend to dismiss it and hat is not fair. There have been books published about the scene and from respected DJ's, and there's never any mention of Centreforce.

I'm a big supporter of British house music and its DJ's. I don't like the American stuff. I don't like that they come over for 20 or 30 grand. But it's a sham that so many of those DJ's don't credit Andy and Centreforce for what they did. It's wrong especially as Centrforce is pivotal in the history of house music in the UK.

I was only young, about seventeen, when I got involved with Centreforce. I used to play rare groove and funk and soul on a pirate radio station based in North West London and I got introduced to it by my brother and my cousin Darren. They had a sound system called Twilight and they'd be doing stuff all around London. I started on that radio station and I became the youngest female DJ in the country to play on a pirate. And then I discovered house music.

I started collecting house records and would slip in some of them, even though some people still thought it was the devil's music. I also started deejaying in some right 'dug outs', really pitiful places and then I met Andy, which I think was at some rave somewhere. Andy then invited us (me and my sister Rochelle) up to the studio and we did a set. The response was massive and after that we found ourselves doing weekly shows on Centreforce.

I didn't really know what I was doing. I listen back now to some of the recordings of them shows and the mixing is horrific. But those days were some of the best times of my life. Going to secret raves around Hackney Marshes was just brilliant too.

I have other memories of playing sets on Centreforce that lasted for hours. I didn't mind. Then there were the thoughts 'are we going to get shut down'. But that's just the way it was back in the day.

Lee Priest 'DJ LUST'

'I originated in the early days of pirate radio. I set up Shakedown FM, was involved with Conflict FM, Force FM and Unity FM, but back in the day it was Centreforce that I listened to, that was the pirate that I looked up to. I think Andy (Swallow) found me by watching some of my live feeds on Fuzion live and the next thing I'm getting invited to do some sessions on Centreforce. For me, getting the opportunity to work with Centreforce was a dream come true. It's been overwhelming getting the call to get involved with Centreforce as one of the resident DJ's. I can't stress what it means to me.

I'm from Hornchurch, Essex way, originally from Harold Hill and back in '89 we were all out raving. I was at the summer of loves. I was still only sixteen/seventeen then too and like so many others back then, was travelling up and down the motorways and getting lost. I remember listening to Slipmatt and being blown away and once I started to DJ too I played at boat parties and a range of events and also worked alongside DJ Slipmatt and it means a lot to know him now and be friends with him.

Back then Centreforce were the leaders. I think every station has come off the back of Centreforce. They were the station to listen to, they played the tunes we wanted to hear, they had the top artists, were linked into the top raves. I think when Centreforce went off air they left something behind that other stations built their own on. As far as I'm concerned Centreforce are the true roots of the pirates.

Things have moved on a lot since 1989. Digital is the way forward and I'm behind Centreforce 100% as they get their digital licence. We all know there's nothing on the FM anymore, we all have to accept that sooner or later it's going to go.

I loved the music and the whole point of the name Lust is about my lust for the music. It really is a love for this music.

Tony Wilson
'Andy (Swallow) did their thing on the Saturday night in Echos and we did our nights called Adrenalin was on the Friday. This was in 1989. Echos was the posh club in East London at the time. It was a good size with two floors. A decent bar and a VIP area and I think the venue had a capacity of about 800 people and we'd get that many people turning up too.

I started deejaying in the early 80's. I came up through the soul scene and then the rap scene and then I got into house, which was after Steve 'Silk' Hurley's Jack Your Body came out. I was working with Paul Oakenfold in the Project club in Streatham. Johnny Walker was also part of it and that was the first club in London where Alfredo played. The Project Club was where the Balearic scene was born really and then the rest is history.

I started going out to Ibiza in 1983 and then I lived out there. When I came back I started playing at the warehouse parties around East London. I got to know the Centreforce people but I wasn't ever a DJ on the station. What can be said is that Centreforce was very important at the time and it was needed to help advertise the various do's and fill the airwaves with house music.

I've been keeping an eye on what Centreforce have been doing on Facebook and it's good to see that young people are getting involved with it. And it's really important to see the young people getting into it.

Steve Proctor
'I moved down to London in 1987 and by this time the style of music I was playing became known as Balearic. It was a mix of alternative, high energy, hip hop and rap. When Jack Your Body came out I thought right I'm having it. I thought it was brilliant. I then started to pick up house records. And then Pete Tong sent me a copy of Love Can't Turn Around. I already had a version, the one with the female vocal. I told Pete that I wanted to mix the two together. This was around the time that house music really started for me.

I had been into northern soul, punk and I had been into New Romantic. When I came to London it was all about rare groove. For me house music was a natural progression. Paul Oakenfold then told me about this club night he was going to start up and he explained to me what he wanted and this was a night full of alternative and Balearic music-just like Ibiza and I thought that was right up my street. That was the Project Club. I went on to play at early Boys Own parties and Shoom and all over the place including raves put on by Sunrise.

When I started out playing those house records it was even called acid house but it was the most exciting music for me. The music that was coming out of Chicago, Detroit and New York was amazing. To be part of the new thing that was happening in the UK was really exciting too. There were DJ's, myself included that were building the vibe. It was good to be part of that.

And then the pirates like Centreforce came along and they were needed too. They helped build the crowd and the vibe. They were very important and I saw that lots of people were tuning into them to listen to the music and to find out about the raves. They were really helping to spread the gospel so to speak.'

Peter Poyton

'I was a listener of Centreforce back in '89 but my history with being a DJ goes back to 1981. I started out on the Mod scene, then Northern Soul and I use to run my own nights at the Regency Suite (which I stole off of Eddie Pillar). That was my roots. I'm from Plaistow but at the time of the Mod all-dayers I was living in Ilford, people like Big Bob Morris was involved with that. And then we followed the bands that were around back then: The Chords, Purple Hearts, The Jam.

After this period, I got into the Soul and Funk thing, played at Caister and DJ'd on a few soul stations. And then the house thing kind of came along and that's exactly what was needed because the clubs were getting a bit tired at the time and in need of something new.

I started buying house records around 86 and 87, the likes of Marshall Jefferson and that Chicago sound. Then by 88/89 it just sort of exploded. Centreforce then came on the dial and that was it. I was going to Echos so I knew Andy, but I already knew Andy because of the West Ham connection.

In 1988 I found myself on holiday in Ibiza and ended up getting a residency out there, and I stayed in Ibiza doing that for two years. I had my pals coming over to visit and they'd bring me vinyl and the local Spanish DJ's at the time were coming to the smaller bars and picking up on the music that we were playing. So, we liked it that we were getting the music before they were getting it. This sort of thing doesn't get mentioned in books about the rave thing. We were nobodies, but a lot of the bigger DJ's got their records through us.

I then did some guest shows with Centreforce and then it dropped off the airwaves and disappeared for a while. I went on to work with other stations like House FM and then a few years later Centreforce came back on 88.4 and I found myself straight back on it.

During the second time around, I got asked to cover for a soul show that Chris Phillips was doing on there. I agreed because I still had all my soul records. It was after this that we formed the Soul Syndicate and those Saturday and Sunday shows were absolutely massive by the time we went over to Time FM. We did a few gigs and they went down well and so I found myself properly back into the soul scene again.

We then did the Summer of Love revival raves with Andy and that was massive to do too. And now it's happening all over again, only this time it looks like it's going to be even bigger.

The Soul Syndicate is back doing the Sunday sessions on Centreforce. The first session is arranged for 5th November. We have the old guys back on board plus a couple of new guys. A couple who run the tribute nights to DJ Froggy are also involved. That's called the Frog March.

What I like about Centreforce coming back, just like it did the second time around, it embraces over genres of music too, it's no longer just a rave station. I think this make Centreforce even more special. There's talk about reggae shows and Mod shows and this all good and keeps it moving forward and the right people are getting on board.

Nicky Brown
'I had buying vinyl and being a DJ in around 1988 and used my friends decks because I didn't even own a set myself. I learnt how to mix by going to lots of warehouse parties that were going on around East London. I remember leaning over a DJ's shoulders just looking at what he was doing. I must have watched him for about five hours that night.

I then started to get deejaying slots at parties and bars and I also stated going to Echos. I also found out about Andy (S) doing parties and putting on nights in clubs and also doing Centreforce.

It was my mate Bud (who came onto Centeforce with me) who got in touch with Andy telling him about me and about how much I wanted to be on Centreforce. Andy came back saying 'yeah yeah, I get it all the time' and nothing happened. But I kept chipping away and then Andy got a message to me asking me to take my records down to a club (Faces) that was in Homerton High St. It was a Sunday night, a sort of a wind down night following hard raving all weekend.

I went down to the club and played an hour's set. Afterwards Any came straight up to me and said 'mate, you're on Centreforce tomorrow.' This was going to be Monday. I was quite shy back then and a bit unsure about doing any talking so I asked my mate Bud to come along with me. Bud had the gift of the gab so I knew he'd be fine. So, we did the Centreforce show together under the name Nicky B and the man like Bud.

At the time Centreforce had a studio in some industrial units in some factory type building in Stratford. I remember the mast was set up on a tower block on the main road. We had to let ourselves in and find the right place. It was like a maze.

There was a bit of a dodgy element around too and I remember someone stole the decks. I even recall that at one stage we, the DJ's, had to chip in to buy some new decks. I think I handed over fifty quid. Yeah, there were certainly a few dodgy and light-fingered characters around at the time.

I don't recall the first record that I played on Centreforce but I do remember playing one record in particular. This was because the DJ that came on after me, who I looked up to, told me that he'd been listening to my show in the car on the way to the studio and that he really liked that record and asked me about it. That really sticks in my mind. The record was Krafty Beaver by Mark Imperial.

I'm now back on Centreforce after twenty-eight years and it's a lovely feeling. It makes you feel happy to be part of it again and you can feel the love that people have for Centreforce. It's a great feeling!'

Jazzy M

'The thing was that at the time there wasn't really much else entertainment wise other than Centreforce. At the time I was working in a record shop and it went from being a normal pop shop into a rave shop and this happened literally over night. One day Andy Swallow and Gary Dickel walked into the shop. They came in sometimes to buy records and, on this occasion, they asked me if I wanted to come and play on Centreforce. I didn't know much about it but said 'yeah go on then'. I'd been a resident at Labyrinth and places like the Camden Head but Centreforce really helped my career.

I remember doing the show at some place but it wasn't in a tower block, but I did go to a tower block and that was near the Blackwall Tunnel. The tower block was a really tall thing that made you feel sick when you looked out. If I had to describe it I'd say it was a bit like a squat really. There were cigarette butts on the floor even though there were signs on the walls asking the DJ's to keep the place clean. But DJ's being DJ's were more interested in keeping their records clean. I was just kind of thrown in the place and it was a matter of just getting on with it. It was straight into the deep end.

I was the DJ in the studio when it got raided by the police. By that time, October 1989, the station had been going for ages and had managed to not get shut down. It was a Friday which was not my usual time. I had been doing Saturdays, literally going straight from working in the shop or straight from deejaying in Labyrinth or some club or bar. I didn't get any sleep and I don't know how I did it.

When the studio was raided there was me and my mate Nigel, who would drive me about. I remember hearing a noise outside the door and I moved away from it. The police had put some sort of pressure device against the door, because all of a sudden it crashed in and nearly flattened me. The next thing the police were piling in like it was some sort of drugs raid. I think they were armed too.

It happened quickly but I realized it was a raid and I threw what I thought was the box, part of the equipment out of the window, but it was the wrong box. I also remember that the last record I played was Hill Street Blues and saying something like 'that'll be all folks'

As a result of the raid the police confiscated my records. I wanted them back and I knew that Tony Wilson had also had his records confiscated at some party and hat he'd hired a brief in an attempt to get his records back. I hired one too and they managed to get my records back saying that I needed them for my work and I got my records returned to me.

But I still had to go court and being the cocky sod that I am, when the judge asked me if I had anything to say I replied 'yes, we should be able to broadcast what we like and play what we want- freedom to dance!'. And with that I asked the judge how he wanted the fine paid and went to pull it out of my wallet.

After Centreforce I had a break but then got back into deejaying and producing and I had my own record label called Red Rose Recordings that I set up with Tony Wybrow and Ian Hughes. We put out a lot of UK Garage artists like DJ Luck and MC Neat.

And now many years later I'm back on Centreforce and the first show I did was amazing. I'm used to a large listenership but the response to my first show was out of this world. It's just great for an ex-pirate station to get cast across the net like that. What's happening is unbelievable.'

Andy Barker (808 State)

'I started deejaying in a youth club when I was fourteen, I was playing hip hop and electro and whilst this was going on house was slowly creeping in. The youth club was like a night club for us and everyone was all around the same age. There were a few break dance crews around and then it became a sort of natural progression to go into house music. This was around late 86 going into 87 and I was automatically attracted to it because of the electronic side of it. I started getting hold of import records so was playing records that people hadn't heard. After a while house became the music that we predominately played in our sets. People then started to twist it and turn it into acid house and this was the next natural progression.

By the time I was eighteen and allowed to get into night clubs I knew what I was doing because by then I had quite a bit of experience behind the decks. I would then be in the Hacienda almost every night. My big brother, Eric, was always in the Hac and he was well-known in the Hac and because I looked so young at the time I used to leave a tenner with the girls who used to work on the door. I then had to go inside and find Eric and then take him back to the door and he'd get my tenner back and say that I was eighteen. So, I always ended up getting into the Hac for nothing. I loved it!

We then started to do warehouse parties in Manchester. We did the very first one which was just across the road from the Hacienda on the City Road. The building we did it in was an old warehouse. There were a lot of old warehouses in Manchester at that time and they would have To Let signs outside them. So, we spotted this one near the Hacienda and thought we'd go and check it out. We broke the pad lock on the door and replaced it with another pad lock and we kept checking it throughout the week to see if it had been changed. But by the following Saturday it didn't look like anyone had checked the building, so got in there with a generator, spent time sweeping up and set up a bar which just sold like Lucozade and Coca Cola-there was no alcohol at all.

And then that Saturday night people went down the Hacienda and after that shut at 2 o clock people came to our party, which was just over the road. It was good, it was great-the first one was fantastic. The only problem was the doorman didn't let in some undesirable, so he decided to phone the police. The police arrived in big riot vans but my brother went out and told them that it was an office party adding that it was a leaving party for one of the girls. He assured them that there were no scum bags or toe rags in the party and the police, who back then didn't have a clue what an acid house party was just allowed us to carry on. We then carried on until 10 o clock in the morning.

The second warehouse party we did we called Sweat It Out. This was held in an old railway arch. It was big and long and could probably hold about five thousand people. Whereas the first one had just been word of mouth for the second one we actually had a flyer, which was just something hand drawn.

Around 86 there was some pirate radio stations. They were mostly based in the Moss Side area and didn't have very big transmitters, so you had to be in that area to listen to it. As soon as you went into city centre you'd lose the signal and you'd have no connection. I knew one of the DJ's on one of the stations and I did some of the early mixes for him, which he used to play on cassette. The pirates just didn't last that long because they got busted.

Pirate radio was quite small in Manchester. What we had more of was community stations. We started our 808 State show on a community station called Sunset Radio. You can actually hear some of those shows because they've been added to the 808 State website.

Sunset Radio was the first community radio station in Manchester to get a licence. It was set up by a DJ called Mike Shaft and he was quite important in Manchester because there was a station called Piccadilly Radio and he had a soul funk show but he started to play dance music.

There's a place just outside Manchester called the Mersey View. People used to gather up there in the cars and listen to Sunset Radio because that was where you'd get reception. We'd be on a Tuesday night and Mersey View would be full of cars surrounded by people dancing to what we were playing and we'd play the latest imports that came in from the States or Europe. We'd get records from Eastern Bloc Records because we'd play their records which meant they were an advert for what they had to sale in the shop. This meant whatever we played on a Tuesday night the Bloc would have loads of kids going in asking for the record.

At the time there was us 808 State, A Guy Called Gerald and people like MC Tunes. We were all part of the same crew when we first started out. 808 State started out of a gang of different groups. Most of us were into hip hop and we'd all meet in Eastern Bloc Records on Saturday afternoons, where we'd listen to new tunes. Eastern Bloc then told us they were thinking about setting up their own label and asked us who was going to come up with the goods. All of us then went off and started banging off our own stuff. This led to an EPbeing released, which was called Wax On The Melt By Hit Squad MCR. There was a track on there with MC Tunes. Another track was very early 808 State.

We then got access to a recording studio and at night we'd go in and record stuff. Some people drifted off and who was left kind of became 808 State. There would be nights when Gerald was in the room next to us making Voodoo Ray and we'd be making songs of our own. We'd then take cassettes down to the DJ's in the Hacienda and they'd play them. It all started to evolve from that and we did Pacific State, which was an underground hit before it started to get played on Radio One. We then started to get a lot of interest of major labels and this came with lots of money offers. It all got a bit serious then and went from just messing around to it becoming our job. Factory Records offered us a deal but we went with a different label because we thought the PR machine would be better for us. We then did Top of the Pops, eight times in all.

When I started going down south I got to know about the pirate radio stations around London. When I drive into London I'd put the radio on, press search and it would pick up a pirate. It was always interesting to hear what they were doing and you could see the differences-after all-we invented it!

I know Mike Pickering came to play in London and played at Shoom. He played acid house and got booed. All he was doing was playing exactly what was playing in Manchester at the time and in the Hacienda. We knew what we liked. Our summer of love was in 1988. We didn't know whether it would actually last for more than one summer, so we made the most of it, we even had a swimming pool in the Hacienda. It was bonkers!

Wayne Anthony
'For most people it was amazing. Even at the end. It didn't get moody for everyone. We did the Freedom To Party rave in Radlett. We crashed the building and before people even got there we had to face a massive police riot squad. It was mad because we looked out of this window and saw them all down the road. At this point there was only about thirty of us in the building. The warehouse we had was on some industrial estate and the road leading up to it was just lined up with police. But then behind them I could see hundreds of people. We ran out of the warehouse and started shouting 'come on'. The police nicked our lighting and sound equipment so organising the things we needed for the party had all happened late in the day. We had at least 10, 000 people at that rave. I had to be smuggled out of that building in a boot of a car. Once the police turned up they didn't go. They stayed there all night and, in the morning, we had to drive through them.

There were different stages in the evolution of the pirate radio stations and the way that we, us promoters, actually used them. In the beginning we didn't actually need them as a means to help promote the events, but in terms of listening to the music, that was where pirate stations like Centreforce were really vital. I mean when we'd come home from the clubs to be able to tune into a pirate radio station that was playing the music that we'd just been listening to was a major thing and a huge leap forward for us. Back then very few of us had that music. It was the early days and that music was hard to get hold of so the pirates made that music accessible for people. This was really important. We were all pause pushers back then too so we would listen to the stations and record the music onto cassettes. This was how we put our mix tapes together.

In the beginning we were doing the events but we weren't doing them in what could be called a commercial way. It was underground. But what the stations like Centreforce did was help us reach people and this started at the time when our parties started to get stopped. For us, we needed a certain amount of bodies in the buildings for us to then be able to stand up against the police. And this was where the pirates became vital for us and they came into their own strength.

Using the pirates to put out radio ads really helped too, so we made our own radio ads. So we started to utilize radio stations to help us get thousands of people to our events.

The police would really come out in force. They would find our meeting points and search a ten-mile radius in an attempt to try and find our venue for the rave. And without the pirates we would never have been able to move the amount of people that we did from area to another in a really short amount of time.

The Police Pay Party Unit commander Ken Tappenden has talked about those days. He says that he wishes promoters like us were his lieutenants because we were able to move a huge amount of people from one area to another very effectively and in a way that the police and army couldn't even do back in 1989.

Once we moved our parties out of the inner London streets we really needed Centreforce and the other pirates. They took care of getting people to the venues whilst we concentrated on the delicate procedure of setting up the lights and sound system before the police found the building.

I'm an East End lad and grew up on a council estate in Hackney where I witnessed a lot of violence. For me the major shift came around in the way people's attitudes changed. Back then people didn't hug one another. Most mates didn't hug their mates or tell them you loved them. But what I saw in the rave scene was how people became more open and found a way to express emotion to people who you cared about. And this shift happened in me and has stayed with me today too. I see this in other people too. Nowadays people hug and kiss-even the tough people and it all comes from that period.

For me, the unity that the rave thing provided was also something special. The reason why I started doing acid house parties in the beginning was because I loved seeing everybody in one space. Up until then events were held in venues where there'd be lots of rooms and they'd all be isolated from each other. This meant that everyone was quite separated. But I wanted everyone to be together and be able to see one another. I wanted people to be able to witness the same thing at the same time-have the same experience.

Getting to the parties was also another thing that stood out to me. Once we'd gotten to the stage where we were putting phone numbers on our tickets things got very busy. We'd be on the motorway at a certain time and we'd recognise all these other people who were heading to the same place as us. We'd end up in these massive convoys. We were lucky because the other promoters would provide us with the information as to where the party was going to be. They knew that we were trustworthy. And to be fair we were well known and respected as being one of the hardest working teams out there.

And we did graft. And I worked with everybody from Energy to Sunrise to Biology and Pasha (Andy). Now with Andy you just knew that he was always going to be successful because he was a real grafter. Andy was prepared to do whatever it took to get the party going. And back in 1989 that's what you needed. There needed to be a team of people that weren't just workers, but people that could respond and think on their feet. There were many times when Andy would come up to me and say 'right, what do you need done?' I would tell him and it would get done. He didn't mind getting dirty.

When Andy and his team launched Centreforce he brought something in with an explosion and he made it work. Centreforce made a huge impact in the east end and they launched so many DJs.

And that was another thing about Centreforce, it launched the careers for so many people. Centreforce were a force to be reckoned with and this was partly because they were working class lads who loved to play house music. And at the time if you told any of them that they'd be respected DJs many years on, they'd say 'fuck off.'

Roger the Doctor

'I used to DJ at a pub on a Friday night. It was around that time that people started to tell me about this pirate station they were listening to called Centreforce. I started to listen to it and straight away I was hooked. People then started to encourage me to go on it and within a few months I had spoken to Gary Dickel and was doing shows on Centreforce.

The first place I got taken to was very top secret. I had no idea where I was going. I had to meet someone who then drove me to some flats. It was a Wednesday, which was the night of my first show and then I kept that show about six months. It was from twelve to two. I just played what I had been playing in the pubs. This was a lot of late disco and early house. As the weeks went on I would spend more money buying up house records but my show wasn't pure house only.

Before Centreforce I hadn't done any radio at all. I found it pretty easy to grasp. Things like pagers were just coming in so people would page in their requests and what have you and you'd get your name mentioned on the radio. It was pretty basic, just decks, a monitor, speakers and an 80's Sound Lab mixer.

Things just went from strength to strength. I got to know other Centreforce DJs and got to play at various parties. I'd been hanging out with DJs the Kenny Ken and Jumping Jack Frost. DJ Randall was a very big influence on me. Kenny Ken, Randall and me became known as the Three Amigos and we did quite a bit of stuff around London. We also went out to Ibiza and did a tour out there that took in clubs like Amnesia. Being involved in Centreforce was the best thing that's ever happened to me in my life. And have to say that Andy (Swallow) was so supportive. We needed Andy to be pushing the station and Centreforce was a properly run station.

I stayed with Centreforce for about a year which was right up until it got taken off the air. It was legendary. I remember being out on holiday in Tenerife and when people heard that I was about they came down to a night club to talk to me. They made me feel like a super star. Up until then I never really knew how important us Centreforce DJs were to people. They'd be telling me that without us they couldn't party and it meant a lot.

Those times were great. I played at Woodstock, which was the biggest crowd I ever played to. There was something like 15,000 people there. The illegal raves were great. The amount of enjoyment that people got out of them was incredible. There'd be convoys of cars driving through fields and parking up at petrol stations and listening in to us. We all knew it wouldn't last but it was something we just went along with at the time. It really was the best times of my life (before my kids were born) and if it wasn't for Centreforce Radio I wouldn't have done the things that I did.

Daddy Chester

'I grew up as a dancer so whatever music was out there I was into it. When it (rave) started pumping out it was late 88. I got to know Adam (Adamski), who at the time was living in Camden above the Paradise Café, which was just across the road from Camden Palace. At the time Adam was playing in a band with his brother and another guy called Johnny and they were called This Chord That Chord and Every Other Epping Chord. I ended up doing some gigs with them and they were nuts. But that band split up and after this Adam got a keyboard and started to learn to programme. Adam and me then done a warehouse party and after this it took off and we got booked for lots of raves.

Going into 1989 I was just doing my ting and raving all the time. I didn't even see the stuff I was doing as an MC and dancer as a job-I mean I wasn't getting paid anyway. I also ended up living with Adam.

Doing the raves was brilliant. It was a good time and put it this way I didn't get much sleep. In 89 I probably got about three months sleep. Raving was great in its day. The thing about 89 was that it converted everyone. If you was a goth or punk or a reggae man, you got into raving.

For me it wasn't just raving at the weekends, Adamski and me were out doing all the clubs throughout the week. This meant that I got to know what was going on. But lots of people didn't and that's why they needed the pirates like Centreforce. Centreforce also had their parties. We may have played at some, but it's hard to remember because there was too many to mention.

A highlight for me from 89 would have been being on stage with Adamski at the Brixton Academy on New Year's Eve. Adamski was promoting Live and Direct and I would get time on the stage too. This was at the time when some people thought Adamski was the name of the band and that I was in the band. People would say the same thing to Seal too when he came along.

At the Brixton gig the track called Don't Need No Acid almost didn't get played. Now that was a track I rapped on and people loved that track. It never got a proper release and when Seal came along he got the single instead. But in the end, we did do it and people loved it. It was the best feeling being on that stage that night and it was all good whilst it lasted.'

Gary Dickel

'When we started up Centreforce there were a few of us that made things work and at the time it was something special. I knew Andy from football and then started going to a few raves and got into the music early on. I started buying records from Black Market and City Sounds and Andy talked about doing a club night and we did nights at places like Faces. This moved on to doing some illegal raves and this led to Centreforce starting up.

We got some fella in to set up the equipment and got the station up and running and after a couple of months it got quite professional. We started taking ads and things like that and when we went to raves we'd get treated like royalty.

I was the first person on Centreforce. It was a bank holiday weekend. We'd been doing an all-dayer at Echos and whilst that was happening the rig was being put up. I got a call saying I should get over to some flat in Hackney. This was the first Centreforce studio. I remember the doorman from Echos took me over there. I had my records. In the flat was Rodge the Dodge. He was one of the geezers that set up the equipment. There were just two old decks, a mixer, a mic and a pager because without the pager it wouldn't have been any good. It was a real buzz being on there and people getting in touch. It didn't bother us at all that we had an illegal radio station. We were all ex-football hooligans and had done illegal raves and it just didn't enter our head.

I think it was Grant Fleming who came up with the name Centreforce. I remember he did the first banner for us and it had Centreforce written on it. I'm sure it was Grant. People said Centreforce was to do with the ICF but it wasn't, far from it, we'd all got out of that football thing by that time. When we went out, yeas we'd go out ten-handed by we'd have our wives with us. There was no connection to the ICF.

Seeing what Centreforce is doing now is really good. I went up the Dovecote the night Keithy Mac was on and it was just blinding. There were people coming up and shaking my hand and this and that. It showed that Centreforce meant a lot to people.

It was just different back then. We would be in places with Millwall fans and these would be people we used to fight with. But we'd be off our heads and just talking. It was a mad, mad scene at the time. I think what me and Andy and the other Centreforce DJs did was amazing and it was special. It's hard to put into words really. It was like a family. Andy was Mr Sort Things Out. Nothing was ever a hardship for him and he was a good leader of things and he loved the music.

Things started to change going into 1990 because there were people earning big money out of the rave thing. There'd be guns around too. We did a party at Brands Hatch and there were loads of problems after that with people wanting money. But we used to stand our ground and mostly people never used to bother us. But things did change and end.

Perry K

'Me and Jack Bass had been doing stuff for a long time and we had that Raindance connection and I knew Andy through football and also when the station was doing things with Time FM. I would go to the studio and there'd be people like Kenny Ken there. This was how my association with Centreforce came about.

There was talk about me doing some shows for the station and I sent them a demo, but this clashed with work as I had just started to do the Knowledge and because of this I didn't end up getting any shows.

I then started seeing the Centreforce live streams and got talking to Jonny C and I got the invite to do a live show. I found the live stream thing to be very different to what I had done before. When I have done radio before there's really just you and the studio, but the live streams mean there's a camera on you all the time. It's a bit strange because that means everyone can see you, but back in the old days the listeners didn't know what you looked like. Back in the old days we wanted to keep a low profile and didn't want the authorities knowing our faces.

There's definitely a positive vibe around what Centreforce are doing at the moment. I think getting the DAB is a good thing for the station. People at our age can't really step out of line, so going the legal route is better for us.

I also think that what Centreforce is doing is good for the scene. I think the scene has got really fragmented. It started off as just house and garage and then it turned into other things and although it evolved and changed it also lost something too and that's what Centreforce are bringing back.'

Danny Swallow

'For me it's pretty amazing to see that despite all the years that we've been off air, we've come back and made such a massive impact. It's amazing for me to be able to work with such big name DJs and get a lot of credit and respect of big names in the industry, like Chase and Status and Andy C and these are people that I kind of look up to in the music industry. These people have been telling how good we've been doing here at Centreforce. You just can't

191

make it up. One minute I'm sitting there with nothing to do, the next I'm talking to Chase and Status and Andy C. It's been a great journey so far.

From ever since I can remember music has been in my life. My dad brought me up on music. My dad started up Centreforce and he had Public Demand Records, so my journey with music started by being around those things. And then there were the various parties. As I got older I'd speak to my dad's friends and I would get to hear about the early days of Centreforce and the parties that he used to put on. I never knew how big all that stuff was back in the day and how influential Centreforce was for the rave thing.

Since Centreforce has been on air and I've been working on this project, the amount of reach and diversity of the people listening is very amazing. We have people listening in from Canada or Ghana and all around the world.

Every week now we are setting a new standard. Tonight we have MC Creed down and he is one, if not the biggest MC on the garage scene. The whole thing is getting bigger and better. But the thing that really makes it worthwhile for me and for the other DJ's is the reaction that we are getting from the fans. The comments are outstanding. They, the fans, are the reason why we do it.

I started deejaying when I was thirteen, I played a lot in a nightclub near to where I live in Epping, but I got bored with playing warm up sets and sort of stopped for a while. But now coming back to deejaying and being on Centreforce I'm enjoying it and I'm not taking anything for granted. Whenever I get behind the decks now, I don't want to get off.

Our Centreforce moto is 'Taking you back from the past and into the future' and we have a lot of exciting things coming up in 2018 and these will include a lot of new and upcoming DJ's and this is what we want to go forward. We want to bring in new listeners and we want to be the biggest and the best.

Colin Hudd

'In 1988 I was doing Spectrum that then changed its name and went into Land of Oz because of the bad press it got. I became aware of Centreforce after that. Up until Centreforce there'd really only been soul stations but then Centreforce came along and was the only one that played just house music. Centreforce existed because of house music and the rave scene. It was born out of it.

By 89 I was guesting on Legends on a Saturday night and was going to raves in Slough and doing Sunrise parties. I also did the first World Dance. I think they secured some field that was owned by Boy George's brother or cousin.

I came up through the soul and funk route but started listening to house music in 1986. There's a mix cloud recording of me playing house music in 86. I didn't play it all the way through my sets. Back then it had to mix up with other stuff from jazz funk to soul. It would be tracks but the likes of Marshall Jefferson. Attitudes varied when it came to house music. People like Paul Oakenfold were into playing hip hop and weren't into the house thing at that point. But I remember playing 'Oakey' a load of stuff in 1987 and it was after that that he asked me to come and play some house music for him and this led to Spectrum.

It was the tempo of house music that grabbed my attention. Back in the disco days I had liked those records and a lot of the gay stuff. I really got the faster tunes so when house music came along I knew that was for me. 120 bpm was a good tempo for me and house music was away from the norm and it seemed so fresh at the time.

By 1989 there were so many good house tunes coming out. There'd be loads of new stuff week after week. I was buying new records every week. It was great. And then the hip house stuff came along and I loved all that too. That was fun and not like the moody hip hop stuff.

I don't think I went to any of the early Andy Swallow parties because by that time I was working in different places. I was doing Monday nights for 'Oakey' and then I started doing the garage night on the Friday and Saturdays I was down at Legends. There'd be occasions when I'd leave Legends at 3 or 4 o clock and go to some rave. On one night, whilst on the way to a World Dance rave, I remember passing the chaos in the streets and the bridge where the Marchioness had just gone down. And then Limelight started on the Sunday and I was just busy all the time.

Another thing that I liked about that 1988/89 period was that there weren't all these pigeon holes. There wasn't any of this happy house. No one said this is that or that is this. It was just a matter of saying 'that's banging' and that was enough for us. My rule of thumb was if it sounds good I'll play it.

By early 1990 it changed. I remember my mate asking me to go with him to the Freedom To Party rally and I said to him 'they've just stuck a fucking landing strip in the Falklands, do you think the government are going to do anything for you and your right to party?'

By 1990 it did start to get moody. I started to hear stories of people, nice people, who were putting on parties but were getting threatened and told to hand over money. There was a heavy-duty element of guys coming in and they wanted some of what was going on. Also, cocaine became the drug of choice. Cocaine held the wall up because people just stood around propping the wall up and looking at each other. I saw the love go from the parties and I knew it was all over, but it had been good whilst it had lasted.

Jack Bass

'I started raving in April 88 when I started going to Camden Palace. When I worked on the council there was a bloke there who'd come in to work still out of his nut. He told me about these parties he was going to in places like Spectrum. I liked the sound of that and that was how I ended up going to Camden Palace. Two of us went out to this thing and at that time we were known as outcasts really-we were the people who took these strange things called ecstasy tablets. And then about four months later there'd be fifty or sixty of us going out and finding the parties put on by the likes of Rat Pack and of course the Andy (Swallow) nights.

I was already part of a sound system called Third Generation and we did parties like the one that Andy put on near the Blackwall Tunnel approach. That was called the Library and a few parties were done there. I got into the sound system thing because of two blokes I knew called Colin and Owen. They'd been involved with Jazzy B but split away. Jazzy B formed Soul 11 Soul and Colin and Owen formed Third Generation. I got involved and we started doing warehouse parties in places like Clinks and we also did the first all-night party in the Michael Sobell Centre. This was all in 1989 and I've still got the decks and mixer that we used back then.

I got involved with Raindance because I was working down Jenkins Lane and heard about it. Sometime after that I was World Dance down the Docklands and got approached about playing at one of their parties. I agreed and that was twenty-one years ago. I think I've played every party, all bar six, since.

Back in the day Centreforce was very important. It's what we'd have to listen to because they gave out the information about the parties and the meeting points. I already had a Centreforce connection because I knew Andy through the football and the ICF. I used to travel with them all over the country.

I'm going to be doing a Centreforce live session this December and to see them back and going forward is brilliant. There's a wide range of music that's going to be coming on there and DJ's too, people like Olas Boss. It's ideal for Essex too because there's no dance orientated station out in that area.

Adamski interview

I started off by asking Adam how important were the pirate stations like Centreforce for the rave scene back in 89? To which he replied 'Very important for promoting events ...and letting people know how to find events...providing a great 24-hour soundtrack for getting ready to go out, travelling to and from and between parties...also reinforcing the sense of unity amongst the rave revolutionaries...'

This prompted me to ask if he felt a station like Centreforce helped promote your music and support what you were doing? And he responded with 'I can't remember if they played my music. I did a live set on Sunrise radio once though that led to me playing at the legendary Dungeon club in East London n other good stuff.'

I was interested to hear what 1989 was like for Adam and asked him to describe it. He came back with 'It was an amazing year and I was very excited to be deeply involved in a massive socio-cultural shift. I went from unemployed and living in a bedsit above a kebab shop to playing my own music to 1000s at some of the greatest parties of the 20th century in a matter of weeks.'

And wanting to find out how Adam got into house music I asked how and why did you get into house music? To which he said 'Funnily enough through another pirate radio station, LWR in 86/87. I always loved mechanical music and I always loved trippy music...my passion intensified in Ibiza in 1988.'

Lastly, I asked do you have a fave rave that you performed at and why? And he answered with 'Sunrise 5000 at Santa Pod racetrack. It was just so spectacular and loud and tribal and futuristic and back then I used to just plug my gear into the mixer in the DJ booth and wasn't being gawped at. People didn't all face the DJ's then. They were all just looking at each other. Also, the anticipation building up to it was so exciting and the whole aftermath continuing to party with hilarious and inspiring friends across the countryside and back into Soho for Sunday night. It's a toss-up between that and the opening night of Amnesia, Ibiza '89...which was a night club so dunno if that really counts as a rave...'

Images of the State ballroom by Bobby Parry!

Specific State 89, the writing's on the wall, back in time to acid reign, courtesy Snowball. The 80's really set the scene, people making shapes, Liverpool was on the map, a place for great escapes.

"Can you feel it" was the cry, in every club in town, the Bank on Scotland road was rife, with tablets we would down. Ecstasy was all the rave, the dance was new to me, with acid house I took my dove, to set my spirit free!

Liquid gold from Images, to send me round the bend, then go the state to just indulge, cloud cuckoo was my friend. Beads of sweat on every head, that walked in to the room, my tee shirt soaked with rush and beer, a real life sonic boom!

"Please don't go" my favourite tune, or maybe "Ride on time", the house was proud with birds galore, my life was pure sublime. The chill out room was not for me, control was in my pill, to lose my mind and dance on fire, was mine and I would kill!

Electric legs to generate, the moves that I would make, to dance away my latest trick, while I was off my cake! Every beat was to a tee, the party was allowed, to mix it up with everyone, a face within my crowd.

Simple minds for simple minds, INXS would 'Kick', music of the likes which finds, it stopped me being sick. Big Audio were Dynamite, the DJ's done their bit, I loved to go on Friday night, the birds were fkn fit!

82 to 89, the years I made my mark, times were great and I was fine, no dancing in the dark. But now they have reunions, I'm yet to take the plunge, like old school time communions, I'll soak it like a sponge.

The Killing Moon I believe it's called, this could be my time, to have a beer and feel enthralled, some words I'll have to mime. Echo & the Bunnymen, ringing in my ears, yes I think it's time again, to give in to my fears

Fk it man I'm on my way, tickets in my hand, I am out and off to play, I hope you'll understand. That even though my knees have gone, I'm up to bleedin' rave, The State is tops and number one, I'll dance on any grave!

Every week would be the same, but better than the last, compared to all the shite today, my life was such a blast. Upon a cloud of ecstasy, completely off my box, with other places to indulge, the famous Paradox!

Sweat and steam for all to see, but no one seemed to care, the hazy days of little doves, was great and I was there. Floating like some holy ghost, immersed in spirit form, to take the floor and call my own, was probably the norm!

'Quadrant Park another gaff, the centre of my rave, with topless birds just getting down, to quench the lust I'd crave. Free love was a better way, of putting it about, the end of night was morning time, and deffo my last shout!

The hit man was a miss for her, Michaela she was fit, but waterman was just a freak, and Clive was such a tit! Dapple down I can't believe, a fucking funny farm, I'd watch as I began to chill, induced by inner calm!

Oh the days of ecstasy, will never come again, with shit they pedal now no good, just causes too much pain! GBH or magic dust, is such a silly joke, the shit they mix will never be, as pure as diet coke!

Live the dream of acid house, the trappings of my youth, the class A's all before me now, my testament of truth! But I would never change my days, of being in this state, my favourite club with memories, of shocking times so great!

Smiley times of mega raves, still lurk within my mind, the ballroom that became my home, I know I'll never find. The magic that it gave to me, I have to put in words, so thanks to all my raving friends, the loonies and fit birds!

Lightning Source UK Ltd.
Milton Keynes UK
UKHW03f0932260318
320045UK00001B/21/P